C000179906

Masquerade

Dear Michèle,

Thanks so much
for all your dear
support, help
& understanding
Lots of love forever,

xx

'This fast moving story takes us back to life between the two World Wars in the old Cardiff Docklands's community of Tiger Bay and Harlem, New York. It follows the fortunes of one mixed race family as the light-skinned central character leaves to find a better life in New York. Anna Corbett successfully combines a very engaging human story with historically accurate details of life in these two very different communities. Particularly striking is the hardship and dangers faced by new immigrants arriving in New York and the precarious existence, driven by dreams of a betterment, that passing for white entails.'

Professor Chris Weedon, Cardiff University

'A man looking for escape. A man with dreams. In this assured, tender and moving debut, Anna Corbett has created a complex and intriguing central character who takes us from the docks of Tiger Bay to the dives of New York on a journey that explores 'in betweenness' in relation to intimate relationships, place and identity, against a sound-track of Harlem Renaissance-era jazz. Moving through city-scapes rich in colour, sound and texture, where – and with whom – will he find 'home'? I listened to the music, cared about the characters and was kept wondering till the last how it would all turn out – story-telling at its best!'

Dr Jackie Goode, Sociologist &Visiting Fellow
@ Loughborough University, Leicester

'Anna Corbett's engaging novel delves headfirst and very directly into issues of race, belonging, family, and discovery. An enthralling read with very relatable themes taking you with the protagonist on his transatlantic, transcultural life odyssey from cold Cardiff to the seething cultural melting pot of Harlem. With the burgeoning Harlem Jazz and social scene providing fresh stimuli and a fertile environment, George finds his place in the world, and in the end, redemption?'

Gordon Wedderburn: Jazz Radio Presenter and Promoter, Co-Founder:
GW Jazz, London.

'Anna Corbett's vivid portrayal of the Tiger Bay community in Cardiff during the 1920s and '30s is both truthful and tender-hearted, yet the discontented George decides to reject it all to follow his dreams to America. There he discovers that those dreams come at some considerable cost.

The many interesting characters who accompany him on his life journey are deftly woven into an engaging story of love, identity and redemption. Set in two multicultural communities separated by the Atlantic Ocean but united by the rhythms of music and life, Tiger Bay in Cardiff and Harlem in New York City, Masquerade is an extraordinary debut – a smart, sensual and witty novel that is deeply informed by archival research and Anna's extensive, lifelong passion for Jazz music.'

Jeremy Rees, Radio Presenter & Jazz Show host at Radio Cardiff

MASQUERADE

Anna Corbett

'Identity [...] a never completed process of
becoming—a process of shifting identifications'.
Stuart Hall,
Familiar Stranger: A Life Between Two Islands

Eulipion

Copyright © Anna Corbett 2020
First published in 2020 by Eulipion
#14 London SE13 6PA
http://www.eulipionpublishing.com

Distributed by Gardners Books, 1 Whittle Drive, Eastbourne,
East Sussex, BN23 6QH
Tel: +44(0)1323 521555 | Fax: +44(0)1323 521666

Apart from a few well-known historical figures the other characters in this
book are fictitious and any resemblance to actual people, living or dead, is
purely imaginary.

British Library Cataloguing in Publication Data
A catalogue record for this book is available from the British Library.

ISBN 978-1-9162862-0-7

Typeset by Amolibros, Milverton, Somerset
www.amolibros.co.uk
This book production has been managed by Amolibros
Printed and bound by T J International Ltd, Padstow, Cornwall, UK

Acknowledgements

Many thanks to my uncle **Harry Ernest,** a patriarch of **Butetown**, the place previously known to many as **Tiger Bay** in Cardiff. He has generously shared with me his anecdotes, childhood memories and knowledge of **'the Bay'**, where he continues to be a valued and respected member of that community.

★

Thanks also to **Loren Schoenberg, Director of the National Jazz Museum, Harlem, New York,** who kindly spent time talking to me about early American jazz, and even let me sing a song while he accompanied me on Duke Ellington's piano!

For Natalie and Annette

Chapter One

May, 1923
Tiger Bay, Cardiff

George Hodges managed to get permission to slip out a bit earlier that afternoon. His shift down the docks didn't finish for another hour but he wanted to go home and wash up before going out. It was a crummy job, loading and unloading coal from the big ships that came in from all around the British Isles and certainly not what he intended doing for the rest of his life. It was hard graft and filthy: his hands were rough and dry even though he rubbed grease all over them every night. Sliding away out of the docks trying not to get noticed by any of the lads was no joke. Some bright spark would be sure to make a comment if they'd noticed him.

He had gone to his boss and told him his mam was sick and he needed to go uptown to get some special medicine for her. Didn't say that the real reason was to go to Howells department store to collect something. It wasn't the kind of swanky shop he usually frequented but hey, why not? Needs must after all. He'd thought of it a few months ago when he was wandering around with nothing else to do one Saturday afternoon.

He just had to get out. Driving him mad. With Mam so

1

sick, the whole house felt like a funeral home. They said it was TB. Of course, it was a terrible thing. Of course, she was suffering. Of course, he was sorry; it was difficult for them all. Everything had changed since she took to her bed a couple of months before.

He had been paying off for the scarf for quite a few weeks. The chap in the gents' department said he could do it that way. White silk it was, with a fringe which stroked your neck when you put it on. There was even a faint swirly design woven in if you looked up close.

He walked all the way up Bute Street into town. The centre of Cardiff. Striding along St Mary Street, James Howell's imposing white stone building rose into view, with its curved corner, fancy sculptures and carved stone flowers inset between the huge windows. He paused for a moment to gaze up at the pillars; he'd read somewhere that the different styles had names, Doric? Ionic?

Some poncy word ending in '-ic' anyway.

He savoured the moment before going inside and looked around. Away to his left, the walls of Cardiff Castle stood commanding the city, safeguarding its worthy inhabitants. A couple strode past him and went into the shop, the woman all done up in a feathered hat and some long blue get-up which swished around her ankles as she moved. Her escort, in a sharply pressed suit, trilby hat and leather spats carried a cane. Although that was obviously just for show, judging by the way he marched along with his head up in the clouds.

Arrogant sod.

Pushing open the big heavy doors gave George a real buzz dressed in his best trousers and a crisp shirt. The salesman recognised him as he approached. Stopped dusting the white china face of a head which sat on the counter displaying a black trilby.

Might save up for one of those next.

'Good afternoon Sir. Nice to see you again.'

Ready to eat him alive with that slimy smile.

'Uh, yes, good afternoon to you too. I've come with the last payment…'

'…on the silk scarf. I remember Sir. Thought you might come in today. I've got it ready for you.'

He reached under the counter using his hands as if he was playing a rare violin or some such. Flapping them about.

Bloody twerp.

'Thanks.'

George opened his wallet and took out a shilling, the final payment. Tried to make it look as if it was no big deal, hardly glancing at the money as he handed it over. The salesman unfolded the payment slip.

'Mr.?'

'Hodges, George Hodges.'

'Oh yes, that tallies with the name on the slip.'

Course it does, idiot.

He stroked the scarf for a second before folding it up. Then he stopped. Gave George a studied look.

'Actually Sir, before you go, I'd like to see it on you one more time.'

'Alright, if you think that's a good idea.'

The creep came out from behind the counter, with the scarf draped over one arm like a waiter about to serve some fancy dinner. He adjusted a long mirror and stood close by, his head to one side.

Too bloody close.

George took the scarf; weighty and luscious it gleamed under the shop lights like a silver fish. The fringes flopped about between his fingers as he threw it around his shoulders.

Gazing at his reflection he saw the beginnings of how he wanted to look in the future. Like a man who could go anywhere in the world. Like a man with confidence running through his veins. Like a man who knew how to treat a woman. He ran his fingers through his hair; it was a trifle too long, but women seem to like it. Matched with some smart trousers, a sharp shirt with a button-down collar and black bow tie he'd be the real works. Tall and lean and ready to take the world by storm. Twenty years old. Raring to go.

'You can really carry it off, if you don't mind me saying so Sir.'

Too damn right.

Trying not to look at himself too long and hard.

'You'll certainly attract the ladies now with your Mediterranean looks. Although I don't suppose that's a problem for you Sir... very handsome if you don't mind me saying...'

'Well, I'm not actually Mediterranean as such but...anyway... now you mention it', with a little laugh.

The bloke was giving him the heebie-jeebies.

'Would you wrap it up please? I'm in a bit of a hurry.'

Getting back to his post, the shop assistant folded the scarf and put it into a shiny bag before George could say knife. Handed it over with a smirk.

'Of course, I understand Sir. Have a good weekend.'

He picked up his duster, turned away and started sweeping the counter in slow circles, without looking up.

George walked home feeling good. The segs he had nailed into the heels of his best shoes rang out on the pavement as he strolled through the last rays of the sun into the early evening. He nodded to a man turning the 'closed' sign around at Lerman's tailor shop on Bute Street. The man nodded back as he locked and bolted the door.

He could picture Ruby's face when she saw what he had bought. That would cheer her up. Things had really moved on for her since that horrible job in the rag factory when she always came home in a foul mood. She and the other girls had to stand in a smelly basement room sorting out the different clothes and fabrics which were chucked down through a hole in the ceiling.

She would come back in the evenings and go straight to the scullery. Scrubbed herself red raw, she felt that dirty. After a couple of years, she got a nice little office job in Lerman's. She was much happier then and looked so smart when she stepped out for work in the mornings. Used to like making a fuss of him too.

She went out with her friends occasionally. They all got themselves settled after a while, engaged or married. It was a shame she had to give everything up when Mam took to her bed. After all, she was going on twenty-three. Since she had to stay home to look after Mam, she could get into a state over nothing. But seeing him looking all fixed up like one of those guys in the films would surely put a smile on her face. She might even start taking care of her own appearance again.

He heard her banging about cooking supper. Didn't even turn around when he went into the kitchen.

Here we go again.

He went to squeeze her shoulder, friendly-like but that didn't work either. So, he took the scarf out of the bag and tossed around his neck.

'Ta-da! How about this then gal?'

She turned then. Looked him up and down. Nothing.

'Well, do you like it?'

She took on that scrimpy look.

'And how much did that piece of frippery cost?'

'Five bob.'

'Five shillings! That would feed this family for a month. What were you thinking of?'

'Oh, come on Rube, can't you be pleased for your kid brother? I've been paying off for this little beauty since after Christmas.'

'Don't give me that kid brother rubbish. You're only three years younger than me…that don't cut no ice with me anymore.'

'You know me Rube. I like to take pride in myself. Not like some I could mention,' looking her up and down with a sneer.

She stopped for a minute, grabbed a big fork and started mashing the potatoes as if she was mashing his face.

'Who do you think you are anyway, flippin' Rudolf Valentino?'

He dragged off the scarf and threw it back in the bag. Standoff. He stomped off upstairs to see Mam.

The room smelled of sickness. His nostrils twitching, he went across to open the window before getting close to her bed, even though Dad had put an old blanket across the sill to keep out the draught. The stuff of years was everywhere: family photos hung on the wall alongside a fading picture of overblown roses competing with those on the peeling wallpaper and there were ornaments on every available surface. Mam's dressing gown hung from the handle of the wardrobe, although she was unlikely to ever wear it again.

She was sunk into the middle of the old mattress, dozing on and off, intermittently opening and closing her eyes. Her red hair lay like strings of grease across the pillow and her face was damp and pale. She opened her eyes as he came close.

'Well now, there's my lovely boyo.' Her voice thin and her breath coming hot and sour.

'Well now, there's my lovely mam.'

They always said it. Every time. Words fragile as paper. She was lovely once. And the only one who really understood him. Her golden boy, an unspoken knowledge shared. George grinned at her, but his upper lip felt twitchy.

Then she spoke soft, 'You want to comb my hair like you used to love?'

'It's alright Mam, you rest yourself. Anyway, Ruby's got supper ready. I'd better go down and eat before I get into trouble.'

It was as if she couldn't hear. Either that or she wasn't listening.

'My little Lord Fauntleroy you were.'

'I still am. Look what I came to show you, Mam.'

On went the scarf again. She smiled, reached up and touched his cheek.

'There's handsome you look.'

He tried hard to swallow what was rising up in his throat; her teeth were yellowing, the corners of her mouth crusted with dried saliva. Slimy stuff hung between her lips as he kissed her cheek. He walked towards the door; when he looked back her eyes were closed again. He heard Dad's key in the lock and then he and Ruby talking.

Better go down and face the music.

★

'Where's George?'

'Think he went upstairs to see Mam.'

'I didn't see him after work, did he come home early?'

'No, he came in a few minutes ago. Heard him in his room this afternoon. Came in and then straight back out. Went shopping.'

'Shopping? What shopping?'

'You'll soon find out.'

She drained the cabbage and started slicing up the boiled ham. If cut thinly enough there would be enough left for their sandwiches the following day. There was always bread on the table as well to fill up their bellies. Loading and unloading those big ships was hard, heavy work. Dad was used to it, but she often wondered how George managed with his namby-pamby ways. But at least he got out of the house every day. Lucky sod.

'Good day, Dad?'

'Hardly call it good…slaving away for the big man.'

She shook her head and turned back to the stove to finish up the supper, putting a little mashed potato aside in a small bowl for Mam, mixed with cream from the top of the milk to give her when she woke up.

★

Samuel went into the scullery out the back. He was a well-built man, handsome and dark. His frizzy hair was receding at the temples and greyer around the edges than it had been the previous year. Aged forty-three, he looked about eight to ten years younger, despite the air of melancholy defeat which hung about him like a wet rag.

He reached up and adjusted the chain on the gas light. A mean flame quivered about the dark walls as he washed his hands and face at the sink. Glancing through the window he noticed that the old tin bath was hanging by one nail from the wall in the backyard. Needed to be made more secure or it would fall and get dented or may even split apart at the sides. It was probably time to buy another one anyway, he couldn't remember how long they'd had that one. His wife's soiled sheets hung on the washing line like broken bodies swaying in the breeze, with maps of faded blood crawling among the folds.

★

Friday night was family bath time when the kids were young. It took forever to heat up all the pots of water to fill it up. When they were small, Bernadette put both kids in together. As they got older they all took turns: George first, followed by Ruby, then Bernadette and finally himself. The kids always had to be reminded not to pee in the water, but he was never quite sure if they did or not. He would hang a curtain hung across the middle of the parlour on four ceiling hooks put there specially to afford some privacy. Although George would run in and out or pull across the curtain to peep in on his sister. No matter how often he told him off, Bernadette would just laugh and say it was nothing. On the odd occasion they would get in the bath together after the kids were asleep. Good times.

★

He thought about the night they first met. It was New Year's Eve and the turn of a new century. Between the last moments of 1899 and 1900 his life also took a new turn. He had never been a hard-drinking man, but when two of his workmates persuaded him to join them for a drink that night, he was happy to go along.

He noticed her almost immediately they went into the pub, the shiny red curls around her face giving her the appearance of a flaming angel in her green dress. She looked about eighteen, sat in the corner with an elderly couple. He glanced over in her direction several times during the evening, and she met his eyes each time before they both quickly looked away again. His mate Tomos noticed his distraction and kept teasing him, saying he should go across and offer to buy her a drink. But that was not Sam's style; being a shy twenty-year old man he had had little experience or success with girls.

She and her two companions were sitting at a table quite near the gents' toilet. The old man was well away on strong ale well before midnight while the two women were on lemonade and looking embarrassed every time he burst into song, his favourite clearly being The Mountains of Mourne.

The evening progressed and several stouts later Samuel had occasion to pass by their table once or twice. The third time happened to be just as the landlord rang the bell to welcome in the new year. The whole pub erupted into cheers; there was a lot of hugging and kissing. Someone started off the singing: Auld Lang Syne. The old man jumped up and pulled the two women to their feet, putting his arms about them both as he pitched from side to side. Before too long, everyone held hands with crossed arms as they sang, and Samuel found himself holding the younger woman's hand. Her smooth skin was cool to the touch and he held on for a few more moments after the song was finished.

Tomos persuaded him to take advantage of the opportunity and on the first day of the year 1900, Samuel took Bernadette Jones for a walk in Sophia Gardens. He found out later that the elderly couple were her grandparents, visiting from the west of Ireland. Apparently, her mother had become pregnant as a young girl and was sent to England to have her baby to avoid bringing shame on her family. When baby Bernadette was born, she was adopted by a Welsh couple from the valleys and grew up in view of the regal Pen-y-Fan, one of Wales' most stunning mountains. As a child she had no idea that her surroundings echoed the wild beauty of her biological mother's homeland, who had disappeared soon after her birth.

The child's grandparents had spent many years regretting the loss of their daughter and their grandchild. They sought help from The Salvation Army who were finally able to track her down, only to lose her again to tuberculosis. Bernadette had enjoyed a quiet life in the farming community with her adoptive parents but was ready at eighteen to explore the city. She decided to move to Cardiff and began her nursing training at Lansdown Road Hospital. And then she met Samuel.

Her grandparents were happy for her to have met such a hard-working and kind man as Samuel and they returned to Ireland happy after their visit. But her adoptive parents were cautious, their constant refrain being that it was all very well falling in love with a coloured man, who, admittedly seemed like a 'decent enough chap', but what would people think when the children came along? Their decision to marry was met with bad feelings and over the years they ignored their daughter's letters, choosing instead to lose all contact. They refused to visit and had never seen their grandchildren.

A few minutes later Samuel returned and started laying the table. He took off his boots and threw them into the corner ready to be cleaned for the following day. Ruby put her arms around him and held on tight for a minute while her father stood upright and rigid as a board.

Samuel looked across at George as he ate. He could tell that there had been conflict between him and his sister again, as his son stabbed away at the ham and tore his cabbage into bits. Whatever had happened, he was obviously trying to hold it down. Samuel had been worried about the boy ever since he was small. About how charming he could be when it suited him and his way of fooling everyone. About how he would say inappropriate things as a small child and listen in on adult conversations when he should have been doing whatever other kids do. About the way he could still captivate his mother.

Bernadette had always doted on him and made it obvious. Poor Ruby hardly got a look in when they were kids. His wife was fading away day by day and the family was falling apart. The boy was too full of himself and one day it would catch up with him. Samuel sometimes heard other men down the docks teasing George after work when he made a big thing of scrubbing his nails and combing his shiny curls through with grease before walking home. Being quite a private man Samuel tried to ignore them although he thought that before too long he would have to sort one of them out. After all, George was his son.

'Did you hear about the accident on last night's shift?'

George didn't look up as he answered. Carried on eating.

'Yeah, one of the chaps told me.'

'Serious it was. Fella lost his arm,' said Samuel. 'A piece of the lifting machinery fell as they were loading, and apparently what happened was…'

'Yeah, I know, Dad. Johnno told me.'

Samuel watched as Ruby put down her knife and fork and stared at her brother.

'The bosses need to do something quick about that, or there'll be a stink. Some of the others are all for making a proper complaint,' continued Samuel, 'but I told them to keep their heads down or there'd be nothing for any of us. There's plenty of men out there queuing up for work in the mornings. Feel sorry for the chap though. That's him finished.'

George finally looked up from his plate: 'Lose our jobs? Jeezus, that's all we need. The wages are crappy enough as it is. Idiot should have been more careful.'

Ruby started clearing away the table, banging the dishes in her disgust. Samuel left the rest of his food, left the room and trudged upstairs to sit with his wife for a while. George was left to finish his meal alone, before he disappeared outside to the lavatory. An hour later the house was quiet again after he had slipped out through the back door onto the dark street.

Chapter Two

Ruby got things out of the kitchen cupboard to clean their boots ready for the morning. Back in the parlour, she wound up the gramophone and put on Mam's favourite: 'Nobody', sung by Bert Williams, a coloured man from America:

When life seems full of clouds and rain, And I am full of nothin' and pain. Who soothes my thumpin', bumpin' brain? Nobody.

Such a sad song but Mam liked it. The gramophone took pride of place on the sideboard. Dad's friend Jimmy Jacobs had got hold of it on his travels and left it at their house while he was away. Samuel never found out how he came across it and made sure not to ask. They had an understanding that when Jimmy was ashore he could board with them at a reduced rent in turn for letting the family enjoy using it. Seemed like fair exchange, even though they only had a couple of records to play until Jimmy turned up with a few more. It was a monster of a machine made of oak with a big horn on the top. Mam dusted it every day before she became ill.

As she polished, Ruby thought about all those times when Mam would sing along with Bert Williams. Sometimes she would try to persuade Dad to join in too, but he maintained that listening to a coloured man who made his living by blacking up his face and talking in 'plantation speak' onstage to please his white audience was to be pitied more than praised.

And then there was the time when one of the men down the docks gave him a battered copy of *The Whistling Coon*, telling Dad he would probably like it because the singer was 'a coloured chap' like himself. He put it on one evening after supper. When the song was finished, silence fell over the room. Bernadette got up to clear the dishes and Samuel picked up the *South Wales Echo*. She and George were both young then, but Ruby understood that the singer's lyrics accompanied by his jolly whistling were a sad reflection of something which made her feel ashamed. Why would anyone want to sound happy after describing their own features and dark skin with such disgust?

All her little brother could remember was the clever whistling. In bed later, she could hear him practising the tune, trying to improve his own whistling skills. When George asked for it a few days later the record had disappeared.

★

Dad came back downstairs to join her, and Ruby turned down the volume. Samuel picked up his boots and started to clean them while she did George's. It was quiet. Almost companionable.

'Mam sleeping, is she?'

'Yes...don't think it'll be long now, Ruby. Do you understand?'

'Yes Dad,' rubbing hard at the same spot over and over. 'You kids haven't done so badly, have you?'

'No Dad, we've been very lucky...until now, that is.'

'I know your brother doesn't always think so. I mean, you know that me and your mam love you both, don't you?'

She had never heard Dad use that word before. The love word.

'It was different for you though, Dad, wasn't it? Growing up where you did.'

He clammed up again. She was afraid she had lost him and wasn't sure how to continue.

'You mean the Cowbridge Road Homes?'

He had not talked about his childhood for years, Ruby thought.

Not since she and George were children. Even then he didn't reveal very much.

'Well, yes.'

'What was it like?'

'I suppose it wasn't so bad really. Some of the staff there were really kind.'

'Did you have friends?'

'Suppose I must have done. Can't remember.'

'What did you do at weekends?'

'We had to help with the chores on Saturdays and went to church on Sunday mornings. It was OK.'

'St David's? On Cowbridge Road?'

'That's the one. It was nice and peaceful sitting there listening to the vicar. Although we couldn't tell what he was going on about half the time. Remember one year he gave us all an Easter egg.'

'Were you happy, Dad?'

'It was alright. At least we kids were all in it together. To be honest I don't remember that much until I went to the Industrial School.'

'That was up Ely way too wasn't it? I didn't know you went there. It's been closed down for years hasn't it? How old were you then?'

It was a relief to hear him talking more openly than ever before. She wanted to find out more.

'About ten, eleven. All the boys were sent there to learn a trade and the girls did sewing.'

'What did you learn?'

'Oh, lots of things: carpentry, tailoring, shoe-mending. That kind of stuff.'

No wonder he was so good with his hands, she thought. He could fix anything at home. Once he got hold of a job lot of linoleum and created a beautiful floor for the hallway out of the different pieces. It was a kind of collage featuring nautical symbols. She and George used to take turns to polish it on Saturday mornings. And he could sew. Dad could turn the collars on his shirts even better than Mam. She looked at his hands as he rubbed at the steel tips of his boots. Strong. Rough. With long fingers. She read once that this was a sign of creativity. Although the index finger on his left hand was bent and shorter than the others following a work accident from years ago.

Dad had always been a quiet man. Quiet, dignified, and somehow closed off to everyone. Except for Mam. Sometimes Ruby could hear them talking during the night. Dad's voice deep and murmuring. Mam's occasional interjections, her tone soft, sympathetic, reassuring. Ruby couldn't hear the words, but they must have shared things he didn't disclose to anyone else. Her eyelids pulsed as she thought of Mam lying prone in her bed. In no fit state to engage with anyone very much. To hear her father open up to her was precious.

'You're so good at practical things, Dad. Why didn't you get a job doing carpentry or something like that?'

'Couldn't find anything regular, so I had to do bits and pieces. Pick up a bit of work wherever I could.'

'What about loading? On the ships?'

'Well, as you know I can only get casual work there now. Mostly goes to the white chaps. Closed shop.'

'Yes, but George has got a permanent job there, so why…?'

Dad looks up from his cleaning: 'Why do you think? Looking like a white man…'

Ruby put down her work, 'Shall I make a cuppa, Dad? And a piece of fruit cake? I made it earlier for you and George to take with your sandwiches in the morning.'

He continued as they stopped to drink their tea. Dear God, she thought, please let me get through to him. Just like Mam used to.

'When I married your mother, I needed to get some money together, find somewhere to live. This house came up for rent. Been here ever since.'

16

'Is that why you went to sea? Sounds exciting.'

'There was nothing exciting about tramping around the British Isles with ship loads of coal, believe me. But at least the money was regular.'

'That's when you were a stoker?'

'Yes, shovelling coal down in the engine room. Man, that was hot work. It was steady for a while. Sometimes I was away for weeks at a time.'

'So why did you stop?'

'That's when you made your appearance, my girl. I was needed at home.'

'Oh Dad, I didn't realise that.'

'Your mother's always been a bit frail. She couldn't cope sometimes. Especially after George came along too.'

'How did you manage?'

'That's when we started taking in boarders in the back bedroom. Mostly West Indians. And of course, we still have a couple of guys sleeping in the hallway occasionally if they're only ashore for a couple of nights.'

Ruby clicked her teeth. 'Yes, some of the lodgers are easier to put up with than others, that's for sure.'

They looked at one another and grinned. Dad held up his boots against the light, 'Don't look bad, considering they'll be filthy again in ten minutes once I start work tomorrow.'

Ruby held George's boots up too and raised her eyebrows in enquiry. Dad rubbed his chin and shook his head in mock solemnity.

'And that's when you met Jimmy?'

Dad smiled, shook his head from side to side, 'Me and Jimmy go back a long way, despite our age difference. Turned up here from Antigua when he was not much more than a kid. Lied about his age to get aboard ship I believe. Good chap he is. Bit rough round the edges, mind, but he's got a kind heart.'

She looked at him, his head bent over as he put the cleaning rag back in its box, his bald patch on top shining with sweat. No wonder he got fed up. No wonder he pushed them both so hard at school. No wonder he used to take them to The Bute Library whenever he could. He still went by himself sometimes and usually borrowed books about the sea or a romance for Mam. She used to enjoy what she called a 'good family story' if she was in the mood. But those days were gone.

'That's why I'm so proud of you Ruby.'

Proud. All this on top of the L word. She didn't know what to say.

'Proud because you are the brains of this family. When you got that job working for Mr Lerman I was the proudest man in the street.'

The job wasn't that much of an achievement really. Using a typewriter occasionally, adding up a few columns of figures and making tea at the back of a small tailor's shop in Bute Street was hardly a move into the world of big business. Although Mr Lerman did have some rich clients who came from the other side of town to have their suits tailor-made. She enjoyed getting ready for work every day and sometimes talking to her boss and his wife, Rebekah about books and other interesting things. To think that she used to imagine herself running her own business one day. Yet there she was with no job and going nowhere. Most girls her age were married with children if they were not working. Anyway, it had been worth spending all those evenings teaching herself to type on the old Remington that Dad had got cheap from one of his workmates.

'You never said. I didn't realise.'

George had the beauty, she had the brains. It was always the same. She threw down the first boot and picked up the other.

'Well, you're a credit to me. And to your mam. I know it wasn't easy for you having to give all that up to stay home and look after her.'

She thought of the little jacket that had been hanging on

the back of her bedroom door for the four months. Dark green, fitted, with covered buttons and a peplum which played around her waist as she walked. She reached up and tightened her head-wrap as she thought of the efforts she made each day to create Marcel waves to one side of her hair before leaving in the morning. Waves which frizzed up again if she stayed too long in the steamy kitchen.

'I remember when you told me how you got your name – Samuel. After your grandfather wasn't it?'

He wore a little half-smile. And sighed.

'That's right. He was brought here by a rich man from Antigua whose wife couldn't have children. To be a companion for her while he counted his money.'

'Oh yes, I remember you mentioning something about that. How come he was so wealthy?'

'Well, think about it. It was 1807 when slavery was abolished. I worked it all out once. I think he was probably making his last trip to Antigua to wind things up and brought back Samuel, who would have been about seven at the time.'

'He was a slave merchant?'

Samuel nodded, 'Yes.'

Ruby stopped her cleaning.

'What happened to all the money?'

'I've never been able to find out. Somewhere along the way the boy must have squandered it all after the old man and his wife died.'

'Who did he marry? Who was your father?'

'I don't remember my parents. They gave me up when I was just a baby.'

'Crikey Dad, why didn't I ever know all this before? Haven't you ever wanted to find out?'

'What's the point? Too late now anyway.'

'Does George know? What does he think?'

'That's enough now my girl. Enough.'

Samuel sucked his teeth, a habit picked up from the Jamaican men off the ships. He gathered up the cups and took them out to the kitchen.

There was heavy knocking at the front door. 'That must be Jimmy. I heard that the Toledo Star came in today. Thought he might turn up.'

Jimmy had obviously come from the pub; he always came in singing the same words when he'd had a few: When life feels full of clouds and rain…Samuel opened the door to greet him.

'Good to see you again, Jimmy.' The two men clapped one another on the back.

'Yeah, you too, man. Don't suppose your lovely daughter could make me a cuppa tea?'

'Of course, man. Come in. There might even be some supper left. Here, give me your bag.'

★

Samuel could hear Jimmy's chatter and Ruby's quieter responses as he went back up to see his wife. He took up a glass of water and thought she might even be able to try some of Ruby's cake. He opened the door, put the tray down beside the bed and then looked across at her. He saw the trickles of blood on one side of her mouth, down her chin and across the front of her bed-jacket. She was sleeping deeply, her breathing coming in short, quick bursts. He knew it would not be too long before she would be gone.

Gone home.

He kissed her damp face: 'Not long now, love…no more pain, no more sorrow.'

★

'So, Miss Ruby, how's life treatin' you?'

Ever since she had known him, Jimmy had called her Miss Ruby. He'd been boarding at their house about five or six years, since Ruby was about eighteen and Jimmy three or four years older. He had finished his supper and they were drinking tea near the fireplace. They always enjoyed a chat when he turned up. There was no knowing when he was going to come. Sometimes they didn't see him for months. The previous year he only came once and then it was only for a couple of days. But Dad always kept his room free. If other visiting seafarers came along they had to sleep in the sitting room or even in the passage.

Jimmy was easy to listen to, a natural storyteller. He often regaled Ruby with tales of his life on the tramp steamers ferrying coal around Britain, his shipmates or anything that was happening in the wider world. And he always managed to make her laugh. But that evening it felt different somehow. Serious. He sat opposite her, his gaze intent.

Ruby pulled down her cardigan and crossed her legs at the ankles. Tucked her head-wrap more comfortably about her ears. She used only to wear it at weekends, at the market, like a lot of other women, but since she had finished work she wore it most days.

Market day was Saturday, when she bought vegetables for the week. Dad sometimes brought home some meat; he got it from one of the chaps at work who had a contact somewhere or other. When Mam dished up their meals at suppertime, she used to come out with the same standing joke,

'If anyone finds a bit of meat, they have to give it back!' Ruby and Dad would laugh or finish the last three words of her sentence while George sighed. That was the thing about Mam. She always tried to stay positive no matter what. Safe, predictable days they were.

★

Ruby spread her hands, shrugged her shoulders, 'Oh well, you know. It's hard seeing Mam like this. She seems to be getting worse every day no matter what I try.'

'You're a diamond for looking after her the way you do Rube. You're a good woman, you know that?'

'Well who else would take care of her if not me?' her voice sharp. Jimmy reached across and patted her arm. Twice. The second time he let it rest for a moment.

'It's alright Rube. You can always talk to me. That's if you want to.'

'I know, I'm sorry for being such a misery.' She shuffled around in her seat.

'I'll make another pot. Or perhaps you'd like a drop of rum? Think Dad's got a bottle stashed away somewhere. He hides it away so that George doesn't pinch it.'

She went over to the dresser. Rummaged around behind all the old papers and Mam's special things, pulling at her clothes again as she moved, conscious that Jimmy was watching. She was tall for a woman, tall like her father. And well built, strong looking and curvy. She found two of Mam's best glasses and poured them both a small tot of rum.

'Here's to you, Ruby.'

'Thanks Jimmy. Ummm…think I'd better go and check if Dad would like some. After all it's his rum.' She made a move to go towards the door.

Jimmy touched the back of her hand and she let it rest there without moving.

'No worries Rube. I'll nip out and get some more later. Make him res' with your mam before he turns in for the night.'

He held his glass up to the light before taking a sip.

'Man, this reminds me of back 'ome. Plenty a rum there.'

He winked at her and she smiled for the first time that evening.

'We had some good times back home in Antigua. When I was a little kid.'

Ruby settled back in her seat, 'I can't imagine how lovely it must be to live in the sunshine. What did you get up to?'

'Oh, all sorts… After school, I was supposed to go straight

home and sweep the yard for Mama, but more often than not I'd hang about with the other kids down at Nelson's Yard.'

'What's Nelson's Yard?'

'It was the place where you get big boats comin' in. You know, travellers. Wealthy yanks. That type.' He whistled, shook his head, 'Man, some of them boats were real fancy too. We boys would hang about to show folks where they could find the best rum joints nearby. Earned a few dollars that way.'

'Rum joints eh?' Ruby pretended to be shocked, waving her hands in front of her face.

'Had to be done, Rube. Not much money around in those days.' He paused.

'Or we would offer to carry their bags onto the smaller boats that took them on trips around the island, to see Jolly Harbour or Dickenson Bay.'

'Sounds a bit dangerous to me, Jimmy.'

'Yeah, it was certainly dangerous when a fat American lady slipped and fell as she was climbing into a fishing boat to take a little trip.'

'Oh, my goodness. Who fished her out?'

'My friend Horace tried to reach her and slipped between the boat and the harbour wall. Bashed his head. The fisherman got them both out in the end. But Horace was never the same after that, I tell you.'

'That's sad…poor little boy.'

'You know Rube, sometimes the visitors would throw a few coins on the ground and we would scramble to pick it up, all happy like a crowd of grateful puppy-dogs.'

They both went quiet.

'The big man used to get mad when he saw that. A local man he was, like the king of the dockyard to us boys. Used to chase us away. Said we had no pride. But that didn't mean nothing to us kids.'

Ruby took another sip of her rum, rolled it around in her mouth, hot and fiery.

'And what did your mam say when you got back late?'

'Say? She didn't say nothin'. Just give me a clip around the ear as I went to pick up the yard broom.' He laughed, nodded at her and smiled across the rim of his glass.

Ruby grinned and tutted as he chattered on. Jimmy was a stocky man, a bit shorter than her. She noticed how his shirt buttons strained at the seams when he moved. The shape of his thighs as he sat: rounded and firm, his knees large and knobbly-looking, the small bones on his hands rising and falling as he talked. And his face: compassionate, thoughtful, alight, excited, all things at once. A face that her dad would describe as 'a good countenance'.

'…and then, you know, on special days we even climbed all the way up to Shirley Heights. We'd take a picnic too, some fried fish or chicken all wrapped up nice in cloth with bread and bottles of water or home-made lemonade. Rum for the grown-ups. From the Heights you can see all over the island. You can pick out the harbours, the inlets, the beaches, see the fishing boats and the green all around…Yeah man, we did have some good times in beautiful Antigua. My homeland. Perhaps I'll take you to see it all one day, Rube.'

★

Ruby turned around to see Dad standing at the foot of the stairs. She went over to him, searching his face.

'How is she now, Dad? She was very fretful before you came home. Asking for you she was.'

Samuel briefly closed his eyes and shook his head. Then, looking over at Jimmy, 'Any more of that golden stuff left, my brother?'

'Of course, Dad, we've only had a drop…'

Jimmy chipped in, 'Yeah my man, I'll go and get another bottle before I leave. *Toledo Star's* not sailing again 'til Monday, and it's nice to be here enjoying lovely company while I can.'

He glanced at Ruby as he spoke while she busied herself with the chair cushions. Dad smiled and nodded at them both.

Chapter Three

Two months later, the night before the funeral, and Bernadette's coffin was in the parlour, set on top of a wooden trestle. She was dressed in what looked like a white nightgown with lace around the neck, an unlikely outfit for someone who liked to look good despite financial constraints. She was a dab hand at sewing and could make something stylish out of any old hand-me-down. One of the neighbours once gave her an old coat and she cut it down to make a cape with a matching muff for six-year-old Ruby. Family life was measured by the time before she got sick and then everything else afterwards.

Ruby tried to move the stiff lace away from Mam's soft face and neck. The people at Beston's Funeral Parlour had done their best but she didn't look the same. Peggy came in from next door to help add the finishing touches. She carried a little bag full of creams and make-up. She was always called upon at such times down the bay. She began by applying dabs of cream under Mam's eyes, working it in as she talked.

'Want your mam to look her best don't we, Rube?'

Ruby stood back as Peggy opened a tub of bright red grease.

'Yes, you're right Peg. I'm not so sure about that red stuff though…'

Peggy carried on working.

'Oh, don't you think so? Thought we could use some on her lips. She always loved bright colours your mam.'

'It might make her look a bit…you know.'

Peggy stopped then, put down her things and held her arms out to Ruby. It felt good to be hugged so tightly.

'You're right love. Not so good against her pale Irish skin. Have you got anything we can put on her hair? Make it a bit shinier?'

Ruby went off and came back with George's pomade. Peggy opened it and sniffed.

'Um, smells a bit rich. Only the best for your brother eh?'

Ruby took Mam's comb from the vanity set on her dressing table and started to comb her mother's hair. Very slowly.

'I always wanted Mam to do my hair like this. You know, gentle like.'

'You've got your dad's hair, thick and curly. And his dark colouring. Not like George.'

Ruby nodded, 'Yes…and getting my hair plaited for school every day was a flippin' nightmare.'

She applied some pomade – not too much – and kept combing.

'Mam and Dad called me Ruby because they thought I would inherit her red hair when I was born. But within a few weeks it got darker and frizzy.'

She dropped the comb on the chair went across the room to the chiffonier. Peggy picked it back up and watched as Ruby gazed in the mirror, turning her head from one side to the other.

She spoke as if to her own reflection, 'I would sit between her knees as she struggled with my kinks. She used to whistle sad Irish tunes, that she had learned at school. I could feel her breath on my scalp. When it was finished she usually made a little sigh and told me to get my coat.'

Peggy listened. 'I like the Marcel waves you've put in today though, Rube.'

'Mmm, thanks.'

She continued, 'And when it was George's turn she usually just ran her fingers through his curls before shooing him away. With that special smile.'

One of the men from Bestons struggled to quieten two white horses pawing at the ground as the tall feathers on their heads swayed in the sunshine. The carriage which would carry Bernadette Deirdre Hodges to her rest was draped in black and bunches of flowers lay on the pavement ready to be set around her.

Inside the house the family gathered to say their last goodbyes. Mr Beston himself waited quietly near the parlour door waiting for an appropriate time to screw down the lid on her coffin. Ruby looked across to where Dad sat beside his wife, inert and silent since the early hours of the morning when the last of the visitors left. Neighbours had called during the previous evening to pay their respects. A few of the older men stayed on to talk and reminisce. Ruby didn't have the heart to ask them to leave. She knew the importance of funerals as social occasions. Her father had hardly slept in forty-eight hours. She noticed Mr Beston glancing at his watch.

'Don't you think we should go soon, Dad?'

George chipped in, quick as a flash, 'Yes Dad, think Mr Beston needs to get us on our way.'

Samuel finally lifted his head, looked at them both one by one and nodded. He stood up, leaned over and kissed Mam on her stiff lips. Ruby kissed her cheek. George paused, then stroked her hair. Turning away he left the room and stood out in the passage as Mr Beston covered Mam's face for the last time, with Ruby and his father standing by watching. He looked back to see them holding hands and weeping without sound. Ruby took her handkerchief and dabbed Dad's eyes.

He stood quite still as he observed.

Jeez, can't stand this. What will they be like by the time they get to the church? Last night was bad enough, with Dad just sitting there and not talking to anyone. And Ruby running around like a blue-arse fly dishing out the food as people brought it. This morning even more food turned up. Booze too, for the wake.

The carriage and horses look grand enough. Flowers all over the place. And that heavy silence of the women. Mam's certainly getting a good send-off. Wonder where Dad found the money. Perhaps you can pay off for funerals like you can for new clothes.

He remembered how it used to be with himself and Mam. She loved it when folks commented on his looks. Whenever Peggy from next door dropped in he'd have to stand up on a chair and sing All through The Night. He was one of the few children in his class who could remember almost all the verses in Welsh: Ar hyd a nos.

But she'd shush him if Dad came in: 'That's enough now my love.'

He couldn't understand why at the time. When she took him and his sister up to the market she would gently push him forward. Presenting him to the world. He could still feel the sensation of her hand against the small of his back. Ruby would hide behind Mam's coat when he started showing off. Sometimes he didn't feel too good about it as he got older. Especially when he saw how his sister's life had changed over the last few months.

He was tired. And all for what? When Mam was well she kept him going. It was her love and attention that made him feel good. When she took to her bed, it became increasingly difficult to maintain that sense of strength, power and pride that only she could give. He knew that some people held a dim view of him and all of them thought he was full of shit. But they didn't understand, he had dreams, aspirations. There was a lot more to life than working down the docks. The world was a big place and he was determined to see it. With Mam gone and he was on his own. Ruby had Dad, who did he have?

Nobody. Just like the song.

Once Mam's coffin was on the carriage, Mr Beston led the way as the procession started to walk towards St Mary's Church. Samuel and his family walked behind, and people fell into place as they progressed. They had only gone about twenty yards when

Mr Beston stopped. He held up his right hand and put it to his ear with a theatrical flourish. Music could be heard from a little further along the street.

Despite the sadness of the day, a sigh of pleasure laced its way through the crowd. They all wondered when it would happen. After all, funerals down the bay were renowned for it and the leader of the marching band was well known. It was said he had even spent a few years playing at the famous Cave of the Golden Calf in London until it closed down. Tommy Pinkerton, known to everyone as Pinkie, had duly risen to the occasion. A self-taught guitarist, he wore his signature black tailcoat and a colourful cravat. He was the only man, apart from Mr Beston of course, who could wear a top hat with such style. Although his funeral outfit certainly looked as if it had weathered many such occasions, being more of a dark, faded green than black. He was an imposing- looking man, his skin smooth, tan and shiny and he took his role in the community as seriously as was expected.

He opened with a long introduction of some basic blues chords. Two trumpeters added a simple theme. Another guitarist, a violinist and at the end of the line-up a man wearing a large drum all took up the tune. Someone in the crowd produced a pair of spoons from his pocket and joined the rest of the band. The blues grew into a march of sad joy, interspersed with flying solos as the drummer's assertive rhythm kept them all in order.

Pinkie and his band marched at the front. Street doors opened and whole families joined in all the way up to St Mary's Church. Children ran alongside and most of the mourners walked in time to the music. Some elderly couples, being unable to walk the distance to church, danced a dignified two-step on the pavement as everyone passed by.

Once they got to church, Pinkie took off his hat and bowed low before Samuel and his family. Later the hat would be passed around so unobtrusively that unless you knew the tradition you would almost think you'd imagined it. Everyone loved a good funeral, especially when Pinkie took centre stage.

The coffin was taken down from the carriage. George and five other men lined up in position and carried Bernadette into church, followed by Ruby on her father's arm. The band stayed outside until the coffin was set in place and the congregation was seated. One by one each instrument grew quiet and stopped until all that could be heard was Pinkie playing his singular, original blues refrain.

★

The house was full. There were even folks sitting or standing around on the pavement outside. Lots had brought their own chairs and were settling down for the long haul. A festive atmosphere developed as late afternoon turned into evening. The domino players formed a little group a short way off and others got together to chat or sing. Pinkie was always happy to take requests. There was seemingly no end to his repertoire. Two elderly sisters who lived nearby, famous for their lively renditions of popular songs sang Wait 'til the sun shines Nellie. Ruby smiled as 'Mr Spoons' ran off to get his instruments from his jacket pocket, so he could join in too.

An elderly couple who had been dancing as the funeral procession went by earlier were sitting in quiet dignity in one corner of the parlour being plied with rum punch. Pinkie went across and bowed low before inviting them to dance a quadrille. Only a few of the local elders could still remember how to do it, but they were soon joined by three more couples who rose stiffly to their feet with plenty of encouragement from everyone else. Pinkie began the first few notes of Hill an' Gully Rider and started to sing. Before long the other musicians joined in, the drum supporting with a soft mento rhythm in keeping with the gentility of the dance. When it came to the words at the end of each line he paused so that people could sing out: Hill an' Gullee.

The dancers conducted themselves with grace and proud smiles. Each man held one arm behind his waist as the women pinched their skirts and twirled in sedate manner until being approached by their partners. It was no coincidence that they were all dressed similarly, the men in red sashes and the women's full skirts in bright Jamaican plaid with their frilly cotton petticoats on show. The quadrille was an echo of the slaves' quaint mimicry of the minuet as performed by plantation owners and their wives in the relentless heat of the Caribbean sun not so many years previously.

After their first dance a man sitting in the corner started to sing another favourite: Dis long time gal me never see you. Before too long the dancers were persuaded to stay on the floor as the musicians picked up the accompaniment. One old lady had to sit down half way through and Ruby rushed across to flag her face with a newspaper. The show over, Pinkie and his band followed on with some twelve-bar blues and a couple of men took turns to add their own questionable lyrics about the wiles of fickle women before making way for a young Irishman straight off one of the ships who sang a sad lament.

Ruby was busy serving food and drinks while Samuel sat alone. If folks went up and spoke to him he would chat and nod, but mostly they understood his need just to sit. He chose to be quite a solitary person, but he was well known and respected as an honest man who kept a good home. But as for his son, there was often a lot of gossip.

The domino game ended in much back slapping and laughter. One of them, James, came up to where Sam sat in composed silence and put his arms around him.

'We just goin' off down the pub for a while brother, but we soon come back.'

Sam responded with a tight smile and touched James' hand. As the domino players went through the passage and outside to the street, their loud voices resonated off the walls of the old houses until they faded away.

★

George first noticed her talking to old Mr Lerman. He could see she was not like any of the girls he saw down to the bay on Saturday nights in any of the many local drinking places. There were loads of pubs in the area, practically one on every corner and they were all busy, their patrons being seafarers from across the world. And plenty of women looking for some excitement. George had had his share of girls over the years. He smirked to himself as he thought of the sweet little thing he'd met a few days previously. Meek as a lamb. And a sucker for a bit of flattery.

But this one was different. Looked as if she might have a few bob too judging by the way she was dressed. Wearing some long slinky get-up. Even though it was quite loose you could see her shape and glimpse her legs clad in silk stockings as she walked across the room right in front of him. Not so much walked as swivelled. The dress was trimmed with fur around the neck. She had taken her hat off and threw it on the windowsill. Big job it was and that was trimmed too. Didn't seem to want to talk to the other women much either. Could mean she was either married, engaged or some such. He wondered what she was doing at Mam's funeral.

Worth a try anyway.

'Hello, can I get you a drink?'

She turned as if surprised,

'Oh yes, thank you. I'll have some lemonade please.' Her voice like a bell and seriously posh. Her hair, her pale skin, her smile…

Hell's bells – like a bloody film star.

'Nothing stronger?'

She put her head on one side and touched his lapel, 'Oh no, a lady must keep her dignity at all times.'

Man, she was really something. Not quite sure which way to go with this one.

'Of course. You sit there and look pretty,' as he fetched a chair. 'Won't be long.'

He went into the kitchen and found one of Mam's best glasses, gave it a quick rinse and filled it with lemonade. There was an apple nearby, so he sliced off a couple of chunks and put them in too.

A bit grand like, for a bird like her.

When he got back she was sitting down with her long legs crossed to one side.

Miss Smooth and Shiny. Classy.

'So, Mr Handsome, I'm Rachel. And you are…?'

'George.' He shook her hand. 'I saw you talking to Mr Lerman. Have you got other friends here?'

'Mr Lerman? That's my father. I didn't know anyone else here. But now I do, don't I?'

She was openly staring at him. Looking him up and down. The way a man looks at a woman.

'And what about you? Do you know anyone?'

Have to be a bit smart now.

'Umm…a few people, yes. It's quite hot in here. Shall we go out for some fresh air?'

'That sounds like a good idea. All rather grim in here don't you think?'

She put her hat back on as they went through the passage. Ruby was passing through with a tray of sandwiches and he averted his face as she approached. He could feel her watching him as he put his hand on Rachel Lerman's waist and they stepped outside.

★

Most of the funeral guests had left when George came back several hours later. Ruby and Peggy were clearing away the dishes and a couple of men were still talking in the parlour. A dice game had been set up, so there was no knowing how long they would be staying. Samuel had gone to bed. Ruby heard the front door. She came out into the hallway and stood at the bottom of the stairs with her arms folded before he could creep off to his room. She looked tired. Her mouth tight with disappointment and distaste, she looked him up and down. For once he didn't even try to placate her.

She spoke quietly, her voice a monotone, 'You know who she is don't you?'

George's eyes slid about, 'What do you mean, course I do.'

'Rachel Lerman. The daughter of my old boss.'

'So? Do you know her?'

Ruby shook her head, 'Of course I don't know her. Just met her the once. I only worked in the back office. Remember? My job? The one I gave up to take care of Mam?'

'So, you never knew her then?'

'Why would I? She was Miss High and Mighty who had been sent off abroad to study. Pictures of her all over the desk in the old man's office. She'd be hardly likely to talk to me anyway. And you left your mother's funeral to go off with her. That's overdoing it even for you.'

George flushed and started to take off his jacket, 'I just couldn't take it, Rube, and…'

'You couldn't take it? You sad bugger. And how do you think Dad feels? And me?'

He leaned against the wall and put his hands up to his head. Nothing to say.

She's bloody right. As bloody usual.

'And you, Mam's little golden boy. This was the last thing you could do for your mother. Being there. For her.'

'Oh, that's not fair, Sis. Look can we talk tomorrow?'

'Fair? Fair? What do you know about what's fair?'

He stepped past her and started upstairs. Ruby went back into the kitchen where Peggy put her arms around her, 'Your mam had a good send-off anyway Rube. We all made sure of that. You've done well, lovely.'

Within half an hour, the clearing away finished and the last loiterers gone, Ruby retired to bed. Too tired to sleep and too tired to cry any more tears.

Chapter Four

Rachel was certainly fun. She enjoyed taking George around to unfamiliar places. He was in his element as his hometown took on a new dimension. Sometimes they walked around the gardens of the castle before crossing the street to the Angel Hotel. There they would sit upstairs in the grand coffee room to take afternoon tea, complete with pieces of cake accompanied by tiny forks. At least George learned what to do with the fork. The first time they went he waited until he saw Rachel use it to cut her cake in small pieces as she ate, while making frequent dabs at the sides of her mouth with the starched napkin.

He remembered the impact that building always made on him when he could only view it from the outside. Tall and cream, the pillars at the entrance challenging the unworthy to walk through its portals. He would pass by slow enough to glance inside at the marbled floor until the doorman looked hard at him and he slunk away. As a fifteen-year-old he had walked uptown to watch troops from one of the Welsh regiments parade past the hotel and through the city as they returned home from The Great War. That was probably the first time he had seriously considered the world outside of his own narrow environs and he knew then that one day he would see it. He would see it all.

★

One Saturday in early August Rachel arranged to meet him earlier than usual on the corner of Queen Street opposite the castle. Told him to wear his best clothes because she was taking him somewhere really special. He saw her leaning against the wall as he walked up; she had turned to one side and didn't notice him. He noted the gentle swell of her hip under a dress covered in a design of yellow and blue flowers. She wore lace gloves; her arms were bare, and she carried a small yellow bag of some shiny fabric that shimmered in the early evening sun. She took off her hat and shook her hair from side to side, then smoothed it as if she were stroking a kitten. George had never seen her look so beautiful. Even so, one way or another he knew it couldn't last. Regardless of her being so affectionate and lovely.

She chattered away as she led him towards The New Theatre. 'Oh, darling George, I just know that you will absolutely adore what we're going to see this evening.' She had a way of talking loudly when excited, interspersed with little laughs and 'oh my goodness-es'. People passing by probably thought she was nuts.

'Sounds good to me my dear. You're the lady in charge,' his voice stilted, awkward.

The only time he felt completely relaxed in her company was when they were alone. He knew exactly how to keep her quiet then. Not that they had much opportunity to be on their own. He had been to her house two or three times when her mam and Dad were not at home, but not often.

Not often enough dammit.

Her family lived up in Llandaff. Their big house was set back from a quiet road with a smooth sweeping lawn, closely attended by the gardener. She wanted for nothing, whereas George was fast running up credit with the creepy bloke in Howells for more expensive clothes in order to keep up with her style. He brought them home and hid them in the wardrobe. When he got ready to go out he tried to make a quick exit in the hope that Dad or his sister might not notice what he was wearing. But, of course

Ruby caught him out sometimes. Kept reminding him how Mr Lerman used to talk about his daughter and how she was the apple of her father's eye, and God forbid if he ever found out that his darling girl was slumming it with the likes of him.

At the theatre, they followed the steward upstairs to their seats, went through a door and into one of the small balconies overlooking the stage. There were four chairs, with plush red seats and gilded golden arms. Rachel must have paid for all four tickets, because nobody else came to join them and the stalls below were full of people talking quietly and rustling their programmes. They looked like posh types who were used to the theatre: well dressed and confident. The air was palpable with muted excitement as they waited for the curtain to rise. George looked around him as they waited. The dark red velvet swags and the gold painted flowery motifs on the walls were unlike anything he'd ever seen. He settled back into his chair and raised his eyebrows at Rachel.

Man, this is the life.

The curtain rose on a grand piano set centre stage. The audience fell silent until the great man himself strode on and stood beside it. Jelly Roll Morton. He was a tall light-skinned brown man, his hair slicked back and stiff. Dressed in a sharp suit with a high collar and a bow-tie. He introduced himself as the man from Louisiana who had 'created jazz'. The audience went wild, clapping and calling out and some even got to their feet. And all this before he even sat down to play a note. George was fascinated by his southern drawl, his stage presence, the effect the man had on them all.

He acknowledged their response, slowly sat down at the piano and was quiet and still for a moment or two. He named his first tune: King Porter Stomp in that rich voice before his hands began to dance across the keys. George knew he was experiencing something which he would always reach out for in his life. Jazz.

The following piece was a blues. The tune, the chords and the slower tempo reminded him of Pinkie's playing at Mum's funeral.

Jazz. He whispered the word to himself saying it just as Jelly Roll Morton had. Rachel couldn't keep her upper body still while he tried to measure out the rhythm of each tune on the sides of his chair. The power of the chords and the ripples of the higher notes bounced around in his head as they left the theatre. Rachel studied him, held his hand and smiled.

★

Wherever they went she always paid the bill; it was an unspoken agreement. At first George didn't quite know how to accept her generosity but it soon became the norm. She often regaled him with stories of her adventures in Italy, France and Switzerland. He decided that she could well afford to pay. It gave her a lot of pleasure after all. And he certainly knew how to please her in his own way. He only had to smile in her direction and she was his for the taking. Occasionally they went to the pictures, the Capitol or the newly opened Park Cinema to see Hollywood films. America had sold itself to the world as the promised land and George yearned for its magic.

Chapter Five

Ruby was washing down the draining board. It had been over two months since Mam's funeral and Dad had hardly got out of bed. It was as if all the breath had been sucked out of him. His job was beginning to look risky, because he wasn't getting out early enough to queue up down the docks every morning. She didn't have the heart to tell him that money was running short and she was having to economise even more than usual to make the food go around. As for George, he was worse than useless. When she approached him he just kept saying that he had his own debts. She'd seen the fancy clothes he stashed away in his room and how he sneaked out every evening all done up like the cock of the walk. He must think she fell off a bloody Christmas tree. He was still seeing Rachel Lerman no doubt, but it wouldn't be long before Miss High and Mighty put two and two together.

Thank God Jimmy turned up when he did a few days previously. He saw the whole picture. She didn't have to spell it out. He made an off-hand comment about Mam's favourite cup and saucer that stood on top of the dresser, gave her a wink and touched the side of his nose. He managed to persuade Dad to go to the pub that evening and told Ruby to make sure she dusted Mam's top shelf while they were gone. That's when she found two ten-shilling notes in the cup. The following morning Jimmy and Dad got up early and went down to the Pierhead Building to the shipping office. Apparently, Jimmy went into a private room with one of the officers while Dad waited outside. God knows what they talked about in there, but the other bloke came out looking none too pleased. The upshot was that Dad got his job back, provided he pitched up on time every morning without fail.

When Ruby asked him the next day about what had happened behind closed doors, Jimmy responded by saying that he'd told the boss how respected Samuel was among the other men. And how it looked bad for the company that there had recently been yet another serious accident.

'It didn't do no harm to remind the big man he could be on dangerous ground.'

She was not sure what to make of his comment but thought it best to leave it. Plus, Dad got a bit shirty when she started asking questions.

It had been five days since Jimmy came. And a couple of months since the time before. He would probably be gone again soon. She had thought about a lot of things since his last visit. The way he looked at her, the sense of his touch on her arm, her hand. As if she was seeing him for the first time. Really seeing him. He was a good man. A kind, thoughtful man. But what if his kindness was simply that and no more? She didn't want to come across as desperate. And she certainly didn't need any man's attention out of pity.

Since Mam went, her time had been taken up with taking care of her father. She was tired. More than that, she was weary. Weary of trying to make sure he ate regularly. Weary of trying to coax him out of bed and go to work. Weary of trying to engage him in conversation while she jabbered on about nothing at mealtimes. Nothing seemed to motivate him. Nothing. That was until dear Jimmy pitched up and took up the reins.

Peggy from next door had been dropping hints about Jimmy for months. Told Ruby to sort herself out and it was time she got herself a man. Told her she 'could do worse' than Jimmy. Whatever that meant. Peggy was a good sort, but maybe she should look at her own marriage; her husband Charlie was at the pub every night and up to no good by all accounts. She shook her head. Having unkind thoughts about someone else didn't help.

★

She recalled a night, years ago when she and George were young. She must have been about twelve and George was nine. Her brother was sleeping but she couldn't settle. She lay in the dark and listened as Mam and Dad put on some music. The tune was one of their favourites: I wonder who's kissing her now. Mam started singing along with the introduction in that shaky voice she used when she wanted to sound like a real singer. She heard Dad giving one of his quiet, deep laughs but after a while he joined in on the chorus, his warm, bass voice alongside hers. When the singing stopped Ruby could hear Mam's slippers shuffling across the floor. She got out of bed and looked through the banister railings and watched as her parents held each other and danced.

She dried her hands and switched on the gramophone for the first time since the funeral, hunted around and found what she was looking for, 'A Good Man is Hard to Find'. She put it on and stood there smiling as she listened to the lyrics advising any woman who had a good man to hold onto him.

The front door slammed, and she heard Jimmy and Dad talking in the passage. Quickly turning off the music she returned to her chores.

Dad came in and put on the kettle, while Jimmy wandered over to the gramophone.

'So, Miss Ruby, you takin' in some nice music while you work eh?'

She felt the back of her neck getting hot. 'Yes…just thought Dad might like to hear some of Mam's tunes. Might cheer him up.'

'Yes he loves his music, doesn't he? And you too?'

'Yes, we all do. Thanks for letting us use your gramophone

Jimmy. And bringing us so many lovely songs. It brought Mam so much joy.'

'My pleasure, Miss Ruby.'

Chapter Six

It was a warm night for September. A noise from downstairs disturbed Ruby from her sleep. She lay still for a moment and listened again. It was probably nothing. She took a sip of water from the glass beside the bed, turned over and tried to get comfortable. She had been finding it difficult to sleep over the last few weeks. Ever since Mam's passing. There was so much to think about: her brother's behaviour, Dad's grief and thoughts about what may lay ahead for her.

She got out of bed as raw daylight began to seep through the windows, pulled at the curtain and looked outside. The street was quiet except for a few men going off towards the docks to queue up in the hope of getting some loading work for the day. With their heads down they hardly conversed, each one thinking his own thoughts and carrying his own pain. The sound of their boots echoed across the street. The only other noise was that of gulls' plainsong as they drifted about the vast steel hulks. Bird and man searching for scraps.

There it was again. It sounded like the squeak of the under-stairs cupboard being pulled open. She stood on the landing, looked over the banisters and watched as George dragged a bulky bag from the far reaches of the cupboard before turning the bakelite handle with care to close it again. Then he paused. Unsure if he heard her step, she hid behind the wall and peered out quickly. He took a handkerchief from his pocket and rubbed at the dust on the bag, straightened his jacket and looked at his reflection in the hall mirror, turning his head to one side and adjusting his collar. Ruby began to walk down towards him and he stopped. Neither of them spoke.

She went up close and re-arranged the scarf around his neck and lifted some of the shiny tassels in one hand. Used them to dab her eyes. He touched her face and went to the front door. Their eyes flickered together for a second before he turned the key in the lock and was gone.

Ruby stared at the door; she picked at the paint peeling around the edges of the frame until her nails were thick with the dark red colour of it. Like dried blood. The ledges around the four rectangles were layered faintly with dust brought in from the street. Why hadn't she noticed that before? Mam would never have let the place get so dusty. She went into the scullery, found a cloth and dampened it under the running cold tap. Minutes later, her father appeared on the landing. He watched her for a moment and then slowly came downstairs and stood up close behind her.

'Ruby? Why you doing that now, girl, don't you know what time it is?'

She did not turn around. The dust gone, she scraped at a patch of paint, wiped it down and moved on to the next. Scraping, then wiping, scraping then wiping. She worked in silence, her shoulders shaking.

'What's going on? Where's your brother? Ruby?'

She turned around and the cloth dropped to the floor as she put her bloodied hands on his shoulders and wept.

Chapter Seven

It had been more than three weeks since George went. No explanation. No note. Nothing. Ruby relived that moment of his leaving over and over. The look on his face when she saw him: guilty, sad, yet he still wore that slight upturn at the edges of his mouth. Almost a sneer. Selfish pig.

Dear God, what happened? Why couldn't she have guessed what he was planning? Why hadn't she noticed the bag at the back of the cupboard when she got out the dustpan and broom? Why in heaven's name had he not talked to her?

They used to be close when they were younger, even though Mam clearly favoured him. She enjoyed helping to take care of him when he was just a small, lively boy with a knack for pleasing people. Even quite proud of him sometimes. It saddened her to think of the man he grew into. But she always had Dad on her side. She knew he valued her brains and loved it that he noticed when she tried to be kind and helpful. Kept her going that did when George went too far and made her feel like a dark, ugly lump.

So bloody nice of George to wait until Dad was back at work. Every time she tried to talk to him about George he clammed up or started slamming things about. He probably got a lot of stick from the other chaps down the docks too. And just when he was getting himself together again thanks to Jimmy, who helped her too in the few days he had stayed last time.

Jimmy had persuaded her to write to Mr Lerman asking if he had any work. She got a nice letter back saying that he would arrange for her to come in for a chat. Said he was thinking of expanding his business and might have some typing work. But after George went she heard nothing more. It must have all come out about his daughter's shenanigans. There was probably hell to pay. And she was sick of people asking about George in the street, in the market, even when she was scrubbing the front step on a Saturday afternoon, for God's sake.

★

'So, how you coping then, lovely?'

Peggy was sitting opposite Ruby in Dad's chair, legs tucked up beneath her, hands wrapped around the teacup, her lean frame sunk into the cushions. She had always been thin, even as a small child. Thin and pale. She scampered and scuttled through life, her blue eyes constantly darting about, seeking to alight on anything worth further investigation.

She was making herself comfortable for a long visit, by the looks of her.

Ruby detected a hint of pleasure in her friend's consoling words. Peggy's funeral voice she called it. Maybe it had become a habit, since she was always the one called in to help fix up dead female bodies in the neighbourhood. Good at it she was too. Although she could be a bit heavy-handed with the rouge.

Their friendship had been through various stages since they were kids. They were in the same class at South Church Street School. In the playground, six-year-old Peggy was the one who sat on the wall showing other girls how to do finger knitting. One day she came into school with an extra cotton reel for Ruby. She'd got her dad to put four small nails around the hole, so it was ready to use. She'd also brought an extra length of wool for her. They would sit side by side making long woollen snakes which curled around their ankles and feet, while the boys raced about slamming into one another.

Then there was the Whitsun Treat when all the Sunday School children went out for the day. She never knew who organised the lorries which collected them from outside the church. The open trucks were loaded up with church pews and Sunday school chairs. Rows of excited children gazed out as they were trundled along through the dull streets and out into open spaces or parks and brought back again in the early evening. Tired and happy. Some children had eaten their ration of a sandwich and a Welsh cake bun in a paper bag before they arrived at Lisvane where they would race and play all day. Peggy was the one to go to if you got stung by a nettle. She collected dock leaves to rub on the sore spot and soothe away the pain.

Ruby recalled how it was when they were both working in the rag factory before she got the job at Lerman's. All girls suffering together, in the same boat, female comradeship, having a laugh despite the odds. All that malarkey. Then Peggy's whole life changed in a year.

Her mother, who had always been regarded as a quiet, mousey sort of woman suddenly upped and ran off with an English man who was in Cardiff on business for a couple of weeks. It transpired later that they were sharing a bungalow somewhere near the sea on the south coast. In a place called Margate. And apparently, she was very happy thank you very much and told her husband so in the one letter she wrote from her idyllic new life. Peggy's father disappeared soon afterwards. Whether it was in search of his wife or perhaps due to the nasty rumour which quickly spread about the unhealthy interest he began to take in his daughter after his wife's leaving, nobody knew.

Then Peggy met Charlie. They got together and married quite quickly, but their baby boy died in his sleep one night when he was only days old. Peggy had had a difficult pregnancy and delivery and couldn't have any more babies. She and Charlie both went off the rails after that. Down the pub most nights, Peggy all done up in heavy make-up and laughing loudly with the men, while Charlie gazed a bit longer than he should at other women.

That was when one of the girls remarked on her make-up and asked if she would help tidy up her once glamorous granny on the day of her funeral. Make her look nice when folks came in to pay their last respects before the coffin was nailed down. That was how it all started, and Peggy ended up doing it for other families down the bay thereafter. Ruby noticed how much her friend enjoyed being indispensable. Death gave her a role in the community, fell into step beside her and kept on walking.

When Ruby first got the job at Lerman's, things changed. Peggy wasn't that interested and was often too busy if Ruby suggested they take a walk up to the park or go to the pictures. But when Mam got sick, Peggy was in and out of the house, bringing soup, kind words and solace, her position secured. She rarely mentioned Charlie, whom it was rumoured had been seen with a pretty girl who came down from the valleys every weekend to drink down the bay with the boys. Then the girl suddenly disappeared and there was talk of a baby on the way.

Peggy was probably wondering how she could carry on helping after Mam's passing. She'd been a bit short when Ruby told her how kind Jimmy had been.

'Jimmy's been so helpful, but you know Peg, got to carry on. Can't do more than that.'

'So, what are your plans? Do you think there's any vacancies in the rag factory? We used to have such a laugh, didn't we, Rube?' Her voice an octave higher than before.

'Oh, I wouldn't go back there. Not anymore. Those days are over.'

Peggy shifted her legs, sat up straighter, put down her cup.

'Well you can't go back to Lerman's can you? After everything that's happened with his precious daughter and your brother... Although, I'm sure Mr Big Man Jimmy will have some bright ideas.'

'Yes, he did suggest I should write to Mr Lerman to see if…' She paused. 'What with George gone, me and Dad were wondering what could go wrong next. Then a letter came from Jimmy. Addressed to me. Will I show you what he wrote?'

'Alright, go on then. Let's see what Mr Clever-Dick has to say for himself.'

'It's the first personal letter he's every written me.'

'Is that so? Go and get it then.'

Ruby went upstairs to get the letter from her bedside drawer. Peggy was definitely being touchy. After all they had been through together. Ruby held out the letter. Peggy took it quickly and read it just as fast, pursed her lips and handed it back.

Dear Miss Ruby,

I hope this letter finds you and your dad both well, although when I heard about your brother's leaving, I could not believe it. What is wrong with that boy? I don't want to say too much because he is your kin but, man wait until I see him face to face. Ruby, you have been on my mind. I have seen you grow into a brave and lovely woman and I want to help you as much as I can. Not just because of what happened to your mam, but because I have strong feelings for you. You must have guessed that by now. I know I'm not as clever as you, but I would be honoured if you could find it in yourself to have feelings for me too. There, I've said it, Lord help me.

When I lay down in my bunk last night I was thinking, maybe you should drop in and see your old boss. Just check if he have any work for you again, even though he didn't reply to your letter before. Might be different by now. You're a clever girl and deserve to be working, using that clever brain of yours. Don't try, don't get Miss Ruby! Forgive me if I'm being too forward, but maybe you might consider all what I have said.

All good, Jimmy xx

PS: My letter-writing not too good, but don't be too hard on me girl! And don't you worry too much about that scatterbrain brother of yours, he soon come back with his tail between his legs. JJ.

'Alright for some, I must say. Looks like we'll have you married off in no time.'

Peggy got up and went to the window. 'Think I'll be getting back now. Charlie will be home soon for his tea.'

Ruby reached across and touched her on the forearm. 'Why don't we have a slice of that cake you brought first, Peg? And I'll put the kettle on. It's still early.'

A few minutes later the two women were sitting in silence with their tea and cake.

Chapter Eight

Ellis Island, New York

Downstairs to steerage was to the voyage from hell; George hardly talked to anyone much of the time. He lay in the belly of the ship feeling sick, sleeping and trying to hold on to his bag. Wasn't going to let any of those dirty bastards touch his things. Three long weeks of other people's sweat and anxiety making him retch every time he moved in his bunk. They all stank and by the end he did too. So much for trying to keep himself nice for his big adventure.

It was mid-morning on Ellis Island. George looked up from the pier to the grand entrance of the Immigration building. It bore an imposing looking welcome, but he had to admit to himself that he was scared and confused.

Shit-scared.

For two pins he could have cried. His legs were trembling after being on the crowded barge which had brought them from the Adriatic to the pier. Different voices and languages echoed and shouted across him. A woman beside him tilted into his shoulder before falling softly at his feet.

What's her problem for God's sake?

He and her man picked her up. Grabbing her steaming armpits making him flinch, his nostrils stretching against the smell.

Jeezus, like rotting fruit up the market at the end of the day.

Two little kids were clutching at her clothes, making him think of hugging Mam when he was small. He used to love smelling her sweet skin. Centuries ago.

The crowd carried him up the stairs into a huge high room: The Registry Room. He mumbled to himself, trying to remember that every step would bring him nearer to his dream. One step at a time.

'Men this way, women that way.'

Strong American accents shouted instructions. Loud, sharp, nasal sounding. Big tough men who had marched west and conquered the world. Made him think of voices he heard on the wireless.

You would almost think they were putting it on, arrogant sods.

'Leave all luggage here, take the steps to your right.'

A big man, bigger than George in a brown uniform pushed his shoulder into line. He took a deep breath and looked away.

Big bastard.

Then the same woman as before was beside him once more, scanning the crowd for her family. She stumbled again, anxious, fearful; a man in medical uniform took her to one side and marked her clothes with a piece of white chalk. George tried to catch her eye to give her one of his killer smiles. It didn't work; she was blank as a caged puppy. The man started to lead her away. George tried to grab her other arm as she shook and cried. Her children, her man started wailing, a long ribbon of sound which flickered into rags before settling on their shoulders. Where were they taking her? What did the white chalk mean? The man looked at George and shook his head as he tried to comfort his children.

Glancing back down through the banisters he saw his bag being thrown onto a pile. People were huddled together on long benches around the room, some trying to offer each other quiet encouragement. George kept his head down for a minute, closed his eyes and smelled his own fear before looking up at a man behind a desk.

'Wait for your name to be called. Is that your wife?'

'No..but…'

'Speak up, can't cha?'

'I…I'm sorry…'

'She'll be taken care of anyways. Stay there in line.'

The desk was high, like a church pulpit.

Guy certainly thinks he's a bloody god.

He looked through some papers before giving a brief nod and a puzzled squint. George's eyes felt big and dry as he approached.

'Single? Money? Dependants?'

'Yes, single. I have money and I want to work. No, no dependants. I am fit and strong.'

'That's for us to decide,' the man says, without looking up.

'Medical test and mental test done yet?'

'No.'

'Pardon me?'

'No Sir.'

He sat down to wait for the medical inspection.

Shit, if the guys at work could see him now they would have a bloody good laugh.

A small, grizzled man beside him shoved at his arm and gestured towards the sounds coming from the medical room to their left. Cries of pain. Sharp. Sudden. The adults quick and shocked. But dear God, the children. Their whimpers and cries a mixture of perplexity and sadness.

His neighbour began to whisper in his ear, his breath hot, his accent clipped and hard. Probably German or some such. He told George what he had heard about the eye test for trachoma, the dreaded eye disease.

Jeezus. a bloody button hook. Christ Almighty.

George's stomach flipped over like a dying fish. Hours passed, the same questions being asked over and over. What was his status? How much money did he have? What were his plans in the great country?

'Hey you.'

'Me? Where do I go next?'

'Yeah, buddy, you. With the curls.'

The man sniggered as he led George into the next room for the Mental Test. He showed him a picture and asked him to talk about it. Rivers, streams, a railroad cutting it in half and engine steam drifting across the scene.

'OK, what does this picture tell you?'

'Um, it's mountains, grass and there are trees.'

'Yeah, and what else?'

What did they want him to say?

It's just a big-arse picture. Of a big-arse country.

'There's a railway line going down the middle and a train.'

'Can you see any people?'

'No, I can't. But there must be people, because they made the train and the tracks.'

He sounded feeble, even to himself. His mouth was dry, his lips quivering and his tongue falling about between his teeth. The man on the other side of the desk stood up, dismissed him with a curt flap of the hand and turned away. Waiting and more waiting. And more instructions barked and shouted thrown and spat at everyone who only want to better their lives.

★

By about four in the afternoon, George finally emerged into the last mean rays of October sunshine. A greedy wind blew off the harbour. His money had been changed into dollars. Forty-seven dollars to be exact. He held onto the one-dollar lunch in a brown paper bag which he had purchased on the island. Forty-six dollars.

He walked along the street, asking different people how he might get to someplace where he could find accommodation.

Most of them simply ignored him. Others shook their heads and hurried on. Across the street a coloured man was emptying a rubbish bin into a handcart.

'Excuse me, I'm looking for somewhere where I could get a room.'

The man stared hard right into his face, 'I know what you want, brother.'

George stepped back, unsure sure how to respond.

'I guess you might like Harlem,' the man continued.

'Thanks. And how do I get there?'

The man pointed, 'The subway station's that way. Go up to 135th Street.'

'Harlem. 135th Street. Thanks.'

Harlem. He liked the sound of the word: rolled it around his tongue.

The shaky ride on the subway was long and noisy. He was scared as he went down below the deep of the city, trying not to panic, trying to look casual like everyone else. He stared at the grimy walls rushing past and the assorted collection of people who took little notice of him. Falling into a tired slump he dozed off for a few stations. Waking up he noticed that the occupants of the train were different from those who got on and off earlier down the line.

They were all coloured.

A man next to him touched his arm, 'Where you goin' man?'

'Harlem.'

'Well, this is it, like it or not.'

George thanked him and noted the sign on the tiled wall from the window: 135th Street. Once outside he looked for the nearest street name: St Nicholas Avenue. Wandering into the cold he was surprised to see the steep grassy ramparts of a park across the way. This was not what he had imagined. During the months leading up to his departure from Cardiff he had often pictured himself stepping into a taxi and heading straight for a gilded sexy bar where he would sit on a high stool with a fancy drink in his hand.

Cock of the walk. He shook his head. Stupid sod.

He climbed the concrete steps halfway up to the top of the park and looked down at the street. The buildings were dirty and shabby, people shuffled along in the early evening dusk as if the world was coming to an end. He sat down on a nearby bench, opened his bag and ate the last scraps of his lunch.

★

Something skittered across his lap before rustling away into the bushes and woke him up.

Bloody hell, a rat.

He didn't mean to fall asleep. All he could remember was laying his head on his bag to rest his eyes for a minute or two. He sat up, rubbed his aching neck and felt in his breast pocket for the stiff edges of the card with his thumb. His Immigration Card.

It was dark.

And cold.

And he was alone.

In Harlem, New York City.

What next?

'Wait, what you doin' 'ere man?'

He jumped up to see a man standing right in front of him. His skin was dark and shiny, looking almost purple in the evening dusk. He was short, solid, confident-looking and dressed as if going out for the evening, although why he would be wandering around the park was a mystery. His Jamaican accent immediately reminded George of the guys who used to play dice games on the pavement back home. They would talk loudly and clap each other on the back as they played. A St Lucian man, known by everyone as James, would call out a loud 'douce' when he played a two die. He was well known for his gambling skills.

As a small boy, maybe nine or ten years old, George sometimes acted as lookout for them. Watching out for the police. You had to be able to whistle properly if you wanted to be a look-out and he used to practice his whistling skills in bed. If you saw a policeman in the distance you had to whistle: once if they were quite far away, twice if they got closer and three whistles meant that everyone had to run like hell down the street because they were dangerously close. It made his heart rush and jump. Later in the evening the men would drift away to one of the pubs. He made sure Dad never found out, used his earnings to buy sweets on the way to school and kept them hidden from anyone at home. When George grew up and started work he hurried past the gamblers on his way indoors, anxious to eat and get washed up before going uptown. He had bigger fish to fry and great plans for his future. Was this it? Either way, it was a relief and a comfort to hear a familiar accent again.

'Can't see a brother sleepin' this way…you are a brother, aren't you?'

George nodded as the man looked him over with a practised eye.

'You might ask what I'm doin' 'ere meself eh? But that's another story.'

He laughed and squeezed George's arm.

'Looks like you jes' come. Am I right?'

George nodded again.

'Yes, I got to Ellis Island this morning.'

'Oh man, I know that place…feel sorry for you,' shaking his head and clicking his teeth at the same time.

'I'm Neville by the way. Come by my place if you want.'

'My name is George. I would like that. Thanks.'

'OK, George, let's go. Looks like you could do with some food inside that skinny frame o' yours.'

Nothing to lose. And he liked the look of Neville. No other choice. He picked up his bag and followed his new friend down the steps of St Nicholas Park.

Chapter Nine

'C ome in Ruby. Come in.'
Mr Lerman got up and closed his office door. He sat back down behind his desk as Ruby stood.

'Sit down, Ruby. No need to be nervous.'

'Umm, I'm sorry to just turn up like this Mr Lerman, I just thought that perhaps you'd forgotten…'

'No Ruby, I hadn't forgotten about your letter. Just been busy that's all. And well, I've had a lot on my mind lately.'

He glanced at the family photograph on his desk: a posed portrait of himself standing behind an ornate chair, on which sat the stately Rebeka Lerman with the dainty, overdressed Rachel on her lap, ringlets and all.

'I understand.'

She understood only too well. Ever since Peggy's revelations about having heard that Rachel Lerman had gone away. Studying abroad again apparently.

Nothing venture, nothing gain was Jimmy's advice. He had her interests at heart and had been so kind since Mam's passing. She owed him. She didn't want to let him down, so there she was in the dark green jacket that had been hung on the back of her bedroom door since May.

'I'm sorry, I shouldn't have come.'

She stood up, patted down her hair, shuffled her feet.

'Please Ruby, sit back down. We both know what you're talking about. Not your fault. Let's start again shall we?'

Mr Lerman took down a big box of papers from the shelf behind him and tipped some of them out onto the desk.

'See this lot? What a mess. That's how bad it's been since you left to look after your mother. You've been sadly missed young lady. Now, when can you start?'

★

Half an hour later, Ruby walked back down Bute Street on her way home. She couldn't wait to tell Dad the good news when he came home from work. Things were beginning to look up. She thought she would drop in to tell Peggy before she went indoors. It was a few minutes until Peggy opened the door.

'Excuse me, I'm looking like a dead rat, Rube. Just washed my hair.'

Ruby sat down and glanced around the parlour. She hadn't been to the house for a while. It was usually Peggy who dropped by to see her. She was shocked: the sink was full of dirty dishes, there were clothes draped around everywhere and a general look about the place which showed that it hadn't been cleaned for a while. A good while too. She moved some things so she could sit down, feeling like a stuffed turkey in her work clothes. Peggy made a big deal of rubbing at her hair as she poured Ruby some lemonade and plonked it on the sideboard near her chair.

'Oooohh, look at you Miss Fine and Dandy,' she swooped. 'Been somewhere special? Or going out?'

'Umm…Mr Lerman's given me my job back. Thought I'd pop in before going indoors. To tell you the good news.'

'Oh, well, good for you I say. Told Jimmy yet? After all, you two are courting now aren't you?'

Ruby paused. 'Not courting, but we've always been good friends, you know that. You told me I could do worse and well, you read his letter the other week.'

'Yes, I did. Well that's you all fixed up now, I suppose'. Her voice abrasive, challenging. This was not like Peggy.

'Look, I'd better go Peg. You're busy with your hair and everything and I need to start getting Dad's supper ready. Drop in tomorrow if you like. If you've got the time.'

Chapter Ten

George followed his new friend through the dark streets of Harlem. He was not overly impressed with what he saw. Or the people come to that. The whole area looked pretty run down. Neville tried to engage him in conversation.

'So, what brings you to this big ole city then man? And where you from?'

Not quite sure how much to tell him, although the guy seemed genuine enough.

'Um, came from Cardiff. Just wanted to better myself I suppose.'

'Cardiff…that rings a bell. One of my friends from back home went there. Jumped on a ship. Wanted to see the world and ended up in the UK.'

'Yes, that's the place. I used to work at the docks. Loading coal.'

'Loading coal eh? Well, well.' He sucked his teeth, 'You want to better yerself? Time will tell.'

Neville stopped at the wide steps leading up to a three-storeyed brownstone and fished around for his front door key.

George looked up at the windows. They had bars across them: not a very comforting sign. On glancing down the street, he saw that the all the other buildings were similarly protected. Neville unlocked the heavy door, welcomed him in with a mock bow and walked on ahead to the top floor. The dark hallway and staircase reminded George of home. Lots of dark wood panelling, looking like it could do with being varnished or painted. Neville unlocked the door to his room. He gestured to the large armchair. It was large, sagging and brown, with a swirling black design faded to grey in parts. Two big cushions kept slipping as George sunk into it, his neck still aching, his legs heavy. The wallpaper, which perhaps had once been cream was nicotine yellow and stained in places.

'Is not much but you welcome to what I 'ave.'

Neville sat on the narrow bed and looked at him, smiling.

'So, wait, is always you so quiet? A big man like you must have somet'ing to say. You lookin' smart or maybe you just smartin'!'

His large head lurched back as he laughed at himself. His face damp, round and pock-marked in places. George considered him to be about thirty years old, although his hair had already begun to recede. Neville noticed him looking and put his hands up to pat it down, took off his jacket and hung it on the back of the door. He started by apologizing for the food as he carefully put it together. It looked like some left-over chicken with rice and peas which he warmed by placing the plates over pots of boiling water.

Rice and peas. Ruby had cooked that the night before he left. A Sunday treat she said. He had been glancing around the room as Neville made a big deal of getting out knives and forks and finding a tray for him.

The furniture was definitely past it. Apart from the bed and the armchair there was a kitchen chair and a small cupboard covered in papers and dishes. A scratchy-looking wardrobe with ornate brass handles stood beside a window facing the street. There was a chipped enamel sink in one corner with a shelf above on which stood some shaving things, a toothbrush and a spotty mirror. The window above looked out at the damp wall of the next-door building. The room smelled stale but due to the steel bars it would be impossible to open the windows very wide anyway. Too narrow for anyone to climb through. Above the bed in the opposite corner was another shelf holding a few books, a glass jar full of small change, and a crinkly photograph of smiling people, all sitting under a luscious tree and squinting into the Caribbean sun, looking like a younger Neville with presumably, his two sisters and his parents.

Both men were quiet as they ate their food, the plates balanced on their knees.

Neville's look was curious as he studied the younger man before him: the thin jacket, crumpled after sleeping in the park, the slender fingers and well-trimmed nails, the callow face, the fancy scarf which he fingered as he talks.

'So, George, what gives? Tell me everything.'

'Not much to tell really. I've been saving up to come to America. I thought...'

'Thought what? Lookin' for yer fame and fortune?'

George flushed.

'Thought I might find better opportunities here.'

'Is that right?' Neville grinned and shook his head.

George wondered how much he should tell and what to keep to himself. About how hard it was to save money. About Mam, Dad and Ruby. About Mam getting sick and dying. But this guy certainly pushed it, like he caught on that there was more to the story. Kept grinning, nodding and getting on his nerves. In the end he mentioned Rachel just to see what the reaction would be. Neville leaped at the opportunity to get one in.

'She 'elp you then? To get the money together?'

Uh, oh, big mistake to have mentioned her.

'Well I, she was, we were, kind of engaged.'

'Engaged? To be married? Hmm, boy, you work fas'.'

'It wasn't like that. I had to get away.'

'Well, I guess you'll tell me more in yer own time.'

George got up and went over to the shelf above the bed and took down the photograph.

'So, what about you? How long have you been here?'

Neville shook his head, 'I pitched up off the boat, just like you did today. Five years ago.' George shuddered, 'Jeezus, I never want to go through that again. Ever.'

'You talkin' dat man! These people can be bad. Bad I tell you!' A pause.

Neville put his fingers to his forehead and closed his eyes.

'I remember me first night. Got off the boat and found Fulton Street Station.'

George leaned back in his chair. The heat was off him for a while.

'If it wasn't for Grantley, I don't know where I would have ended up.'

'Who's Grantley?'

'Well, he helped me on my first night. That's why I wanted to help you. We folks 'ave to stick together. Know what I mean?'

George looked at his shoes.

Neville continued 'I went straight up to 'im and ask where all the coloured people lived.'

'So, it's not just in Harlem then?'

'No, no. You 'ave some of us live down in Brooklyn. Place called Flatbush. Lots of us from the Caribbean down that way.'

'He didn't mind helping you?'

'No, because dat's what we do. And why I want to 'elp you. To get started.'

He paused. 'Ting is, da coloured folks who live here all their lives have de cheek to call us "monkey huggers". Can you believe dat?'

He shook his head, 'Man, it's like our folks didn't have de same shit history as dem. But at least when we come we 'elp each other. Chu.'

Silence for a few seconds.

'So, what happened next?'

'Told me to wait for 'im in the park while he did some tings. Battery Park.'

'Weren't you afraid that he wouldn't come back?'

66

'I 'ad was to trust him, 'ad no choice. Didn't know where to go next. Just like yerself.'

That was true. If it hadn't been for Neville, where would he have gone? With all his big ideas about fancy bars and pretty women…

'Anyway, 'e did come back. Took me to 'is little room in a brownstone off Fulton Street. Gave me food. Let me sleep at 'is place until I get meself sorted.'

'Are you still friends?'

'Of course. Been friends this last five years ever since I reach.'

George held up the photograph.

'Is this your family?'

'That's right, Mama, Papa and my two older sisters.'

'Do you hear from them?'

'Not so much now,' said Neville. 'My mama died since I been 'ere. My own fault.'

Dangerous ground.

Neville talked on, 'I stayed with Grantley for a while, then got this room in Harlem. Didn't tell my folks, too busy finding my way around I guess. Well, that was my excuse. Grantley was busy and I didn't see him for a few weeks. When I did he gave me a letter from my sister. Mama was dead and buried and I didn't even know. I should 'ave been there.'

George put the picture back on the shelf. 'Can I use the toilet?'

'Sure, just go down one flight. Bathroom's at the far end.'

Neville was keen to continue when he got back.

'You see that little glass jar with me loose change? My mama give it to me when I left Jamaica. It was full of olive oil. I don't know how it survived being thrown about in my bag.

Especially on 'the island'.'

George inclined his head and stared out of the window.

'The funny thing is, some of the oil had leaked over my clothes. I 'ad was to borrow some of Grantley's t'ings for a few days. That was a joke seeing as he's a lot taller than me.'

He grinned. Then went quiet for a moment before going to his jacket and took a slip of paper out of the inside pocket.

'You see dis? The last communication with my ole mama. To go with the olive oil.'

He passed it to George: 'Just look after your skin in that cold, cold place where you gone. I going to miss you, Son.'

Neville got up and started to clear away the dishes. George looked at his watch: it was getting late, well past midnight.

'Um, I wonder if...'

'No worries man. We can sort dis. One of us could sleep on the chair cushions on the floor. Or...'

'Or what?' asked George.

'Me and Grantley spent a few weeks sleeping head to toe in 'is place. OK for you? Warmer for both of us.'

Jeezus, his first night in the new world and he's sharing a bed with a stranger. A bloke, too, for chrissake. Still, beggars can't be choosers as Dad would say.

'Um, alright then. Thanks.'

Neville laughed, 'Let's get some sleep now and tomorrow I take you to see my boss, Mr Manni. See if he can do anyt'ing to 'elp you get a job.'

Chapter Eleven

Neville was quiet and withdrawn. Neither of them had slept very well. The morning was bleak. Queuing up for the bathroom was a nightmare and by the time George had slicked back his hair and washed his hands and face he felt quite sick. More so since he'd had to follow another tenant who'd clearly had a heavy night on the binge. He looked at his bedmate. The cheerful confident man of a few hours previously had closed down all the shutters. Making their way to the station in the cold, you'd think they were on their way to the torture chamber.

Bloody hell, couldn't get any worse.

Neville was certainly stepping out fast and kept glancing at his watch. George found it difficult to keep up even though his legs were longer. They had been walking for about ten minutes before Neville finally spoke,

'Don't worry to say anyt'ing when we reach right? Leave the talkin' to me you hear?'

George raised his eyebrows in agreement, looking about him as they walked.

Neville, noticing, urged him onwards, 'Hmmm, you'll see everyt'ing by and by my friend. Yeah, all in good time.'

The subway ride downtown to Manhattan was full of people who were clearly in a Neville-type mood. Not one person cracked a smile. It was only six o clock and George wondered where they were all going this early in the day. He tried to talk to Neville about his job but mostly got one-word answers.

May as well shut-up then. Wait and see.

They came out onto a street off Sixth Avenue in the middle of Manhattan. Looking around, this was much more the kind of place George had expected of New York. Neville led him towards a tall building with steps going up flanked either side by stylish pillars. He looked up to see a sign: 'Lerner Insurance: Absolute Security Assured for your Business, Home and Family'.

Just as Neville was about to knock, the door was opened by a stocky, red-faced middle-aged man. He didn't greet them but stepped back with a grunt to let Neville inside. He shot out his wrist in front of Neville's face, pointed to his watch and gave a slight frown when he saw George following on behind.

'So, you've brought some company today boy?'

George stopped. Listened as Neville mumbled a quiet reply with his head down. His voice was quiet, different. It was difficult to hear what he was saying except for the 'Sah' at the end. Centuries collapsed as all three men acknowledged the moment.

The man looked at George with a smirk.

'I'm Mr Manni, your dear friend's boss. Isn't that right boy?'

Neville assented and began to walk slowly into a large marble foyer. It was cool and quiet. A white man in a bright blue uniform sat behind the reception desk and pretended to be sorting some papers in front of him. On seeing George tagging behind, he gave Neville an enquiring look who barely shrugged his shoulders. Mr Manni stood to one side and opened his hands as he addressed George.

'You looking for work then boy?'

'Yes.'

'Pardon me?'

'Yes Sir.'

'And what do you call yourself?

'George Hodges. Sir.'

So that's how it is. Bastard.

'Well I guess you could help your brother just for today since you're here. I can't promise anything, but I'll think about it. From your accent, I'd say you're English, right?'

'Well not English as such, Sir, in fact I come from Wales which is...'

Mr Manni waved him aside and pointed at Neville, who was standing a little way off.

'Just follow him, he'll show you what to do.'

He walked off into one of the rooms off the foyer and slammed the door.

Neville stood waiting and then led George down some stairs into the cellar in silence. George tried to smile at him, but he would not meet his eye. Neville took off his jacket and hung it on the wall. George did the same. Neville picked up a pair of overalls, put them on and gave some to him. George did the same. He got two mops and buckets and some cleaning stuff out of a tall closet.

OK, I get the picture.

They spent the next three hours cleaning, scrubbing and polishing: floors, banisters, toilets, the whole works, Neville indicating what he wanted George to do as they went along. There was little conversation.

Every so often, Mr Manni appeared: 'So George, how are you finding the work?'

What did he want him to say?

Oh, it's wonderful, Sir. I just love cleaning up people's shit. Sir.

'Yes, fine thanks.'

'Good. Bet your friend's glad you're here since he turned up late this morning.'

Neville twirled his mop hard into the grimy bucket, as Mr Manni moved off again until the next time.

'Come and see me when you've finished. My office upstairs. The blue door.'

'Ok. Thanks.'

'Pardon me?'

'Thanks Sir.'

The whole 'sir' shit enough to piss anyone off.

They stopped at midday and went back downstairs into the cloakroom. Neville sat down on a bench, stretched out his legs and leaned back against the wall.

George hung up both overalls. 'Um, I'd better go up and see Mr Manni.'

'Yes, you do that brother', Neville answered without looking at him.

'Will you wait for me?'

'Of course. No worries.' He closed his eyes.

George went up and knocked on the blue door. The sign on the front said E. Mankowitz, but it must have been the right one as Mr Manni opened it.

'Come in, boy.'

George stood in front of the desk as the boss sat back down without inviting him to sit. Minutes passed.

'So, George, why are you here?'

'I only arrived yesterday, and I need a job.'

'You think you could work here? Cleaning?'

'Well yes, I…'

'How long have you known Neville?'

'Only since last night. He's been very kind. Helping me out.'

George shuffled his feet.

Standing here like a friggin' lemon.

Mr Manni made as if he'd forgotten, 'Oh, sit down George. You're making me uncomfortable.'

About bloody time. Creep.

Mr Manni got up then and went to the window.

He spoke without turning, 'You know that some people have more choice than others, don't you?'

'I don't know what you mean, Sir.'

'Do I need to spell it out?'

'Sorry Sir, I don't understand.'

He sighed, 'OK, OK. Come in tomorrow, same time. If you finish the week, I'll pay you then.'

'Does that mean I've got a job? Sir?'

Mr Manni returned to his desk and picked up the phone, 'You can go now.'

Chapter Twelve

Sunday night and Ruby was getting her things ready for work the following day. She had polished her shoes, pressed her skirt and replaced one of the buttons on her best blouse. The sandwiches were made. There was nothing else to do. Supper was over, and Dad sat in the corner with his eyes closed. Ruby wasn't sure if he was dozing or not. He'd been spending more time upstairs in the evenings lately, pretending to sort some of Mam's stuff. He couldn't bear to touch it before until Ruby offered to help him make a start one Sunday afternoon a couple of weeks previously. But that evening he was sitting with her. They even had a tot of rum after supper in honour of her going back to work.

He opened his eyes and looked across at her.

'All set for tomorrow then my girl?'

'Yes, Dad. Thanks to Jimmy's encouragement. I couldn't believe it when Mr Lerman said he'd take me back.'

'Well Ruby, if anyone deserves it, you do. And as you say, Jimmy's a good chap.'

'Yes, Dad. He seems quite keen too.' She looked down at her hands wriggling her fingers about in her lap. 'But Peggy doesn't seem to be very happy for me. Why do you think she's being like that?'

Dad leaned forward in his chair. 'Some people are only happy when they see others down on their luck, my girl.'

'But why would she be like that with me? We've been friends since we were little. You'd think she'd be pleased for me. She was so kind, when Mam was sick. And she couldn't have done more when...'

'Yes, I know love, but that's her role. Don't you see? Helping people out at their worst time. Makes her feel good.'

'She's got Charlie.'

He sucked his teeth. 'And look at the life she's got with him. And then there was the loss of the baby. And losing both her parents the way she did.'

'You're right, Dad. I should remember all that.'

He got up and went upstairs. Ruby heard him rummaging around, opening and closing drawers and cupboards. A few moments later, he came back with something clutched in his fist and held it out.

'Hold out your hand and close your eyes.'

She opened her eyes to feel something cool and metal in her palm. A silver brooch, a flat diamond shape about an inch long, inlaid with a smaller 3D diamond shape of what looked like jet: black, shiny and multifaceted. There was a little catch on the back with a safety chain.

'Dad, where did this come from? I've never seen it before. It's beautiful.'

'I found it among your mam's things. I remember when Jimmy brought it back from one of his travels a couple of years ago. Asked her to look after it for him for a while. Said he was saving it for someone special.'

'Someone special? Who?'

He smiled, 'Who do you think? Pin it on your jacket. Wear it to work.'

'You mean me? But this must have cost a fortune, Dad.'

'Well, it was obviously meant for someone special. Like you. Jimmy will be pleased to see you wearing it when he turns up next.'

A pause.

'Do you remember the lovely brooch you bought for Mam? With the little red stone? It was always on the lapel of her big coat. Took it with her to the grave, just like we agreed.'

'Yes, that's right she did, God bless her.'

Ruby held the brooch up to the light and studied the facets of jet shining there, before pinning it on her jacket.

Chapter Thirteen

Once Neville had shown him the ropes, Mr Manni offered George a few hours each week as a cleaner in the adjoining building: City Insurance. George sometimes dropped by to see Neville when he had a few minutes off. If their work shifts were at different times, it meant that occasionally one of them had the luxury of sleeping alone in the small room on 135th Street. It was agreed but unspoken as a temporary arrangement until George became independent. He made himself scarce on the day the landlord came calling for the weekly rent which they split in half. They made the best of the cramped conditions: both of them wondering how long it could last. Things had subtly changed since that first meeting.

When they had the time, Neville showed him around the cheapest food stores, regardless of George's obvious disinterest. Evenings were the worst. One or the other of them made an effort to go out alone. George spent his spare time wandering around Harlem, wondering how he was going to move on. He needed to find a way of getting a place of his own. But the weekly pittance he earned wasn't going to get him anywhere. He decided he would just have to try and be patient and see how things panned out. So it continued for a while.

Neville was shaving one Friday night after they had eaten while George pretended to take a calculated interest in the newspaper.

He glanced up as Neville was lathering his face. Looked like he was going somewhere special, considering the way he was getting fixed up. Maybe he would have the bed to himself for a change.

'Making an effort tonight then? Going somewhere different?'

Neville finished what he was doing before responding. Turned as he was towelling his face,

'Going down to Brooklyn to see Grantley. Wanna come?'

'Oh, yeah…thanks.'

'Some fine women down that way, if you know what I mean…'

George had already started grooming his hair and brushing down his decent jacket.

'Sounds good to me, man.'

Nice to be asked. Perhaps things were on the turn.

★

Maisie's was an illicit drinking club in Flatbush. It would be easy to miss the heavy door sandwiched between two office buildings unless you knew it was there. Directly inside, steep steps led down to a small cellar room. On one side there was a bar with a few stools and on the opposite wall a couple of wooden barrels with kitchen chairs placed around them. Three couples were dancing to Mamie Smith's 'Crazy Blues', from a phonograph on the corner of the bar. Not so much dancing perhaps as lurching together from one foot to the other. One of the men was singing along: a woman's lament about how she couldn't sleep because her man didn't 'treat her right'. His partner tried to quieten him without success; he just laughed and held her more tightly.

Over the next few weeks, Neville and Grantley showed George around and introduced him to their favourite places. The three men spent most of their free time together and it didn't take long for George to adopt their Jamaican colloquialisms and habits. He soon found himself mimicking their way of speaking: a curious hybrid derived from the language of Harlem speakeasies and

Jamaican patois. Listening to the other two talking together felt safe somehow, a small memory of all that he had left behind. He tried not to think about the devastating effect his departure must have been for his family. And for Rachel.

Grantley enjoyed cooking the way his mother taught him back home in St Elizabeth, Jamaica. His cow-foot soup took most of Saturday to prepare and boil. It was a culinary magnum opus even though he had to adapt where necessary when ingredients were hard to get hold of. He was able to recreate that back-home taste and texture leaving their lips sticky, their taste buds quivering, and their stomachs sated. Every week he made two big pots, one for them all to share and one for the other two to take back to their room the following day. After a hard Saturday night at Maisie's, they dossed down on the floor at Grantley's place. On Sunday morning, George and Neville greeted the subway train with the big pot balanced between their laps as they dozed or chatted while hurtling through New York's concrete and steel intestines. The well-scrubbed pot was then returned the following Saturday and thus the weekend ritual continued for a while.

One Saturday night Grantley decided to make his way up to Harlem for a change. Someone at work had told Neville about a small bar nearby. The woman who ran it offered other services too by all accounts. The three of them met up and had a good evening. Neville and Grantley got involved in a dice game while George chatted up the girl behind the bar. The place became their favourite haunt for a few weeks. On one occasion, George stayed for a quick drink before making his excuses saying he had somewhere else to go. The truth was he needed to exonerate himself from a failure of a previous Saturday night. An event which had dealt a fierce blow to his manly pride. He grimaced to himself as he recalled the incident.

★

He had been taking in the air one evening as usual when someone tapped him on the shoulder, 'Hi there, Daddy, you looking for some fun?'

He turned around to see a young woman. She looked about twenty years old, small and lean. Her face dark, smooth and beautiful, conveyed a girlishness which contrasted sharply with the way she was dressed, a provocative style indicating less than childish intentions. He noted the heavy application of rouge and lipstick, the slim curves beneath her thin dress and the strong thighs which rounded under the fabric as she moved to draw him to the inside of the kerb.

'So, what's it to be then, Daddy? You up for it?'

Being completely unaware of the historical significance of her address, George thought she was referring to her childish looks.

'OK. I suppose so. Where do you want to go?'

There was no point in wasting time after all. Thought he might as well see what was on offer. She detected his accent in those few words,

'Oh my, you suppose so huh? You an English gent?'

He changed tack then and imagined how Neville or Grantley would respond,

'Well, you lookin' nice. A sweet gal.'

He wasn't going to be teased by some little tramp. She needed to know what's what.

'Or Jamaican? Whoever you are I guess you like a little sunshine girl. No problem, honey, as long as you got money in your pocket.'

★

'What is it with the scarf man? You planning to tie me up or what?'

She had led him to a small room, in the basement of a brownstone a few blocks away from home. The room was dingy; signs of damp patches slewed across the florid wallpaper and a tattered rug slid across the bare floorboards. There was one small closed window. A rancid smell, redolent of cheap perfume and stale sex hung in the air. Barely stifling a tired yawn, she carelessly raised one slender leg onto the hard, wooden chair beside the bed, rolled down her stocking and drew it off with a weary flourish, looking at him the whole time. Chipped nail polish on her toes offered a faint gleam under the fringed bedside lamp. Did the same with the other leg. She stood up, opened her thighs and raised her arms to remove her bodice. George lay on the flimsy counterpane, squinting at her.

'You like what I got, Daddy? You gonna get some?'

That word again. He wanted to get out, but it was too late. The scarf flopped loosely around his shoulders. He said nothing but waited for the familiar stirring in his loins. It took a long time coming and moving his hand downwards he tried to help things along.

The girl gave a slow smile, 'You want to use the bathroom honey? It's just at the end of the hall.'

'Yeah, OK. Soon come.'

He got up and dragged on his trousers before loping out through the door.

Minutes later on his return, she was gazing out of the window. She started to turn on hearing his approach.

'No, don't move. Stay like that. And don't talk.'

Lowering his head, he lifted her stiff, store-bought hair to one side and kissed her neck before moving across to caress the soft mounds of her shoulders. Gripping her arms tight he flew away into the stratosphere.

Oh no, shit, shit, shit.

Once it was over he stepped back, hands clenched at his sides.

She turned then and laughed in his face, 'Honey, "soon come" is right...'

Still tittering, she held out her hand.

A short time later, with thirty cents less in his pocket, George ambled off down the street. Coming across Slyshots on 134th, he sat at the bar and ordered a large whisky. Man, what a disaster that was.

Chapter Fourteen

After George had left, the two men sat close together downstairs in Mizz Johnson's exotically named Bamboo Bar. Mizz Johnson had converted the cellar room of her imposing brownstone just off St Nicholas Avenue. Nobody knew how she could have afforded to buy the house in the first place. Rumour had it that she was in fierce competition with the well-known queen of the numbers game, a certain Mme S. who was highly respected throughout Harlem.

Others said that a wealthy white English lover from her past took pleasure in his remembrance of their sweet loving by regular gifts of cash and jewellery. Mizz Johnson's curvaceous charms, physical dexterity and enchanting expertise of yore could only be wondered at. What few folks knew was that thousands of miles away in Europe: maybe Paris, Milan or Lisbon, a handsome, elegant and educated young man dutifully wrote a letter to his mother every month. The only time the lady's serenity was punctured was if she was seen reading some missive covered in foreign stamps. Then her black eyes glistened with what one could suppose to be sentimental tears.

Some nights visitors who cared to look might have noticed the swish, swirl and glance of any of the beautiful dark-eyed girls in satin and taffeta as they slipped into one of the small rooms above followed by a man. Folk going down to the Bamboo Bar were rarely able to lock eyes with any of those devotees, who tended to look nervously sideways before sidling along behind the personification of their fervid passions.

The Bamboo Bar, so named because the back wall was covered by a mural of a supposedly tropical scene. A cacophony of bamboo and florid blooms struggled for attention while an unlikely collection of lustrous birds which defied scientific classification flitted among the vegetation. Unfortunately, you would have to look carefully to enjoy the delights of the artist's bold efforts because even during the day the shades were pulled down against the sunlight. At night, lights glowed but dimly conveying a sense of forbidden activity, or even yet to hide the failings of the weary furniture.

No doubt the local law enforcers knew of Mizz Johnson's dubious business practices. Maybe some even availed themselves of her tantalising offerings and acknowledged her part in supporting the local economy. A counter in one corner served bootleg liquor, water or soda. On a good night, clients could also purchase a meal of pigs' feet or chicken with rice, grits and collard greens on the side. A handful of high stools stood proud before the bar, a few card tables and wooden chairs were packed closely together around the remaining floor space.

Sometimes a couple of musicians might stop by and set themselves up in the opposite corner for an impromptu jam session, their precious instruments lurking dangerously close to the drinkers. It was quiet that night, the atmosphere pervasive of a drawling illegality, a shared and secret pleasure. Apart from the tired looking young woman serving the drinks, it was mostly full of men. On occasion, a white woman might stray into the bar on the arm of a confident coloured man. As the couple strolled down the stairs, other patrons looked up briefly before continuing with their drinks or food.

Mizz Johnson sailed down the stairs, imperial as ever. A large woman, she adorned herself in bright, bold prints, daring anyone to question her proud voluptuousness. She wore glittering jewels which to the untutored eye could be regarded as cheap baubles. However, those who knew better recognised that only real diamonds could wink and nestle so brightly within the contours and valleys of her smooth bosom. She nodded briefly towards the two men before retiring again to her lair upstairs beside the front door.

★

Neville, finishing his meal, wiped his plate with bread and picked up his drink. He leaned back in his chair.

'So, what you thinkin' then brother? About George?'

'Well, I don't want to disrespect' the man, but it look to me like he ready to move on. Do 'is own thing you know?'

'And what do you think that thing might be?'

'What do you mean?'

'Well, look at him Grantley my man. What you think I mean?'

Grantley stared into his glass, nodding slowly. 'Yeah, well, he will come to that in 'im own time, that's what. I like him. He's a simple kinda guy', his tone measured and conciliatory.

He paused before speaking again as Neville sucked his teeth and groaned.

Grantley urged him, 'C'mon, drink up man. Let's go down to Flatbush. This place feeling like a grave tonight. I 'ave someone that want to meet you down by me. Jes your type. Full, buxom like.'

Both men laughed and finished their drinks. The girl behind the bar shrugged as they went past. She was tall and slender, her taut body tightly enveloped in a cocktail of bright blue shiny stuff and feathers. A matching bow kept slipping from its rightful place in the big hair above her right ear. Her eyes slid across towards them and lingered on Grantley's generous face. Yet when she spoke, her tone was flippant and dismissive.

'So, we're not good enough for you guys tonight then?'

Grantley leaned across and briefly fondled the strap of her dress before squeezing her shoulder. 'Sweetie, a high yaller gal like you must have a lot of guys on the leash.'

She smiled back at him. Hungry. 'Yeah, guess so. But how do you know what kinda guy I'm lookin' for?'

He patted her arm then, friendly, casual. 'I 'ave to look after me frien' honey. He's getting' lonely since you don't want 'im.'

She looked after them as they mounted the stairs before going off into the night.

Chapter Fifteen

Ruby had not seen much of Peggy since she went back to work. Mr Lerman's pile of papers was gradually diminishing. He'd fallen so far behind with his paperwork after she left five months before and all that as well as taking on some new clients meant that Ruby was kept hard at it. But she loved every minute of her days. She had been into town a couple of times and bought two more skirts and blouses, so she didn't have to wear the same things every day. And Mrs Lerman kindly gave her a big coat which was handy with winter coming on. She spent the evenings cooking supper, clearing up and putting the hot iron through her hair for the following day. She and Dad rarely talked about George. When they did he got snappy and marched upstairs. She still felt guilty that she hadn't realised whatever was going on in his mind. She was happy enough during the day as long as she didn't dwell on her brother's absence.

Jimmy's tramp ship, *The Toledo Star*, had been back to reload a couple of times since she started back at work. He took her down to Da Silva's Café in Bute street one night where Pinkie sometimes dropped in with other musicians for a jam session. Jimmy insisted that she wore a silky blouse he had brought for her. Said he had found it in a little shop in Liverpool when the ship docked there for a couple of days. Just as they were about to leave for the evening, she went upstairs to put on her best jacket.

As she came to the bottom of the stairs, Jimmy looked at the brooch. He said nothing but took his wallet from his pocket and took out a pair of earrings which perfectly matched the brooch. He took her hand and placed them in her palm.

'There you go gal, now you have the full set. Matching. Like you and me.'

Chapter Sixteen

Friday evening. George's shift was over, and he decided to go next door to see if Neville was ready to knock off work. He thought they could travel home together. Things had improved somewhat since he had been out drinking with him and Grantley and he was anxious to return to their previous easy friendship. The doorman grinned and let him in. Neville, complete with overalls, mop and bucket greeted him as he was about to pack up.

'You going home soon Neville?'

'Yeah man, me jes' finishin' up. Come while I get changed.'

Mr Manni came out of his office and saw them both going through the cellar door. He went up to the doorman, 'Was that George I just saw with Neville?'

The doorman lowered his head, 'Yessah, I thought it was OK to let him in through the front, Sir.'

Mr Manni waved his hand and went back into his office A few moments later he reappeared carrying a large bag. He went down to the cellar where Neville was taking off his work clothes and telling George about an evening he'd spent with Grantley.

'Man, you shoulda seen this woman. She was a big gal,' using his hands to demonstrate her attractions. 'And all over me like a cheap suit.'

Laughing over a cup of coffee from Neville's flask as Mr Manni came in, they both stopped as they saw him and looked at one another. Mr Manni briefly acknowledged Neville who busied himself in hanging up his overall.

He addressed George directly, 'Thought I saw you come in George. I want to talk to you.'

The two men waited. It felt as if all the air had been sucked from the room.

Mr Manni continued, 'The guy on Reception won't be back after today and I need somebody to take his place.'

George and Neville only knew the receptionist as someone who barely noticed them whenever they passed by. A white man, big and surly as a rule except if a pretty secretary came into view, when his demeanour changed to one of helpful joviality. He was often over-friendly with them on occasion and Neville heard Mr Manni speaking to him dismissively more than once. Perhaps he'd gone too far this time. George didn't understand what Mr Manni was saying. He stayed quiet and waited.

'Don't you get it, boy? I'm offering you the job.'

George flushed. He looked at Neville who got up and threw the rest of the coffee down the sink. Mr Manni tipped the contents of his bag down on the table. It was the receptionist's bright blue uniform.

'Try this for size boy, you and he are about the same height.'

'Why, thanks Mr Manni but ummm, I'm not sure that I'll know what to do on the desk.'

'You should leave the worrying to me, boy. That's what I'm paid for. Put it on and get yourself upstairs pronto. I'll show you what to do.'

Neville turned away and started looking though his kit bag as if he'd lost a gold bar. Nobody spoke. Mr Manni stood with his arms folded, while George picked up the uniform and struggled to get into it. The trousers looked alright when dragged together with his belt. But the jacket was too broad in the chest. Gold braid and buttons set off the colour. The outfit fell heavily around his shoulders and he rubbed his neck against the rough serge collar.

Mr Manni smirked at them both before going back upstairs. The two men looked at one another. George lowered his head and continued to struggle with the brass buttons.

'So, what you sayin' then man? It look OK on me? The trousers are the right length but the jacket don't feel right.'

Neville mumbled something and sucked his teeth. He emptied his bucket and stood it in the corner with the mop. After gathering the floor wash and polish together he put them on the shelf and went out banging the door, which shuddered behind him. By the time George got upstairs he was nowhere to be seen.

The receptionist had gone and Mr Manni was waiting to show him what to do. He was taught how to answer the phone, welcome visitors and give them directions around the building, being assured that his cute 'English' accent would be sure to go down well with clients. After an hour Mr Manni sent him away with instructions to come in early on Monday morning.

He started off home. As he approached the front door he saw Neville coming out of a local store with a bag of groceries and hurried to join him. They mounted the stairs in silence, George being careful to stand back as Neville unlocked the door, took off his jacket and began taking food out of the bag to prepare dinner. George tried to help and started chopping onions. Neville took the knife from his hands and waved him off, raising the knife high in the air.

'Is OK man. My turn. I got this. Not goin' out so me 'ave plenty time to cook.'

'At least let me help.'

'OK, put on the rice,' Neville's voice low and slow.

A thick blanket of unspoken resentment hung between them. Shuddering waves of tension swept around as they pretended to concentrate on the food. When there was nothing more to do except wait for it to cook, Neville retrieved the newspaper from his jacket pocket.

Shit, the man must have read it a dozen times already.

George lifted it from his hands and laid it on the table. For a moment he thought Neville was going to punch him, judging by the look he gave him.

'Think it's time for me to be moving on man.'

'Yeah, guess so. You's a big man now so you mus' spread your wings and do your own t'ing.'

'I appreciate all you've done for me Neville.'

'H-m-m-m. It's OK man, we 'ave to 'elp each other in dis world. But you have to make your fortune in your own way.' He looked up with a shrug and a tight smile. For a minute George felt like punching him instead.

'Yes, I understand.'

Neville went on, 'You never know, you could do well in this city. Mark my words man, do whatever is right for yourself. You catch my drift?'

He got up and shoved his coat back on, 'Poppin' out for a walk. See you.'

'What about the food?'

'Don't worry yerself. I will eat later. Soon come.'

George watched from the front window as Neville marched along 135th street. He turned off the heat under the food, packed his few things as fast as he could, ran down the stairs and went outside. It was a chilly evening, but the streets were warming up for the night's action. A few men walked past, talking loudly and laughing. A woman with a cigarette huddled in a doorway. An old man leaning on a walking stick, had stopped to rest against some railings.

Out on the street again. And maybe back to St Nicholas Park. He walked down to Slyshots, thinking he'd get a drink while he decided what to do. Just as Neville was coming out.

'Wait, what you doin' man?', noticing that George was carrying his big bag.

'Well, I thought you probably want me to leave, so I packed up my stuff.'

'So, what? You were gonna make a quick getaway without so much as a cheerio?'

Neville shook his head, 'Man, you somet'ing else. A deal is a deal. I couldn't see you on the street before and I won't now.'

George had the grace to look shamed. He had never come across such kindness. Back home the men at work were only too glad to get one in if they got the chance. He had put it down to jealousy, because their lives were simply about loading coal, chasing cheap women and getting drunk. Only to end up with nothing. They would certainly have the last laugh if they could see him now.

He remembered a particular Saturday afternoon when he was coming out of The Angel Hotel with Rachel on his arm. There he was, all dressed up to the nines in his double-breasted suit and button-down collar shirt, courtesy of Rachel. And she was all done up in some shiny pink stuff which clung around her hips with a matching hat. As luck would have it, one of the lads from work was crossing the street with his wife, and coming directly towards them. George's first thought was to wonder what they were doing uptown, especially looking so shabby and poor. He tried to divert Rachel's attention by pointing up at the sky, and frowning.

As the couple passed by, the man sucked his teeth at George then openly whistled at Rachel. His wife cursed and tried to drag him away, while her man laughed. Right in George's face. Rachel was pissed off and more so when she tried to find out who the fellow was as George tried to change the subject. Fortunately, her parents were away that weekend, so they were able to spend a few hours in her flouncy bedroom and he found ways to cheer her up for a while.

Word had obviously got around by Monday when George went to work. The same man called out, 'Hey, Gigolo George!

How was your date?' A load of the other men fell about. Laughing like drains they were. Fortunately, Dad wasn't on the same shift or the shit would have really hit the fan.

★

Neville took his bag, 'Wha'appen? The food cook yet or what?'

'No, I turned it off as I was leaving.'

'Well, we better go turn it back on.'

Neville shook his head and walked on ahead back to their room. They had a difficult few days while George was looking for somewhere else to go. He slept on the chair cushions, so Neville could have his own bed every night. After work he went straight away to find food. Coming in much later he tried to rest. Neville was usually still out but when he came in he made a big deal of stepping around George as he got ready for bed, who kept his eyes shut tight. Things came to a head by early December.

It was as cold and dreary inside as it was outside. Neville came home earlier than usual that night. He banged around a bit then shook George by the shoulder.

'So, you 'ave any luck yet?'

George sat up, pretending to rub his eyes as if he had just woken up, 'No, not yet. Do you have any ideas?'

'Why you don't try the YMCA? The place just a coupla blocks from 'ere. Go out, turn lef' pass by that little grocery store and you can't miss it.'

'Yeah, yeah, thanks. Hadn't thought of that. I'll go tomorrow morning.'

Chapter Seventeen

The White Rose Mission and Industrial Association, Harlem

Sarah Kinsey was in her parlour on the second floor of the imposing brownstone on West 136th Street, Harlem where she had lived and worked for twenty years. Since then she had devoted her life to following in the worthy footsteps of her predecessor who had opened the mission many years before as a sanctuary for young coloured women who found themselves in dire straits.

She was tidying away her sewing for the night; she tried to make something different every Christmas for the young women in her care. She had been embroidering tray-cloths for each girl to take into her married life, every item representing a design in keeping with the nature of the individual. Florence, who loved dancing had musical notes on hers, Erica's design was a big pink cake covered in berries because she enjoyed serving the tea on Sunday afternoons. A picture of a young woman in a doorway wearing a warm smile was for Alice, who was so welcoming and kind to the many frightened girls who turned up at the door of The White Rose Mission, each with their own sad stories to tell. The tray-cloths were embroidered with each girl's name across the top and in the bottom left-hand corner was a small flower with SK in the middle.

There was a knock at the door. She flung an antimacassar over the sewing and went to open it.

'Oh, Alice, it's you. Come in.'

She studied the girl's face. Alice Jarrell had been at The White Rose for four years and Sarah Kinsey had seen her grow from a timid sixteen-year-old girl into a capable young woman. She had come across her slumped on a bench at Penn Station. Shabby and torn, her eyes large with fear and confusion.

Sarah Kinsey had seen that look many times. She could only guess what had probably happened, which was why she often went down to Penn Station. As Superintendent of The White Rose she had rescued many such girls over the years. Most of them had endured a hard life journey and many became hardened and bitter by their experiences. They were the ones who took what they could before drifting away to fall into the kind of life from which Sarah Kinsey tried to save them. But Alice still managed to maintain an optimistic naivety.

She had been grateful for the initial benefit of the Travellers' Aid Fund available for destitute young people and willingly helped out in the sewing and cooking classes. After a few weeks, Sarah Kinsey offered her a part-time position as a cleaner and general help, so she could earn her keep. Alice knew that she would have to hone her domestic skills, since the only paid work available to her would be as a maid. Sarah always shared the annual report with those in her care which re-iterated every year that, 'Negro girls [..] must appreciate that the simple needs of the South are gone. She must learn to labor as well, if not better than the white girls in the kitchen, the dining room, the nursery and the sewing room if she is not to fail here.'[1]

'Everything alright dear?'

'Yes...well no, not really, Miss Kinsey. A girl knocked on the front door a few minutes ago. I couldn't catch her name, she's that upset.'

---

1 See index.

'Oh, thank you Alice. I'm so glad it was you who greeted her with your beautiful smile. Where is she at present?'

'I took her to the kitchen. Erica's making her a hot drink. Think you should see her soon because she's wailing somethin' bad.'

'I know, I know Alice. I'll be right there. Not to worry.'

The older woman rested her eyes on Alice's face. 'Why don't you go upstairs and calm yourself for a few moments, dear? I'm sure Erica will take care of her until I can come.'

Alice shut the door quietly and ran upstairs to the attic room she shared with Florence, who would be back from work anytime soon. Alice felt bad when her friend saw her falling apart like a big cry-baby. But Miss Kinsey understood when that feeling came over her like a swamp mist. That feeling which took her right back to a day she couldn't forget. June 20th 1919. When she first pitched up in New York city. Alone.

Chapter Eighteen

She had finally made her way to Penn Station and sat down on a bench wondering what to do next. People all around. Noise. Scared. And so tired. She wanted to close her eyes for a while but was afraid that someone might steal her bag as she slept. Hungry too. As her mother used to say, her belly was touching her backbone. Thinking about Mom made her mouth start shaking, but she pressed her lips close together and stared at the ground for a few seconds until it passed.

Everyone seemed to be in a rush going nowhere. Except for a coloured man she saw carefully loading some hatboxes onto a little cart for a grand lady in a large dress and hat. Kept his head down as he worked and didn't look into her face as she was waving her arms around something bad and making a whole heap of fussing. Then a big man came out of nowhere. A white man, grey-haired with a slight stoop and a shiny face. He was wearing smart clothes, a tailcoat, a tall hat and he carried a cane. Came right up to where she was sitting.

'Good day. Have you just arrived?'

She wasn't sure what to say, or whether to say anything at all. He looked like an official kind of person.

'Well yes, I have...Sir.'

'Good, well I'm just the man to help you. My name's Harold Parker and I work on behalf of the railroad company. My job is to help young people who are new to the city. People like yourself.'

'Oh, my goodness, I didn't realise. I thought that now I'm here I could just find someplace to stay.'

He briefly held her shoulder. Quite hard. 'I have to make sure you have the right papers to enter New York', his face stern, like his features had been stuck on with cow glue.

'Papers? What papers?'

Her bag slipped to the floor as she stood up. She was too afraid to pick it up, her knees trembling like jelly. She bowed her head and twisted her fingers together. Over and over. Harold Parker sighed. Shook his head slowly from side to side. Took his fob-watch from inside his coat and spent a long minute looking at it. Finally, he nodded towards her bag.

'Perhaps I should take a look at your things to see if you might have mislaid them young lady.'

Alice bent down, conscious of him watching her every move. She grabbed hold of one handle and the bag gaped open. He took it from her and tipped the contents onto the ground. There was a collection of the few belongings she had carried all the way from Georgia. A couple of grubby working gowns, even grubbier underwear, a large tooth comb. And the only photo her family had of her Gramma. Cracked and faded it had stood on top of the chiffonier at home for as long as Alice could remember. He picked it up and held it close in front of her face.

'And who's this in the picture? Your mother?'

'It's my Gramma, Sir. She died when she was the same age as me.'

'And how old is that, may I ask?'

'Sixteen. Sir.'

Images quivered about in her head of the story that was passed on down through the family about what happened to her

Gramma when she was sixteen. A story too terrible to dwell on. Gramma and her friend Eucratia had set off from Georgia to join the underground railroad to the North. The girls had travelled together disguised as young men. Eucratia made it through but poor Gramma didn't. Eucratia managed to get a message to the family two years later saying that they had been hiding in a barn one night. A farmhand, seeing through their disguise had raped and killed Gramma but she had been saved by the kindness of a white man. One of those abolitionist people that Mom had told her about. Mom always used to say that if you thought too much about the bad folk you came across in life, you'd only be harming yourself. She drummed it into Alice that there were good people out there who wanted to help, and that God would be their salvation and save them just like He had saved Eucratia. Except that poor Mom herself ran out of that positivity in the end. She had endured so much.

★

The journey northwards from Georgia was fraught with terror when Alice and her parents struggled to find safety. The great flu epidemic of 1918 had claimed the life of her baby brother, Eugene. After that the family decided to move north in the hope of building a happier future. Their pastor had given them a little money collected by other church members but that soon disappeared. The journey had taken months. When they needed food, they would try to earn a few dollars by doing any labouring work they could find.

It was a brutal time. They often went to sleep hungry in the corner of a field. Alice's father worked for a short while on the Pennsylvania Railroad until a tragic accident took him. She and her mother carried on as best they could, but the older woman's spirit was broken following the loss of her baby and her husband. One evening Alice came back from the fields to find her weary body hanging from a beam in the barn where they had been sleeping. Somehow, she made the last few miles alone.

'Sixteen eh. And what's your full name?'

'Alice Eucratia Jarrell.'

'Well now, Alice Eucratia Jarrell, at the grand old age of sixteen you are supposed to have proper papers to live and work here. Didn't you know that?'

'No Sir.'

'Well, here's the plan. Since I've had a good day and you seem like an honest person, I can probably sort you out with some papers. How about that?'

'Yes, thank you, Sir.'

'You can call me Mr Parker.'

'Thank you – Mr Parker.'

'You will have to come to my office, so we can sort it out.'

She felt like a catfish had just flipped over in her belly. She glanced past his shoulder and saw two railroad guards laughing and chatting a few feet behind him. If she were to run, someone would be sure to catch her. She had no choice but to believe that he would be true to his word. She closed her eyes for a second, calling upon the Lord's help as he made a big deal of looking at his watch again.

'Well, Missy, don't be wasting any more of my time. I'm a busy man. You have two choices. Either you come with me and get your working papers or get thrown in jail as an alien.'

She nodded, scrabbling about getting her things together and followed him as he began walking away out of the station. They walked in silence for a while before he spoke again.

'So how comes you're alone? Where are your folks?'

'My parents have both gone home to the Lord.'

Mr Parker grunted. 'Any other family?'

'No, Sir.'

He grunted again and walked on.

They walked along 34th Street, around the corner and past a huge store with lots of shiny windows. She'd never seen anything like it. But none of that seemed to matter as they continued walking, Mr Parker's heavy hand clutching her shoulder the whole time as she carried her bag in the other hand. A man was smoking in one of the doorways and Mr Parker greeted him as they approached. She thought maybe this would be her chance to run, but Mr Parker lifted his cane and waved it in front of her. Dangerously close to her face. People passing by glanced across at them before carrying on their way.

He spoke to the other man, 'Franklin, I need to collect my parcel from your office.'

The other man didn't say anything. Simply raised his eyebrows slightly and took Alice's elbow on her other side. She was trapped. Sweating and scared. But she had to believe it would all turn out alright.

The office was above a little store. By then Alice was uncertain where they were in relation to the railroad station. They climbed a lot of stairs, Parker in front of her and the other man behind, until they came to Franklin's office. It was quite small and there was a big desk in the middle with a swivel chair and cabinets all around, covered in papers. Mr Parker told her to wait while he collected his parcel from next door.

A few moments later he returned alone. He locked the door and put the key in his pocket, his face blank, fixed and staring. He stood very close, saying nothing. He made no move to find any papers or indeed say anything.

Her voice shaking, she spoke up. 'I don't want to take up anymore of your time, Sir. I will collect my papers and go.'

Still he said nothing.

'I'd like to go now, Sir. Please. If you don't mind.'

She made a move towards the door, but Harold Parker was having none of it. He started to remove her jacket. She was all of a-shudder, arms and legs trembling. He gave her a quick slap right across the face when she tried to speak again. She started to whimper even though she was trying hard to keep quiet in case it made him yet more angry. She put up her arms to cover herself as he wrenched off some of her clothes before flinging her across the big desk, banging her head and shoulders while the backs of her knees slammed against the rolled edge. He climbed on top of her, groping at his pants. She struggled and groaned until he punched her mouth. She froze.

All the stories about what had happened to Gramma crowded into her mind. This is what she had endured countless times before she managed to escape. And still she never made it. Alice tried to call up her strength, willing herself to recall that fuzzy photograph. Long, long ago. She lay stiffly beneath Mr Parker, her body a cold hunk of lead, her mind closed off to his coarse body and hot breath. Probing fingers opened her, hurt her, sharp nails scratched and then came the darting pain. A damp wetness slewed across her thighs.

A few moments later he fell sweating on top of her. Her thighs were wet with blood and other stuff. He started to say kind words to her, but she kept her face turned away and held her lips closed, trying not to breathe in the rank smell of him. He climbed off.

She kept her eyes shut tight and heard the rustling sounds of him straightening his clothes. She stayed very still, too afraid and hurt to move. Heavy, weary and so tired she wanted to sleep, sleep, sleep it all away. All of it. She heard the door being unlocked followed by quick footsteps echoing on the stairs. The street door slammed. Grabbing on her clothes, she looked out the window to see him walking real fast down the street. Without the cane.

Worried that she might see Franklin, she tiptoed down as quietly as she could. Somehow, she got outside and found her way back to the station. He wouldn't dare be there. Not after what he'd done. She found a corner bench and sat down. Shaking. Maybe she could ask the station officer where she could go for the night.

A tall lady came towards her. Her hair was pulled back to show a face round and smooth as a chestnut, dressed in dark clothes and wearing white crochet gloves. She looked like one of the gentle ladies who used to help out at church back home in Georgia.

Alice jumped as the lady touched her on the shoulder: 'Don't worry my dear, I can guess what's happened. My name is Sarah Kinsey. I can help you. You are safe now.'

Chapter Nineteen

Neville sometimes had occasion to pass the reception desk on his cleaning rounds. George always tried to catch his eye but got no response. When he went downstairs for his lunch Neville took the newspaper from his pocket and read it intently as George moved around him organising his food in the cramped space. The situation was not helped by Mr Manni's sickly smile as he addressed him in Neville's hearing one day,

'George, would you step by after your lunch. We need to discuss your improved salary now you're on reception.'

His extra earnings came at a cost. There were no more invitations to join Neville and Grantley on their nights out. And the YMCA had turned out to be a non-runner. A lot of the men were off the streets. They gave George a hard time, asking him why he was there in the first place, begging cigarettes from him or commenting on his fastidiousness. He didn't belong. And those who said nothing gave him filthy looks. The second night he woke up on his narrow cot to find some nutter sitting beside him and staring. He only stayed a few nights. The next morning, he took his bag into work and hid it down in the basement behind an old filing cabinet, not knowing where he would sleep that night. Maybe Grantley would let him doss down for a few days until he could find somewhere. Or maybe not.

★

He knocked on Mr Manni's office door.

'Come in.'

He entered the room and stood before the desk for what seemed like ages before being waved to a seat: 'Sit down, George, don't stand there like a dummy.'

'Thank you, Sir.'

'Yeah, yeah. Now I propose to raise your salary in keeping with your position. After all you're the first person whom clients see when they step through the door. You realise how important that is don't you George?'

'Yes Sir. I appreciate the opportunity.'

'OK, OK, drop the sir. Call me by my name, Mr Mankowitz. Sounds better in front of the clients.'

'Yes, Mr Manni – Mr Mankowitz.'

'I will pay you a decent weekly wage on the strict understanding that you keep your nose clean. That means speaking properly to clients, not being over friendly with other staff and generally behaving yourself. You get it?'

'Yes.'

'Yes what?'

'Yes, Mr Mankowitz.'

'Speaking of looks, you don't seem like your usual smart self today George. What's up?'

As if he didn't know. Drop the 'sir', being called by name instead of 'boy'. Things were changing. He thought he may as well tell him.

'Well?' said Mr Manni, tipping back his chair, arms folded, head to one side.

'The thing is, it's not working out with me and Neville now and I'm looking for somewhere to sleep until I can find a place of my own.'

Mr M. sat forward, raised his arms and rested them on his head. 'Oh great, that's all I need. Look, give me a couple of hours, I'll think of something. You better get on back to your post.'

A few minutes later George saw him going out. He returned at closing time, leaned across and told George to follow him. Took him next door to City Insurance and introduced him to a Mr Roberts. George had sometimes come across him during his cleaning rounds. He stood aside while the two men talked about him as if he was not there before calling him over.

Arrogant sods.

Mr Manni made their intentions very clear: 'Now look, George, there is somewhere you can sleep temporarily. My good friend Ray here will show you where. But take care and listen to what he has to say.'

They both marched off and he followed on behind like an obedient puppy into the storeroom. He was familiar with it because stationery for both buildings was kept there and it was his responsibility to make sure it was kept tidy and accessible. There was a small closet in one corner and shelves all around the walls loaded with old typewriters, pens, paper and other random office items. The space in the centre was piled high with blankets and a pillow thrown on the floor.

Mr Roberts took over: 'You can doss down here for a week or two until you find a room. Put your things in that closet. Make sure you use the restroom early morning before any other staff come in and then get back into Lerner's double quick for opening time. And remember, you're not supposed to be here.'

The stationery cupboard. That would surely give folks a good laugh if they knew. George vowed not to tell anyone. Ever.

'Thank you, Mr Roberts. Sir. I'll find somewhere soon as I can.'

'Good. Once you're inside for the night, that's it. The building will be locked at the usual time If you need food, you'll have to get it during your lunch break and bring it across here. But, don't let anyone see you, understand?'

'Yes, but um, think I might need to pay a month's rent in advance when I find somewhere.'

Mr M. took out a few dollar bills from his pocket: 'Here take this, I'll deduct it weekly.'

'OK, thanks. I won't let you down, Sir.'

Kow-towing to the big man again.

Seemed like that was the way it had to be. Maybe one day he would find the life he wanted, but meanwhile, it was time to put his stuff away and make up his bed on the floor.

★

The foyer area in Lerners was very high and light with a marble floor, just like you see in the films. Probably because it was in mid-Manhattan, the posh part of town. There were paintings on the walls of the company's founders and their colleagues. Grim looking individuals in stiff, starched collars. He wondered how anyone could look so miserable when they had so much money. The reception desk was in front of a tall window. He had to sit behind on a stool and watch who was going in and out, answer enquiries, take phone calls and direct people to the right place using a map of the building. Always making sure to work to a script written out in long hand by Mr M. who sometimes lingered nearby to check that he followed it. If he needed to sign for deliveries of stationery and other office equipment it had to be countersigned by Mr M. He smuggled his food down to the storeroom when he packed it all away.

Clarence occasionally talked to him, but only if George addressed him first. He was a friend of Neville's. Clarence was not allowed to leave his post unless he was really desperate to use the hell hole of a restroom way down in the basement. George found it shameful to listen to him begging Mr M. when he needed to use it. The bosses at the dockyard back home were strict, but George had never known anyone having to abase themselves to that degree.

The storeroom became his home. He was locked in the building every night and had little time during his lunch break to look around. Some nights he lay on the concrete wondering what he had done in leaving home the way he did. Granted life was difficult, especially between him and Ruby, but maybe if he'd stuck it out things might have worked themselves out. Then there was Rachel. He couldn't have kept stringing her along forever.

She had lent him some money as the deposit for a little place of their own after which they were going to tell her folks about their engagement. That was supposed to be the plan. She was prepared to wait a while until he could afford to buy her a decent ring. Fat chance of that or anything else on the wages he earned even if he had been serious about her. He was always vague about his job; making out that he had a job in the shipping office was not such a good idea. And if she ever found out that he was Ruby's brother, all hell might have let loose. Although who knows, she was at Mam's funeral after all.

He was getting tired of having to skirt around his family life if she ever asked him anything personal. Punched above his weight with that one, but man didn't she enjoy a good romp. She was an alright girl really. Been to a good school, travelled abroad, knew a lot about films, literature and other highbrow stuff. She used to lend him books to read and they would talk about them afterwards. She made him feel sort of worthy and encouraged him to make the most of himself but her patronising behaviour sometimes pissed him off. Poor baby didn't realise how much she had helped him to leave her.

Although he never did get to meet her parents. When he asked why she always maintained that they were busy and that it would happen 'all in good time'. In the end he stopped mentioning it. So maybe she had her own agenda too.

Funny how life can jump up and bite your sorry arse.

He never imagined he'd end up sleeping on the floor, hidden from view like some kind of dark, alien secret. He had a lot to think about, that was for sure.

Chapter Twenty

Ruby was in the kitchen making the Christmas pudding. It was late December and she should have made it weeks ago. Mam always made it on the first day of the month so that the rum could soak in properly. By the time it was boiling away on Christmas Day you could get drunk just on the smell. Mam always used the same big pot, kept at the back of the cupboard together with the same raggedy old piece of sheet to wrap up the pudding. She and George would be sent out of the room when Dad boiled a coin to add to the mixture. Whoever found it in their pudding on Christmas Day made a wish and a little speech. It was usually a three-penny piece. One year it was a sixpence. Ruby got it that year. It was still in her drawer somewhere. Mam made the Christmas cake on the same day too, a stiff mixture packed with fruit, nuts and of course, rum.

Then there were the mince pies. They had to be made on Christmas Eve, so that any visitors who dropped by could eat them hot from the oven together with a tot, a glass of beer or home-made lemonade for the children or those adults who didn't drink. Although there weren't many of those. Ruby especially enjoyed helping to make the pastry, stirring in the flour with a little water, usually adding too much, until the sticky mixture was all over her clothes and in her hair. The best part was bashing away with the rolling pin and adding as much butter as the mixture could hold. The resulting pastry was yellow and rich. She and Mam spent a long time scrubbing the table first before they started. And afterwards. George was usually outside with the other boys and came in later to scrape the bowl.

The whole family used to go uptown to the indoor market to get all the ingredients. Dad would come too because there was too much for Mam, Ruby and George to carry by themselves. With Dad there it felt like Christmas had begun even though it was weeks away.

★

But everything was different that year. Ruby was doing it all by herself. She heard the front door open then close with a bang. Dad's voice in the hallway. Loud whispering, Dad's laugh. Footsteps. He came into the kitchen with a grin she'd not seen in a while.

'Just look who I found outside my girl.'

And there was Jimmy following on behind, carrying his small cardboard suitcase.

'Hello there lovely', as he bent towards her.

Ruby shook her head, quickly trying to gather herself. 'Well now look who it is. Turned up for an early Christmas dinner I suppose?'

Jimmy gave her a hug, stepped back and made a show of dusting the flour from his jacket, laughing all the while.

Although Dad knew that she and Jimmy were officially courting, she still felt too shy to show her feelings when he was around. She clicked her tongue, wiped her hands on her apron and turned back to her pudding.

'Hope you two are not going to interrupt my serious cooking now. Christmas soon and I'm all behind with my preparations.'

'Don't you worry about that,' said Jimmy as he looked her up and down. 'Me and your father are going to take you out for supper. What do you think then, gal?'

111

'Oh, my goodness, that sounds exciting. Hang on, I just need to finish off here.'

Dad watched them before he went to fetch a couple of glasses from the kitchen cupboard, so they could give Jimmy a welcome tot. It was heart-warming to see Ruby looking happy. The last few months had been tough for them both. But dear old Jimmy was a godsend, helping them get back to work as well as putting a smile on his daughter's face.

She was a good girl and deserved to be happy. God willing it would work out for them. And that his son would come home to him one day. Maybe he would send a letter or a Christmas card. Although there was hardly any point in getting his hopes up. A man who could hurt his family the way George had was capable of anything. Best not to think like that. After all George was his flesh and blood and darling Bernadette doted on the boy to her dying day. At least the chaps at work had stopped gossiping about it. Not in his earshot anyway. He poured the rum and took his glass out to the scullery while he got washed up.

★

'So, Miss Ruby, are you pleased to see me?' Jimmy noticed his friend's disappearance, put his arms around her, and undid her apron strings.

'Course I am, you silly sod,' she said as she lifted her face up to kiss him.

'Well go and get dressed up, my gal. I'll clear away in the kitchen. Looks like the wreck of the 'esperus in here,' he laughed.

★

A couple of hours later, all three were sitting in Da Silva's on Bute Street. They were just finishing up their dinner of bacalhau. The fish dish was steaming hot, the onions done to a turn and the potatoes sweet and moist. Jimmy and Dad were enjoying a beer and Ruby was on port wine.

Jimmy called the waiter over, 'Can we have three pastel de natas, young man? My lady here has a very sweet tooth.'

'Of course, Mr Jacobs. Right away.'

Dad was puzzled: 'What's a pastel de whatsitsname when it's at 'ome, man?'

Ruby giggled. She was halfway through her second port wine. 'Don't worry, Dad, it's just custard tart to me and you. And if you're not keen, I don't mind eating yours as well.'

She raised her eyebrows and grinned across the table at Dad. He smiled back, although he was probably thinking about the rare occasions when he took Mam there. He used to try and get some overtime at work, so he could give her a special treat for her birthday or their anniversary. You would have thought they were dining at The Ritz the way Mam would be all dressed up to the nines. She could make a plain dress look like a million dollars with a remnant of fabric she bought in the market draped across the front or a few sequins found at the bottom of her button tin. If she were there she probably would have really gone to town in something suitably festive.

It looked like a lot of folks in the neighbourhood had started Christmas early. The atmosphere was alive with loud voices and bonhomie. Annie and Dot were over in the corner. Both in their late forties, the two sisters lived next door to one another just along the street, being well known for their kindness and high spirits. Ruby smiled as she remembered their musical renditions at Mam's wake. They were both buxom women.

That evening they were dressed in bright colours, their grey hair upswept to one side with tortoiseshell combs. If anyone commented on their style, Annie usually responded by saying,

'Yep, we look like flippin' bookends, don't we?' Then she would throw back her head and laugh. Their husbands were seafarers and were often away for long spells at a time. Annie and Dot were very popular and guaranteed to bring good times and joy to any social gathering.

All of a sudden, Annie started singing:

On moonlight bay ...

Dot joined in by the time her sister reached the second line.

They were swaying side by side as if they were on a sailboat, and after a while a few other folks joined in. One elderly couple even got up and started to dance. A gentle side to side step. By the end of the song, Pinkie had come in with his guitar and joined them for the last line, a sweet serenade to the music of love in the moonlight. Everyone cheered and raised their glasses. Annie and Dot got up and gave a lopsided curtsy in unison as they accepted complimentary glasses of port wine from Mr Da Silva himself.

As the dancers went back to their seats, the elderly man knocked someone's drink over by mistake. Within minutes an argument broke out, one man shouting in defence of the old man and the other complaining about his clumsiness. Such skirmishes were commonplace in any of the thirty-two pubs down the bay. People knew what to do. Everyone calmly got up and ambled outside while Mr Da Silva sorted things out. There was a bit more shouting, the sound of broken glass and a chair being knocked over. Dad, Jimmy and Ruby stepped onto the pavement with the rest of the diners. Nobody seemed to be that bothered, surprised or even annoyed.

The last two to come out were Annie and Dot, giggling together with their glasses held high, still half filled. They were met with applause and much thigh-slapping laughter before everyone went back inside and returned to their seats. The pastel de natas or rather – custard tarts were still there and still intact. The two troublemakers, friends again, slunk away into the dark and went off to drink elsewhere.

Chapter Twenty-one

George was used to visitors asking about his accent and which part of England he came from. They seemed to think he should know all there was to know about the Old Country as some of them called it. About the royal family, Shakespeare, history, all that crap. Sometimes he exaggerated the accent if anyone seemed impressed by it. They didn't know the difference; Welsh, English, it was all one and the same to them. Mr Manni found reasons to intervene several times a day to see how he was getting on and to offer quiet advice. But mostly he just wanted to blend in. A couple of the office girls might stroll past, all sassy, sidelong glances and exchanged whispers. As the days passed he became more confident and relaxed in his new role. He was anxious to settle into his job, find a place to live and become a real American.

He should be used to being alone, but it hurt each time he thought about it. As a child he had enjoyed being adored and spoiled by Mam, but it only accentuated the difference between himself and Ruby. She had brought him up to feel so special that he couldn't fit in nor wanted to, at work, at home or in the neighbourhood. Mam always told him he was destined for greatness, but he was still a loner. The outsider. His confidence was frail; he hardly knew who he was any more.

A few days later: Christmas Eve. It was three-thirty in the afternoon and the staff in both buildings were packing up early for the holiday. That meant George would be locked in at City office for at least two days and nights. There was a festive atmosphere in the air. A couple of the more friendly secretaries stopped by to chat as he sat at his post wondering what he was going to do. It had been a busy day with a lot to finish off and no time to go out and get some food to sneak back to his sleeping quarters. He would have to get hold of Mr Roberts and ask him to wait a while before locking up, so he could nip out to the store. Although God only knew how or when he would have the opportunity to ask.

Mr M. came in carrying what looked like a box of stationery. The foyer was busy with people saying their farewells and buttoning up their coats before going out into the cold. Mr M. went right up to George and dumped the box on the desk, speaking in what seemed an unnecessarily loud voice.

'I want these office things taken over to the storeroom. Make sure you pack them away tidy, so I can find what I want when I get back in a few days.'

'Yes, Mr Mankowitz. I'll do it right away.'

'By the way, you may as well finish up now too. Looks like everyone's racing to get outta here and go home. Nothing more for you to do here today.'

With that he turned away and went into his office. He came back out with his coat on and gave George a slight nod before Clarence opened the front door for him with a bow and an overly effusive greeting.

Pathetic sad sod.

But then he considered that his own behaviour was probably creepy too.

Yes, Mr Mankowitz, No, Mr Mankowitz, three bags full, Mr Bloody Mankowitz.

He hastily tidied his desk and took the box next door. Mr Roberts raised his eyebrows, jangling his keys, ready to lock up.

He went straight up to George, 'Did Mr Mankowitz give you the office things to put away?'

'Yes Sir, but I need to talk to you about…'

Mr Roberts widened his eyes at George before cutting him off, 'You better do it right away then. Report back to me in five minutes when you're done.'

George went downstairs and opened the box. Inside was enough food to last him for a couple of days: some bread, cold meats, fruit, nuts and bottles of soda. There was also a book and a short note, 'Didn't want to see you going hungry. Hope you can sort yourself out by the new year. And you might find this interesting reading.'

It was signed, E. Mankowitz.

The book was a battered copy of William Shakespeare's collected works.

George lay on his makeshift bed. It was four o'clock in the afternoon of December 25th. After everyone had left early the previous day, he sat around until he was sure that Mr Roberts had finished his rounds and left the building. He had spent more than three weeks locked away every evening from five-thirty until the following morning and had never felt so alone. He slept a lot in the early evening; after he'd eaten there was nothing else to do. He often woke up in the early hours, when he spent his time wandering from the storeroom to the restroom and back again, or simply lay in the dark waiting for daylight.

When he found it difficult to go back to sleep he concentrated on any familiar object around him, a box, a comb, a pencil, whatever, closed his eyes and tried to focus on it. How it looked and felt to the touch, its shape, dimensions, anything to avoid the memories. Once the working day started he would have the chance to talk to people as they came and went about their business. He had already eaten some of the cold meat and bread and drunk one of the bottles of soda, being conscious of the need to ration the food, unsure how long it would have to last.

Opening the Shakespeare book at random during the evening he couldn't make any sense of the language, so decided to read some of the preface. Rachel was the most educated person he knew, and she always maintained that Shakespeare was the best writer in history. She used to talk to him about some of her favourite plays and sonnets. The stuff had certainly been around a long time, so there must be something in it. She once gave him some sonnets that she had carefully copied out in her loopy handwriting. Must have taken her ages. They were all about love and full of thees, thous and doths. He didn't really appreciate what they meant at the time but kept them in his wallet.

He recalled the play she talked about a lot in which a rich Jewish man called Shylock was having a tough time. Probably because her own family was Jewish, although it seemed to him that they had a bloody good life. Her dad was obviously a clever businessman and worked hard. True, some people didn't like him. Why do folks need to get so het up? Small-minded jealous types who don't want to see anyone making a go of it. Maybe he should be considering going into business himself. But what? He needed to think about it. New year, new beginnings.

He found *The Merchant of Venice* and read it right through, coming across the speech where the same guy talks about being an outsider: 'for suff'rance is the badge of all our tribe'. Although he was as nutty as a fruitcake anyway what with all that business of cutting off a pound of the other bloke's flesh.

Sick weirdo.

And then there was the story of the great soldier, Othello. One minute they were praising him for being so smart and all the while his right-hand man turned out to be a scheming so-and-so. He was a fool to fall for it. Difficult to know who to trust. And then the business about him and Desdemona, she was certainly taking a risk when she got the hots for him. Shakespeare certainly knew what made people tick. One thing was true, people haven't changed for centuries. He read late into the night, having to keep constantly referring to the notes at the bottom of each page to help him decipher the language.

There was bugger-all else to do.

The stories brought him so much: sadness, amusement, anger and often sheer wonder at the beauty of the words. One thing puzzled him: why didn't any of the poor sods in his plays have surnames? Shakespeare had really slipped up there.

Chapter Twenty-two

'So, George, what did you think of The Bard?'

Mr Roberts came down to the storeroom just as he was getting ready to go next door to work. He had hidden away his things; a new year had begun and there he was still having to hide away like a criminal.

Could really do without Mr Smartarse with his damn fool conversation.

He was grateful for the food and everything else, but nothing had really changed.

'Sorry Sir, don't understand,' he says, trying to glance at his watch without being noticed.

'The Bard? Shakespeare?'

'Oh, right. Umm, as a matter of fact I really enjoyed it. Sir.'

'What did you like best? Which play?'

'Hard to say. It gave me a lot to think about.'

'OK, I can see you're anxious to get away, George. I'd like to talk to you after work, about your thoughts and a couple of other ideas I've had.'

He paused for a moment: 'Oh, by the way, I'll leave the back door unlocked, so that you're not seen. About six o'clock.'

'Yes Sir, I'll be there.'

★

'Come in, come in.'

Mr Roberts ushered George into his office. Everybody else had left and the building was quiet. He had slipped out of Lerner's into the cold, dark evening and in through back door as directed, noticing how shabby both buildings looked from the rear in comparison with the main entrances. All done up to impress the clients with their fancy ways.

'Sit down, George. Don't stand on ceremony.'

He was wondering what this was all about and was mentally preparing himself to be told the worst. That he would have to get out. Pronto. He waited. Mr Roberts opened his desk drawer, searched around and came up with a piece of paper. He folded it in half and put it down on the desk between them. Silence. He tipped his chair back, crossed his legs and folded his arms.

'So, tell me, George, how do you see yourself?'

What kind of stupid question was that?

'I don't understand Sir. As a worker? A man?'

Mr Roberts sighed and put his hand to his head.

'What do you think of New York? Are you pleased you came?'

'It's a great city, Sir. Umm, I want to learn more about it.'

'Is it what you expected?'

Shit, shit, double shit. What is going on with this bloke?

'Well, I haven't been here long.'

Mr Roberts stood up. 'My good friend Manni tells me that you're good at your job and manage to keep your business to yourself. The only problem you have at the moment is you're not having any luck in finding accommodation. Ain't that so?'

Jeezus, what a weirdo.

Looked like he was going to get the push. And would still have to pay back the advance rent money.

'Yes, Sir. Umm, there isn't much time during the day for me to go and look for somewhere. I was wondering if I could get a day off, or even an afternoon.'

'OK, I know what you're saying. I have a proposition for you.'

He picked up the piece of paper and dangled it between them both. 'I have the address of a room that may be suitable.'

George stayed quiet. Why was his boss trying to be so helpful? First the food, the Shakespeare malarkey and then...

Oh shit, maybe he's one of those creeps that don't go for women.

Come to think of it, he had been looking at him funny. Plus, it didn't help that they were locked up together in the empty building.

Bloody hell.

The older man sat and waited.

Might as well take the bull by the horns.

'Why would you want to do that for me? Sir?'

Mr Roberts laughed then, 'Don't look so scared. Believe it or not I thought you could do with a break. A guy like you deserves better Do you know what I mean?'

'Well, thanks Sir. I do my best.'

'Don't think my offer doesn't come with, let's say, an understanding between us.'

Right, it was time to tell this guy where he could get off. Sure, he was desperate for somewhere to live, but not if it meant what he thought it meant.

No sirree, no bloody chance.

George stood up and began to back up against the door.

Mr Roberts laughed out loud: 'Sit down, George. It's a genuine offer. A friend of mine has a house up in Yorkville. He's looking to rent out one of the rooms which has just become vacant.'

'But, why me?'

'Well, as I said there's something different about you which I think could be good for business. You're polite, you got that cute accent, the clients seem to like you. You look the part. Do you want me to spell it out?'

'No, Sir. And thanks.'

'Good. I was telling this guy about you. He's looking for

someone who knows how to keep himself quiet, won't go around blabbing his business to the other tenants and most of all, won't invite undesirables to the house.'

'Undesirables?'

'Yes George, undesirables. Like Neville and his cronies. The other people who live in the house are decent, professional types. This would be a good chance for you to think about what you want here in New York.'

He stood up and opened the door: 'Let me know by tomorrow morning.'

Chapter Twenty-three

One morning in early January 1924, a woman by the name of Mrs Feldmann knocked on the door of The White Rose. She was looking for a willing girl who could cook, keep house and care for her two small boys for a few days each week. That evening after supper Sarah Kinsey stopped Alice as she was going upstairs.

'Would you step into the parlour, Alice; I'd like to talk to you.'

Alice stood inside the door, unsure why she had been singled out for attention.

'Is everything OK, Miss Kinsey?'

'Of course, dear, I just need to discuss something with you. Come in and sit down. And don't look so worried.'

Sitting on the edge of the chair, Sarah Kinsey's opening gambit made her feel even more anxious: 'Are you happy here, Alice? And do you enjoy your work?'

'Yes Miss Kinsey, of course. Is there anything extra you'd like me to do?'

'No, it's not that. I'm very satisfied with all you do and don't think I haven't noticed how kind you are to the new girls when they turn up on our doorstep. However, I think it might be time for you to see what's out there in the big, wide world.'

Alice rose to her feet, 'Oh, Miss Kinsey, does that mean you want me to leave? I couldn't bear it.' She started to cry, 'Please, please don't make me go.'

Sarah Kinsey left her seat by the fire and held both Alice's hands in hers. 'No, you've got it all wrong. Sit back down and listen for a moment.'

She continued by telling Alice about Mr and Mrs Feldmann, who had four-year-old twin boys. They lived in East 86th Street down in Yorkville and had a bakery nearby on York Avenue. Their last girl had left and Mrs Feldmann was very anxious to find someone competent and reliable as soon as possible.

'So of course, right off I thought of you. I've recommended you but wanted to discuss it with you first. What do you think?'

Alice paused. 'A real job? Would I be able to earn money to give you Miss Kinsey?'

'Put it this way, my dear. As far as I'm concerned, you've been earning your keep here all this time by doing and being the splendid person that you are. But yes, you would be more independent with a job outside and would be able to pay for your bed and board, plus a few extras. Mrs Feldmann will pay you fourteen dollars each month.'

'Fourteen dollars! Oh, my goodness, I've never seen so much money.'

'That's what I thought. And just think, you might even meet some nice young man one day, get married and have children of your own. And you would be able to save towards your bottom drawer if you had a proper job.'

Alice had never ventured so far south in the city before and she may as well have been setting off for another planet. Miss Kinsey told her to take the Harlem Railroad all the way followed by a quick stroll through Central Park. There had been a slight fall of snow the previous day and the trees looked like monsters looming large and quiet between the huge rocks. As she rushed along the wide path, a grand-looking couple were walking in her direction. The lady wore a swirly blue coat and cloche hat with feathers on the side. Her collar and cuffs were trimmed with dark fur, the sleeves stopping just below her elbows with soft leather gloves in a darker blue coming up to her elbows. She was chattering away and waving her left hand about as she talked, the other holding the arm of her escort who looked very imposing in a long brown coat, a trilby hat and spats. As they passed by Alice tried not to look at him because he reminded her of the bestial Mr Parker.

★

The doorman, a fat coloured man with a friendly smile stood inside the entrance to the apartment block on 86th Street, done up in a tight grey uniform with a pillbox-type of hat. Alice was falling all over her words by the time she reached the right building as she tried to explain why she was there. He directed her to the elevator, but she couldn't shut the gates properly and he was obliged to leave his post to come over and help. Even so she got out at the second floor by mistake and ran up a flight of stairs to the next floor.

Mrs Feldmann opened the door and showed her in with a smile.

'You are Alice, jah?'

'Yes, good morning, Ma'am. Miss Kinsey sent me.'

'Jah, jah, come in, Alice.'

The hallway was a fugue of darkness. Wood panelling, heavy furniture and maroon swagged drapes graced the entrance to the sitting room. Two blond boys were quietly drawing in the corner, lodged between a hefty-looking bureau and a tall window casting a shaft of timid sunlight on their imposing surroundings. They looked Alice up and down and glanced at one another before turning back to their pictures. She was trying to remember what Miss Kinsey told her about being respectful and polite and not to sit down until invited to.

Mrs Feldmann's voice was loud and her German accent was quite pronounced which Alice found daunting. Not wanting to be thought of as a dumb cluck, her head bobbed up and down in mock understanding. Everything was so big, Mrs Feldmann: her voice, her hair, her presence, the room, even the children looked larger than life. At four years old Alice expected them to be smaller and more smiley. Mrs Feldmann took her into the kitchen and gestured for her to sit.

'So, Alice. Tell me what you like to be clever at. What you can do very well.'

The unfamiliar style of Mrs Feldmann's language threw her off key and she couldn't think how to respond. Furthermore, nobody had ever asked her that question before. She knew what Miss Kinsey thought of her but didn't want to appear boastful. Her voice came out like a mouse squeezing through a hole as she shrank into the dark patterns of the rug.

'I try to help people, Ma'am. And I like to cook and sew.'

'Jah, jah, is good. Would you have any questions for me?'

Alice shook her head. The lady must think she was a real dumbo.

'We have a bakery on 1st Avenue. My husband is very busy man because now we are to have another one.' She sat back and laughed. 'My people like our German cakes. Perhaps one day I will bring one for you.'

'That would be very nice, Ma'am. That's if you want me to work for you.'

'Of course, not to worry, Alice. Miss Kinsey tells me you are a very good girl. I will need to be busy too now that we have two bakeries to run. My boys must have a strong person to care for them. Three, maybe four days every week.'

'Yes, I understand, Ma'am.'

'Let us go and talk to the twins, Alice.'

They went back into the sitting room where Mrs Feldmann directed her to a large sofa. The boys were strangely quiet for kids of that age, which to Alice's mind, showed how well behaved they were.

Their mother went over to them and spoke softly in German; taking each of them by the hand she presented them to Alice: 'This is Felix and this Leon.'

Alice stood up as they held out their hands to shake hers, so she had one on either side. They greeted her politely, 'Guten morgen. Wie geht es Ihnen?'

Alice knew they must be asking a question because of the way their words rose at the end. She looked to Mrs Feldmann for help.

'They are saying good morning, how are you,' she said, touching Alice's forearm, 'but it's OK for you to answer in English. They need to learn.'

Alice shook each child's hand separately: 'Good morning, Felix. Pleased to meet you I'm sure. Good morning, Leon, pleased to meet you I'm sure.'

The boys both gave a little bow before going back to their drawings. Mrs Feldmann reiterated the fact that she valued Miss Kinsey's recommendation: 'I know you will not let me down, Alice.'

Eventually Alice remembered to enquire what her duties would be, using 'Ma'am' at the end of each sentence to an exaggerated degree. Back in the kitchen Mrs Feldmann showed her where all the cleaning things were. There was a huge dresser along one wall, with all kind of flowery china in neat rows along the shelves. Alice had never seen such beautiful things and worried about how she would get to dust it all without breaking something.

The older woman stood aside and studied her face, 'Not to worry Alice. You must not touch those. They are too precious to me. Look in here.'

She opened a cupboard beneath which was stock full of thick white china and pots and pans, 'This is better jah? You use these instead?'

Alice nodded. Rich people seemed to need an awful lot more things than other folk. Mrs Feldmann showed her where the groceries were kept and told her that she would leave enough food from evening supper for lunch the following day. It only had to be warmed up.

'And one day I show you how to cook good German food, jah?'

'Yes Ma'am. I would like that.'

Suddenly there came a heap of hollering from the room next door. When Alice and Mrs Feldman went in the twins were fighting and rolling around on the floor. Their mother shouted loudly at them over and over. She yanked them both by the arm and sat them on opposite sides of the room. They hushed up soon enough although Felix still flicked crayons across at his brother as if nobody was looking. Alice's eyes grew big. What happened to the adorable kids of just a half hour ago? Mrs Feldman warned her again that she would have to be firm with them if they misbehaved.

'They are not schlecht very often,' adding that, 'The last girls were all too kind; my boys' behaviour became nicht gut.'

Alice's high spirits at being recommended for the job wavered and she began to wonder if she would be able to cope any better.

By the time Mrs Feldmann showed her out of the front door, her palms were sweating, and her forehead curl was all damp and frizzy. As she left the older woman touched her on the arm. Alice flinched and looked down at the floor.

'You will soon learn. I try to be good mistress, Alice. You come back tomorrow at eight o'clock. Is OK jah?'

The girl's eyes filled with tears of embarrassment as she mumbled her goodbyes and left. She didn't use the elevator again in case she got it wrong, but ran down those stairs as fast as any rattlesnake, somehow found her way back to the subway and home.

Chapter Twenty-four

Alice was taking stock. Things had certainly turned around thanks to dear Miss Kinsey. She'd been in her job nearly two months. Felix and Leon were not easy kids to cope with, but she thought she was getting through. Although maybe it was just because she was still a novelty to them. Time would tell.

A lot had happened since Christmas. She chuckled to herself as she recalled that special day. All the girls were up early to help prepare dinner: chicken, collard greens, grits and rice. And sweet potato pie with homemade lemonade for dessert. They stood for grace before they ate and thanked God for His goodness in providing a safe sanctuary. Afterwards there was singing upstairs in the sewing room. Miss Kinsey played her limited repertoire on the piano, including, 'Jesus loves me, this I know' and 'Lift every voice and sing, till earth and heaven ring'.

Florence got a bit carried away on the second hymn, introducing a guttural, bluesy voice to the proceedings. Sarah Kinsey's hands froze on the keys as she demanded to know where she had learned to sing like that. Some of the girls tittered. Florence thought better of it and decided to help take around the candy instead. When the festivities were over, each girl was given a tray cloth with her name on it, embroidered by Miss Kinsey's own fair hand.

★

Alice peered in the hall mirror and pulled at her bang trying to make it rest nicely across her forehead. She wore a felt cloche hat, which had probably once been black but was faded to a muddy dark grey. Small, dark and curvy with the movements of a small bird, she gathered her bags together. Pulling on her gloves and belting her coat up tight she stepped out onto East 86th Street into the cold twilight. The astrakhan collar added by herself from a piece given her by Miss Kinsey was pulled up around her ears as she hurried towards the station and got the train home.

★

Unlocking the door of number 262, West 136th Street, she was greeted by Florence who also volunteered at the Wednesday evening sewing class. She had some exciting news. Apparently, an anonymous donor had brought a gift of several bolts of ratine crepe fabric during the afternoon. The cloth was glossy and came in a variety of vibrant colours, arousing a thrill among the girls. It had been donated by a woman whom somebody thought might be a famous jazz singer. She had sat outside in a big, shiny car while her driver delivered the parcels. Florence said she was brazenly drinking liquor straight from the bottle and opening her door she was calling out to the girls as they peered from an upstairs window.

'Y'all be good gals now. Maybe I might see a couple of ya sometime when you're out and about.'

Then she leaned back in her seat: a big woman with a big laugh. And a big heart.

Florence said she was definitely The Empress of the Blues, but Alice didn't think that a royal person would be coloured. Nor yet behave that way. At sewing class there was a lot of talk as to how the fabric could best be utilised. It was obviously far too glamorous to wear to church. Those girls who enjoyed a somewhat dubious social life could already imagine themselves dressed in a fetching ratine gown and leaning on the arm of a handsome beau in one of Harlem's speakeasies. Sarah Kinsey came upstairs to the sewing room and gave each of them a dress length in the colour of their choice.

Excitement over, they went back to making gingham aprons for the cookery class. The evening passed. Around ten-thirty Alice mounted the stairs to the attic room she shared with Florence. After saying her prayers she climbed into bed and thanked God for His love.

Chapter Twenty-five

Since the new year George's social life had been considerably less than satisfactory. He wondered why he couldn't seem to find the right girl. He thought about the few occasions he'd been up to Harlem and visited places he used to frequent with Neville and Grantley. He came across them a few times in The Bamboo Bar and tried to engage them in conversation. Grantley was willing enough but Neville made it very clear there would never be any going back to their earlier friendship. When he saw George coming towards them he downed his drink in one and left, followed by Grantley, who shrugged his shoulders and opened his hands as they passed by. He in turn tried to hide his frustration by chatting instead to the girl behind the bar.

The last time he waited until she finished work and they slunk off to her room in the apartment she shared with her mother who was in bed listening to late night jazz on the radio. She insisted that her mom was hard of hearing and wouldn't know what was going on in the next room, but it didn't escape George's attention that their greedy lovemaking was accompanied at times by loud blasts of Paul Whiteman Orchestra's rendition of *Whispering* at crucial moments. Hardly ideal circumstances in which to conduct exciting sex.

They met occasionally after that and he made excuses when she asked to go back to his place. He always arranged to meet her after work so that he wouldn't bump into Neville and Grantley. She was a seasoned lover and did all she could to please him. He liked her lean, dark body and lively ways. But she was too keen, and hardly presented a challenge. He soon gave up on the idea. Added to which he seriously went off the Paul Whiteman Orchestra for a while.

Then there was the secretary from Lerner's who came by one day on the pretext of looking for a work colleague. She was blonde, buxom and liked to make a big thing of flinging her long hair around him when they were in bed. His bed. She confessed to having noticed him looking 'so dashing in his uniform', an expression which made him squirm. So what if she was offering it on a plate, who was he to refuse? That affair didn't last long either, he wasn't quite sure why, although he had noticed her studying his face intently one night when he woke up after a particularly energetic session. Gave him the creeps that did.

★

There was a knock at the door. George had just got in from work. He didn't know whether to open it. True to instructions he'd made a point of lying low since moving into the house near Second Avenue. He'd been there coming on for three months and had met two other occupants, a young man, a student, who lived up in the attic room and a woman on the ground floor who banged the front door when she came home late at night, which was frequently. It was difficult to guess her age, since he'd only seen her face to face a couple of times.

The fourth person, whose room was right next door to his on the middle floor was a man who, according to Mr Roberts worked mostly out of town, just keeping the place as a convenient pied-a-terre. George was not sure what that meant, maybe the guy was French.

He looked around. The room was a far cry from where Neville lived. True it had the standard offering of wardrobe, table, chairs and armchair. But they were in much better condition than he'd seen up in Harlem: new, unscratched and polished. The wooden floor was covered in a bright rug and there was a kitchenette area at one end, with separate storage and a stove that was so clean it might even have been new.

As an added bonus there was the long mirror hanging on the back of the door. He enjoyed going home each evening, catching a glimpse of himself before he set to tidying up and preparing his food. He made sure to use the bathroom very early each morning before he heard anyone else moving around and late at night when the house was quiet. All things considered, he had fallen on his feet.

The door knocked again, and a woman's voice called out, 'Hello, you there?'

He opened it – not too much mind, and put his head outside. It was the chick from downstairs, looking like she'd had an electric shock. Her blonde hair was all over the place and dry-looking; her make-up slithered about her face as if she'd put it on with both eyes closed. She raised her eyebrows when she saw him, started patting at her hair.

She spoke again, this time lower, quieter, 'Hi there, I wonder if you can help me. I seem to have locked myself out.'

George hesitated, 'Um, I'm not sure. I don't have any tools.'

She brightened then, 'Oh, no need to worry about that. Mr Roberts keeps a box of tools down in the cellar. I just don't wanna go down there by myself.' Then, her voice an octave higher: 'Too dark and scary.'

'Mr Roberts?'

'Yes, the landlord,' looking at him as if he were nuts. 'The guy you pay your rent to?'

'Oh yes, yes of course,' George responded, thinking to himself, so old Roberts owned the house. That's why he always insisted that he take the weekly rent from George's salary to pass on to 'his friend'. Said it was easier that way. He couldn't understand why the man couldn't have been upfront about it from the start.

Weirdo.

She was looking at him, her head on one side, 'Look sweetie, can you help me or not? You scared of the dark too?'

George gathered his thoughts: 'No of course not. Just give me a moment.'

She clicked her tongue and started walking back down while he went inside and closed his door.

Shit, shit shit.

Moments later he followed her down.

She carried on chattering away as they went along the hallway. 'I know I've seen you coupla times but seems like you're a very busy guy or just prefer being alone. Is that right?'

'No, just, well, you know, working, coming home.' Couldn't think what else to say.

'So, do you have a name, Mr Mystery Man?'

'George. And what about you?'

'Bonnie, Bonnie Fflett, with two 'ffs' and two 'tts'. And what do you do with yourself? For a job, I mean. Although you look like you could be one of those student types.'

'No, not a student. I work in, umm, for an insurance company.'

'Right, a serious man eh? And what do you do for fun?'

Her questions were beginning to piss him off. 'Do you know where the key for the cellar is kept?'

She opened a little door in the wall, next to the mailbox, 'OK, thought it might be here. There's a torch too.'

She went to the cellar door and struggled to turn the key.

'Here, let me,' he said, putting his hand over hers.

She turned around, giving him one of those looks. Hungry.

Bloody hell, don't need this.

He averted his eyes and concentrated on unlocking the door, switched on the torch and they went slowly down the dusty steps. George walked ahead, while Bonnie followed behind, at one point pretending to stumble and holding onto his waist. A huge boiler grumbled and groaned in one corner and there was a load of old furniture lying around. They hunted about and came across a big metal toolbox. After rooting inside George found a screwdriver and a couple of other things he might need before they went back up. Bonnie made a point of going on ahead, her tight little backside just about in his face. This gal was a tease if ever there was one.

Better steer clear.

He fiddled about for a few minutes and finally managed to open her door.

She stepped inside, leaned on the doorjamb, 'Oh George, what would I have done without you?' Then, her voice taking on that little-girl-lost routine again, 'Don't know how to say thank you.'

He stayed well outside and gathered up the tools from the floor without looking at her.

'No problem, I'll just take this lot back down then get on with my stuff.'

'Oh, OK,' she turned away and started closing the door as he continued, 'It's all done now.'

The door closed.

Had a lucky escape there, boyo.

He replaced the tools, locked the cellar door and went back to his room to prepare his meal.

He bumped into her three times more over the following week. She knocked on the door with a letter addressed to someone with G at the beginning of their first name. It was obviously not for him and had been sent to the wrong address. After all he never received any letters anyway, but she wouldn't have known that. Then he was about to go out one Saturday morning as she happened to open her door to 'check the mail'. The third time she emerged from the bathroom wrapped in a towel, early in the morning. He noticed that she was wearing full make-up each time. The late-night door banging seemed to have stopped too. This bird was on a mission for her next victim and he was determined that it was not going to be him.

★

A couple of days later Miss two ffs and two tts, knocked on the door. Again. This time George was prepared, having suffered a couple of nights of agonising solo activity. She said nothing as he opened the door and raised his eyebrows in query. She ducked under his arm and went inside.

'So Mr George, what's the score?'

'Umm, you know, the usual stuff. Going to work. All that. Is there anything I can do for you?'

She sat down in the armchair, her legs ever so slightly open, while he remained on his feet.

Bloody hell, this gal means business.

'Honey, if you don't know what you can do for me then only God alone can help you.'

Chapter Twenty-six

'For mercy's sake Alice, can't you keep still?' Florence turned over, dragging at her share of the blankets.

Alice was lying on her back, staring into the darkness.

'I'm sorry dear. Just can't seem to get comfortable.'

'Is that so? Honey, you been kicking me in the leg for two nights now. Can't you stay quiet on your side? I got an early shift in the morning.'

Alice concentrated hard on keeping still until her body ached with the tension.

After a few minutes, Florence sat up, turned on the light, reached for her robe and draped it around her shoulders. 'Look, I can tell that you ain't gonna sleep anytime soon. What's up? Tell me quick and then maybe we can both get some shut-eye.'

Alice reached for her own robe: 'It's, well – you said I could talk to you about anything. You're the only one who will understand.'

'Oh Lordy, you ain't gone and got yourself into trouble, girl? You of all people?'

'Oh, my goodness, certainly not. But the other day I met someone.'

'You met someone? You mean you met a man?'

Florence pulled the chain on the gaslight, her eyes alight with anticipation, all signs of tiredness gone.

'Well, well you little minx, Alice Jarrell. Tell me everything. And don't leave nothing out, mind.'

'It was yesterday. I had to go on an errand for Mr Feldmann. Had to take the boys with me of course.'

'Where was it? Were the boys OK? I know they can be little rascals when you take them out.'

'Mrs Feldmann told them she'd bring home a big cake from the bakery if they behaved themselves. We had to go all the way to the middle of Manhattan. We went on the subway. I think they were a bit scared, so they were OK then. After that we had to walk a few blocks through a little park. That's when they got a little skittish.'

'Oh Lordy, you went that far? You know folks down that way don't take too kindly to the likes of us. Hang on – the guy you met – he wasn't like the awful man you came across when Miss Kinsey found you?'

'Oh, dear God, no. Please Florence I don't even like to think about that time.'

'I'm sorry, honey. Go on, I'll try not to interrupt.'

'I had to hand deliver a letter to an insurance company agent. Some business thing. Mr Feldmann told me time and time again that I had to put it directly into the person's hand, a Mr Arkel. It was really important.'

'OK, OK, carry on. I wanna hear about this Romeo that's keeping you awake nights.'

'By the time we got to the corner of Sixth Avenue I was sweating. Steaming almost. You know how warm it was yesterday. Anyway, I found the place alright.'

'Oh, Alice dear, you're so brave.'

'Yes, but boy was I nervous. The twins were hot and bothered. The doorman was grinning like a cat when he let us into the building. He could see what was going on.'

'The doorman? Is that him?'

'No. Just listen, Florence. I need to think how it all happened. How I got this…this feeling.'

'Sorry sweetheart.' Florence lay back down. Settled. Ready to wait as long as it took.

Alice continued, re-running the sequence of events as if chanting a holy mantra.

'Inside it was a huge space, a shiny floor with square patterns on and pictures on the walls of old men in frilly shirts and the like. When the twins heard the clickety-clack sound of their boots on the tiles, they started in jumping and dancing round me like colts in a field. I was that embarrassed.'

'Was there anyone else around?'

'On the opposite side of the entrance hall there was a reception desk with a man in a blue uniform, like the doorman's, but with gold buttons.'

She stopped and looked across at Florence.

'Yeah? And? Oh, my Lord, it's him, isn't it!'

'Yes, it's him. Oh, Florence what am I gonna do? I've never felt like this before.'

'Calm down, honey. Tell me about him. He's a coloured guy I take it?'

'Well, that's just it, I'm not sure.'

'What do you mean you're not sure? Didn't you take a good look at him? After all, seems like you fell for him pretty darn quick.'

'At first he was behind the desk like I said. Then Leon, trying to be smart, started jumping all around the whole place. He slipped and fell. Let out such a squawking right there in the middle of the place. I hurried to help him and dropped my bag with Mr Feldmann's letter in. It fell out and slid across the floor. I felt like a prize fool.'

'Oh, my dear Alice.' Florence reached out and patted her shoulder.

'Then what happened?'

'I sat on a bench and tried to comfort him. Closed my eyes for a moment and quietly sent up one of my arrow prayers to

God. It must have worked because they both stuck their thumbs in and went real quiet.'

'Didn't anyone come to help?'

'Yes, that's the thing. An old man came out of a room at the side just as the guy from behind the desk was coming across to help me. When he saw what was going on the old man went back inside and slammed the door.'

'What did Romeo say? What did he do?'

'He looked down at me and asked if he could help. He had on the same grin as the doorman did. I got a bit cross, even though his voice sounded so different and he looked so nice. I stood up and spoke my best. The boys hugged each other and just stared at him.'

'What was so special about his voice? How did he look up close?'

'I said, I have an important letter for Mr Arkel. Then he said, If you give it to me I can pass it on. Then I said, all proper like, No, my boss requires me to hand the letter to him personally.'

Florence began to laugh, 'Alice you're such a card! But you still haven't told me about his voice. And his looks.'

Alice continued, her voice low and thoughtful, 'He stepped back and said, Whoa, there Miss, I'm just trying to help. Put his hands up but still with that grin on. Then he said, I think Mr Arkel might be in a meeting at the moment.'

Florence stood up and started straightening the bedclothes. 'Honey, come on, give me more.'

Alice, quieter, 'He sounded different from anyone I've ever heard. Just the way he was saying those few words; it was like… like poetry. And his voice, going up and down like he was singing a little song. Had butterflies twinkling about my insides.'

'So, was he coloured or not? You still haven't told me.'

'He's tall and slim, with long fingers, you know, piano fingers my Mom would have called them. His skin is way paler than mine, but there's something about him that's like me and you.'

'His hair? Is it curly, nappy or what?'

'No, not nappy, but big shiny curls and dark, sticking out from under his cap.'

'His nose? His eyes? Honey, feel like I'm wading through a swamp here...'

'He has black eyes and thick eyebrows. Oh Florence, he's so handsome he almost looks like a girl. Know what I mean?'

Florence rubbed both hands across her chin, 'Mm mm. And the voice, the accent, do you think he could be English? Sounds kinda mixed to me. It's all different over there.'

'Oh, yes, maybe that's it. An English gentleman. When he asked my name and I told him he said it back real slow, Alice Jarrell. Do you mind if I call you Alice? Oh my.'

'Well, didn't you find out where he was from?'

'He was asking me about myself. Seemed real interested too. He walked with us back to the subway and he talked so easy. I was a bit shy to start off.'

Florence sighed, got comfortable and murmured, 'Oh well, I guess you'll tell me more by and by. Let's go to sleep now and we'll talk about Romeo again tomorrow.'

'George. His name is George.'

Alice lay back and replayed the rest of the afternoon in her mind. He was so kind. He could see the boys were getting cranky, so he asked his boss if he could get a jug of water for them. She noticed how carefully he knocked on his boss's door and spoke to him, less cocky, and slower, lower. And the same when Mr Arkel came downstairs for the letter.

Just like a coloured man.

How he went across while she was talking to Mr Arkel, crouched down in front of the boys, talking to them softly.

How he picked them up, one on each arm and showed them the view through the high window.

How he pretended to shuffle the papers on his desk but kept glancing across at her.

How he quietly packed up his things at the end of the afternoon and politely offered to walk them back to the subway. Said he was going back that way anyhow. She waited while he went off to remove his uniform and came back looking so smart.

How he took Leon's hand as they walked together up the street with the boys between them.

★

'I'm glad you came in today Alice. Cheered up my afternoon you did with your pretty face.' George was swinging the boys along, chatting easily and taking a look at her sideways.

'Yes, good to meet you too I'm sure,' she responded. She'd always been taught to be polite after all. She felt like a melting marshmallow when he said her name in that charming way.

Occasionally he lifted the boys up so that their feet almost rose off the ground; they laughed and shouted. He was so good with little kids, he must have brothers and sisters at home. Or maybe kids of his own. No, hopefully not. After all, he didn't act like a married man. She would love to know more about him.

'I'm guessing from the way you talk, you must be from England, right?'

He gave a little shake of his head. Don't any of these people know the difference between one country and another?

'No, not England. I come from Wales. It's part of Great Britain. Like America has different states in the USA, we have different countries. Joined together.'

'Oh right. Great Britain. Sounds fancy. You have a king too, right?'

'Yes, King George.'

'Oh, and you have his name?'

'Yes, s'pose so. Although I don't suppose my parents named me after him. It's a popular name.'

'Does he really live in a grand palace and wear a big crown like you see in books?'

'Sure thing. Although I'm sure he takes it off before he goes to bed.'

★

The way she giggled. Even her laugh was attractive, rippling and musical. He wanted to get better acquainted with this little cutie. Much better. He had been studying her all afternoon. Her modest, innocent ways, her compact little shape and her open face made him want to pick her up and fly away with her. She was dressed quite plainly yet even so he enjoyed the sight of her chest when she bent down to tend to the kids and the way she held her jacket around tight when she saw him looking. He noticed the way she tried to lick the sweat from her top lip and wanted to do it for her.

Watch it boyo, can't be seen to get too excited right here on the street.

★

His confidence had taken a bashing since he arrived. The Ellis Island experience was bad enough and from the very first day when he came into work with Neville, he saw how things were for coloured people in this country. He soon realised that the only way you could survive was to keep your head down. And then all that business about having to hide away and sleep in the storeroom. That was too bad. But it was still early days yet. He was lucky to have decent digs, he liked being seen on reception and the comments he got from the clients. It was a start. Who knew what the future might hold?

Meanwhile he may as well enjoy himself. His futile encounters with the Harlem call-girl a couple of months ago hadn't done much for his male pride either. The women he'd come across so far were tough, brash and intimidating. Unlike the soft, willing

145

girls from back home who were like putty in his hands. And then, who should come along but little Miss Alice. A challenge he couldn't resist. Just at the right time.

'What do you do when you're not at work, Alice?'

'I go to church; St Philip's up on 134th Street with my friend Florence. It's quite near home. And if it's a nice day we take a walk afterwards in St Nicholas Park.'

'I know St Nicholas Park.'

He went silent for a moment.

'You're a fine woman Alice.'

She looked down at her feet.

'And where do you live?'

'At the Mission, it's called The White Rose. On 136th. I've been there ever since I came to New York just over four years ago.'

'Where did you come from?'

'Umm, from Georgia, down south. The Mission is wonderful. The lady who runs it is called Miss Kinsey and she is so kind.'

She chattered away happily. On safe ground. She told him all about Bible Class on Sunday afternoons and the Wednesday evening sewing class, how she got the job with the Feldmann's. Everything. After a while she slowed down to a stop. They had reached the subway, Felix and Leon were excited about getting on the train and she had to dash off. George watched as she helped them climb aboard. All three turned and waved through the window and within a blink the train was sucked away into the tunnel.

Chapter Twenty-seven

A fine woman. Alice lay in the dark thinking about how George described her when they met the week before. A whole week. On Wednesday afternoon. And his voice, his way of making it sound like some kind of poetry-music.

'Wanna talk, honey?' Florence put her hand out in the dark and touched Alice's forearm.

'Oh, Florence dear, I didn't know you were awake.'

'Honey, I can feel it coming off you in waves. You still thinking about that guy?'

'A fine woman. That's what he said about me. I've always thought of myself as a girl. Until now that is.'

'Mmmm, mmm, sounds like you got it bad, sweetie.'

'I'm sorry I've been so restless. I expect I'll settle down soon.'

'Don't look that way to me. Anyway, tell me more. What did you talk about?'

'I told him all about my job and The Mission and everything; he looked at me like he was really interested. Even though I felt a little shy.'

'OK, but what did he tell you about his own life?'

'He said that after his mom died, his family turned against him and he had to leave home. Can you believe that anyone would do that to their own kin? It's so cruel. And sad.'

'Why did they do that?'

'His pa and his big sister just straight-up turned against him. Can't think why.'

'Mmm, sounds pretty strange to me. Do you believe him?'

Alice sat up: 'Why wouldn't I? He's such a nice, polite man. So caring.'

'Well, time will tell. Sounds to me like that man could charm the birds off of the trees. You be careful now, honey.'

'What do you mean? He's a very special person.'

'I know, Alice, I know. I'm saying watch your step. That's all.'

★

It was Sunday morning and they were getting ready for church. Or rather, Alice was. She was already up, washed, breakfasted and wondering what to wear. It was eleven days since she met George. Eleven long days and even longer nights. Florence was still in bed. She stretched her arms and yawned.

Alice was fiddling about with her clothes: 'What about my checked percale?'

'Whatever you think, my dear.'

She put on the dress, a good choice because it always made her feel kind of upright and kind. She and Florence had found the fabric in a closet in the sewing room, but Alice had been the one to make sure and ask Miss Kinsey if they could use it.

'Come on, Florence, we don't want to be late. Some of the others left early. And you won't have time to eat anything before we leave.'

'Don't you worry about me, honey. I had a big dinner last night, believe me.'

She smiled, yawned again and then climbed out of bed.

Alice recalled how late Florence had crept in the previous night. She had been looking at her reflection from all angles in the mirror, sighing and whispering to herself while Alice pretended to be asleep. And this morning she looked somehow different. Alice couldn't put her finger on it and didn't like to ask. No doubt she would tell her everything in good time. They had not shared very much in the last few days, not since she had related the story of George's life. Florence obviously doubted his sincerity. Furthermore, Alice was embarrassed about what her feelings for him brought to mind. She'd never experienced such temptation and couldn't tell a soul. Not even Florence.

★

Sitting in church the pastor's sermon droned on as she studied the angels hovering above the high altar. They looked more like graceful women than heavenly beings. Even though made of stone, their long gowns looked like they could be made of soft silk, the kind that would tremble about their ankles as they flew to heaven. She'd never noticed that before and wondered how it would feel to have a silk dress which flickered around your body. Showing the shape of your hips underneath. And your chest.

Florence nudged her. It was time to stand up and sing another of her favourites, with the best lines, when the mists have rolled away, we will understand it by and by. She wished she could understand it all. While the pastor was getting all fired up about the importance of Christian virtue she was focusing on the eagle with its wings spread right across the front of the pulpit. She thought of her Ma, Pa and little Eugene all with their wings joined together as they circled and flew across that huge sky.

Free at last. No more pain, no more sorrow.

At times she felt alone and lonely, despite having a good friend like Florence, Miss Kinsey's kindness and the comradeship of the other girls. And today was one of those times. The service over they stepped out into the bright noon sunshine of Harlem. She and Florence fiddled about putting their gloves back on, linked arms and strolled along W 134th street. It was a beautiful day and they started to make their way towards St Nicholas Park.

'Alice. Miss Alice.' His voice.

She turned around and there he was, sitting on a bench, his

149

legs crossed, one ankle resting on his knee and his arm stretched out along the back. Confident, easy. He smiled, stood up and walked towards her. His high-collar shirt and high-waisted narrow pants made him look even taller than she remembered. He was well-pressed and smart. And oh, those shoes, two-toned in tan and white, looking shiny and new. Even though it was daytime he wore a white silk scarf around his shoulders. She couldn't decide whether he'd dressed up especially for her or maybe it was his English style.

People surged past, talking as they said their goodbyes to other church members before setting off home with their families. He must have been waiting for her. Alice didn't know how to respond nor yet if she even should. She looked at Florence who moved her arm away, patted her friend on the back of her hand and nodded slowly as she began to walk away.

'Hello George, this is a surprise, I didn't know…'

'Yes, I hope you don't mind. I remember you said that you attended St Philip's. I found out where it was, and well, here I am. Would you like to walk with me for a while?'

She smoothed down her skirt as he offered his arm.

Heat emanates from the buildings either side as they walk with a hazy sense of thighs brushing, crossing Eighth Avenue, the warmth of her arm in his. There is a tense yet tender closeness as she involuntarily tilts towards him with a guileless charm, engendering waves of heroism previously unknown, unwarranted and unwanted. Together they glance upwards at the steep ramparts of the stone steps.

Chapter Twenty-eight

Sarah Kinsey closed her bible and got up to draw the curtains. She glanced at the clock: it was past midnight. No wonder she was feeling sleepy. And so much to do tomorrow. Time to think about smartening the place up a bit. The stair banisters could do with a good polish, it was certainly overtime for the annual spring clean. She thought she would get everyone together, so they could organise the rota. Then there were the weekly groceries to order.

Looking out of the window she saw Florence walking up the steps to the front door and fumbling about for her key, her wrap hanging loosely from her shoulders. Showing far too much of her chest. Sarah Kinsey closed her door quietly and went out onto the landing. By which time Florence was creeping up the stairs carrying her shoes and humming softly to herself. She looked up.

'Miss Kinsey!'

'Shhh, please whisper, Florence. You'll wake everyone up.'

'Ummm, sorry Miss Kinsey, I'll be soft as a little bitty mouse.'

'I'd like you like to come in for a nightcap dear? I can make us some tea.'

'No thank you Miss Kinsey, I'm bushed, ummm, quite tired.'

'I think you should Florence. I need to talk to you.'

Florence took her shoes out from under her arm and bent down to put them on, with a sigh.

'Don't bother about your shoes. We need to be as quiet as possible at this late hour.'

★

'Is everything alright Florence? I do worry about you, you know.'

The two women were sitting opposite one another in Miss Kinsey's parlour.

'There really is no need, I'm fine. Absolutely. Nothing for you to get fussed about.' Florence stood up and went across to look at the photographs on the bureau, her back to Miss Kinsey. She picked up one from the middle of the display. A picture of a much younger Sarah Kinsey, arm in arm with a young man. He is tall, wearing a moustache and a military uniform and they are smiling at one another. She turned around, her head to one side, holding the picture up with one hand and raising her eyebrows.

'I've always wanted to ask you about this photo Miss Kinsey. Who is the guy with you?' Her voice challenging, throaty.

'That was long ago, Florence. I will tell you about him another time. But for the moment let's talk about you.'

Florence carefully put back the photograph in its place with another sigh and sat back down. Fiddling with the hem of her dress, she didn't look up.

Sarah Kinsey looked at the young woman before her. She remembered only too well the day she arrived at the mission six years ago. Bruised and battered, and with no belongings she had fallen, sobbing into her arms as soon as the door opened. Sarah had rescued her from a life on the streets. The only life she knew. Her childhood and personal history did not bear thinking about, but Sarah could see that underneath it all, the girl had a kind heart and wanted to improve her life. She paused, wondering how to approach Florence without upsetting her.

'How's Alice? You two getting along alright?'

'Of course, she's my best friend. We talk about everything.'

'When she first came I put you two together because I knew you had a good heart, Florence, and would take care of her.'

'Well I sure do.'

'And what about you? You need to take care of yourself too, you know.'

Florence glanced up then, her face grim. 'I know what you're getting at, Miss Kinsey. I'm not that stupid. Those days are over.'

'Yes, but Alice depends on you. Your guidance and support.'

'If you think I'm going to lead her astray, you're wrong. Sometimes I think you will never forget about…about before.'

'That's not true, Florence, dear. I want you to be happy and fulfilled. Like I want for everyone at The White Rose. I was so pleased when you got yourself that job at the Delaney Hotel. It's a very smart place.'

Florence shook her head, her mouth tight, 'Yeah, as a cleaner. Yippee for me. It's smart alright and the folk that stay there are high and mighty for sure.'

'Well you have to start somewhere, dear. Who knows, you might find yourself in charge of the housekeeping team before too long. And then, well who knows…'

Sarah Kinsey's voice tailed off. She knew how hard it was for young coloured women to get any work other than menial domestic tasks. But hope springs eternal as they say. She stood up. Time to bring their little chat to an end. She squeezed the younger woman's shoulder as she passed by to open the door. Florence sat staring at the other side of the room, trying hard not to yawn.

'Time for bed for us both I think, don't you? But remember I'm here for you, Florence, if you ever need to get anything off your chest.'

'Thanks Miss Kinsey. And I'm sorry to be such a grump.'

She trudged quietly upstairs and into the bedroom, thinking back to her date. She'd had a couple of drinks with a guy she'd met on the street a few days before. The ratine crepe donated by

The Empress of the Blues certainly had the desired effect. The red draped gown which clung to her figure in all the right places drove him crazy. She was feeling good. Or she was until Miss K. appeared on the landing like the goddamn angel of death. She had been careful to wrap her coat around tight when stepping out earlier that evening so as not to arouse Miss Kinsey's suspicions. Not that it was any good in the end.

★

She tried to undress quietly but couldn't help overhearing her friend's pleas: 'Dear God, please give me the strength to face another day', before climbing into bed and facing the wall.

Florence gave her a shake: 'Alice, honey, you OK?'

'Yes, I guess so. It's just so hard.'

'What is? The job?'

'Well, yes. I don't want to be ungrateful, I'm so pleased to have a proper job for the first time in my life, but the twins are awful rude.'

Florence sat on her side of the bed and took Alice's face in her hands, 'You never said any of this before. Tell me now, honey.'

Alice sat up, her eyes big: 'Don't get me wrong, Felix and Leon are getting used to me now. But they sometimes they still give me a hard time.'

'What? How?'

'Like throwing their food on the floor and not helping to clear up the mess. Punching me in the legs when I try to scold them, and other things.'

Florence stood up and paced about: 'What other things?' Her voice brittle, sharp.

'They say stuff to me in their language, in German and I know it's bad what they're saying by the way they speak it. Then they both laugh.'

'Oh, glory be! Have you told Miss Kinsey?'

'Oh, no. She was kind enough to give me the job. I don't want to let her down. Please don't say anything, Florence.'

'OK, OK, don't fret. But make sure you tell their parents and you know you can talk to me about anything. If I can be of any help I will. You're a good friend Alice.'

'I will, Florence, thank you. I have told Mr and Mrs Feldmann some of it. They are decent folk and they do scold them. It stops for a few days after that. Leastways I must be doing something right, or they wouldn't keep me. It's been three months now and I don't think any of the other girls got to stay this long.'

She paused: 'The funny thing is, even though they can be a trial, I'm getting to love those boys. And I think they care for me in their own little ways. Sometimes Felix will come and sit on my lap or stroke my arms when I'm helping him with his boots. He likes to put his fat little white arm next to my brown one and smile up at me.'

'Mm mm, is that so? Anyways, just talk to me in future. Now shift over to your side, I'm getting cold standing here in my nightgown.'

She and Florence lay awake talking long into the night even though she was so tired. Florence talked about her latest lover, a fine fellow from Jamaica, the places they went and the things they did together down to the last detail. Alice was still awake long after Florence was asleep, wondering how it must feel to be so crazy about a man that you would risk all your womanly secrets. She recalled the details of the afternoon again before she finally fell asleep.

★

The boys were getting restless being stuck indoors, so she decided to take them to the Carl Schurz Park. They often went if the weather was suitable. It wasn't too bad if it was cold or even raining a little. She wrapped them up warm and at least it was important to get out for a while. But she soon learned that taking them out on a windy day was out of the question.

155

Especially kids like Felix and Leon. The wind always seemed to make them kind of mad. As soon as the breeze blew up, so did their attitude. They would run, jump and scream like a couple of baby raccoons. There were a few cross-looking clouds threatening rain later on, but it was still quite a mild and bright afternoon.

They had to cross a few big avenues to get to the park and Alice made sure to hold them both tight by their hands the whole time, knowing that as soon as the open space came in view they would want to run on ahead. At the entrance to the park you have to climb big wide steps up to paths between large rocks, bushes and foliage and benches from where you can look out over the East River and see right across to Welfare Island.

Mr Feldmann had told Alice a lot about the island's history one evening and she thought about it every time they visited. It had first belonged to the Canarsie Indians and many people had claimed and renamed it over the years. It had a penitentiary at one time and if you looked hard enough on a clear day you could see the small lighthouse that was built using convict labour. There had also been an asylum on the island which had burnt down and been replaced by a hospital.

She felt sorry that it had been stolen from folks long ago who probably loved living there, growing their crops and looking after their land. But she knew from the history her Mom used to tell her about that there were lots of bad people in the world who steal land and precious things from others. And it was hard to think about the sad, sick folk who came after. It looked so lovely from a distance, and gazing at the water always made her relax, at least for a short while. Curved railings stood at the edge over the river to stop people from falling in, but she still worried about the boys' safety, Leon in particular, who was more active and loved to climb.

She sat on a bench after giving the boys strict instructions to stay within sight. They stood and gazed through the railings at the flowing water, mesmerised by the way it shifted and glittered in the early afternoon sun. She studied them as they chattered away to one another in a mixture of English and German. To be able to speak in two languages must mean that they were very clever indeed and she wondered what the future held for them both. They were good kids really. It probably didn't help that they'd had had such a lot of different girls looking after them. And the Feldmanns, for all their kindness, were very serious about their bakery business. Maybe they thought about that too much, instead of considering the needs of their kids. But who was she to judge, they were sure good to her.

She closed her eyes, listening to the sounds of the river and feeling the soft breeze on her face. Minutes later she heard a child's scream coming from behind. She turned and saw Leon falling out of the thick bushes with a graze on his head which was quickly developing a hard lump as she ran to him. He was yelling and weeping at the same time.

Her stomach lurched as she picked him up. 'Oh, dear God, what happened?' She shouted at Felix who said nothing. He stood and stared at his brother.

'I said what happened?'

'We were playing hiding. He was jumping by the big rock. I didn't hurt him. I couldn't find him.'

He started to cry and kept saying that Leon was being freche. She wondered what had been going on between them. She needed to think and act fast. And oh, dear Lord, what would Mr and Mrs Feldmann say?

'OK, OK. Look, sit here on the bench while I see to your brother. And don't move.'

After a couple of agonising minutes, she managed to find her handkerchief and tried to clean up Leon's injury as well as she could. The walk back home was quiet and slow. The twins were tired and clingy as she considered what the outcome would be.

By the time the Mr and Mrs Feldmann were back, she had bathed Leon's head properly and put iodine on the graze. He struggled as it stung calling out Lassen Sie mich in Ruhe! over and over again until she was finished. Thankfully, the lump hadn't got any bigger and he seemed to be in good spirits after a few minutes. When his mother walked through the door and saw him, she ran to hold him tight, all the while whispering softly in his ear as Alice tried to explain the events of the afternoon.

Mr Feldmann patted her on the shoulder and told her not to worry, his sons were tough and strong. He went and spoke quietly to his wife. It was obvious that he was trying to placate her and they both kept glancing over at Alice who stood like a statue by the door, with her coat on, wondering if she would still have a job the following day. The boys drifted off into the parlour and Mr Feldmann shut the door behind them.

'Come and sit down, Alice. Bitte.'

She sat as instructed, her head down, and hands in her lap. Mrs Feldmann was still on the opposite side of the kitchen.

He gestured to her, 'And you too, my dear.'

She came and sat next to Alice, her hands clasped on the table.

He continued, 'You know that the boys have had a lot of babysitters since they were small, and my wife needs to work with me at the bakery?'

'Yes Sir.'

Mrs Feldmann said nothing.

'You are the best, Alice. My wife and me are happy for you to care for them.'

'Thank you sir,' she replied as she gave a quick look at Mrs Feldmann's blank face.

'I do care for the twins. Very much.'

Her eyes began to sting, and she felt in her pocket for her handkerchief, then remembered that it had Leon's blood on it. Instead she used her sleeve.

Mrs Feldmann turned to her: 'Not to cry, Alice. You are good girl. My boys can be very freche. You must be always strengen.' She took Alice's hand; 'You come back tomorrow jah?'

Chapter Twenty-nine

It had been several months since Mam's passing. Ruby was trying to sort out more of her things without making it too obvious to Dad. If he did a weekend shift she took out a few of her dresses and took them apart, one seam at a time, before putting the fabric at the bottom of her own wardrobe until she could think of what to make with it. Although she had precious little, Mam took good care of her clothes. She sometimes swapped with her friends, putting a new twist on old garment.

Mrs Lerman didn't often come into the shop. According to Peggy, she involved herself in local charity work. Putting on afternoon tea parties for her husband's rich customers to raise money for deprived children or advising young girls who had got themselves into trouble. Peggy seemed to take pleasure in recounting the latter, suggesting that maybe her own daughter Rachel had been in the same boat.

'After all Rube, why did she leave Cardiff so soon after your George went? Thought it was a bit fishy at the time, but I didn't want to say so.'

Ruby got up and started tidying the cups away at that point and Peggy had the sense to shut up. Although, she had wondered the same thing herself. She had been trying hard to get back to the former friendship between them. After all was said and done, Peggy was always there to help, whatever her motives were.

Saturday morning. Ruby dropped in on Peggy on her way home from the market.

'Wonder if you'd like to help me with something, Peg.'

'Course Rube, what's your problem? Your Jimmy giving you a hard time, is he?' With a brittle laugh.

Ruby paused. Started counting in her head, one thousand, two thousand, three thousand. No point in getting annoyed. She needed to find a way of fixing things. Since she'd started back to work at Lerman's she'd been careful not to talk too much about her job, or Jimmy.

'No, it's not Jimmy. I'm thinking of doing a couple of extra things and wondered if you wanted to get involved. Little business idea.'

'Woohoo Rube, businesswoman now, are we?' Her voice took on that now familiar rise in tone. She lit up a Woodbine, her hands trembling as she fumbled with the match. Her hair looked dull, the ends dry and broken. She pulled it behind her ears with both hands, the cigarette trembling from her lips. She'd always been very slender, but Ruby noticed she was looking even thinner. And her face was pale, the circles under her eyes like faint bruises.

The room was heavy with unspoken truths. And no sign of Charley. He usually came downstairs to say hello if he heard her voice. But the house was quiet. Ruby went to open the curtains, still drawn despite it being nearly midday. What was going on? She couldn't take the risk of upsetting the applecart even more. Needed to tread carefully.

'Actually Peg, I need your help. You're a talented seamstress aren't you and I was going to suggest that you help me set things up. I was going to ask Mrs Lerman if I could display a couple of home-made ladies' clothes in the small window in the shop.'

Peggy took a long drag on her cigarette. 'What, you mean I could work with you?'

'We would come to some arrangement, of course, Peg. We

would have to discuss your rates of charges for hemming and umm, the finishing touches.' She tailed off.

'Have to say it for you, Ruby, you're a woman with ambition.' Peggy exhaled long and high into the air. 'Old Clever Clogs you are. Sorry to be such a misery. Shit happening here with you-know-who.'

Over the next hour or two, Peggy regaled Ruby regarding all the aforesaid shit about Charley. Other women, his frightening drunken outbursts, the lot.

★

On Monday morning, Ruby was hunting around for some tissue paper. Surely there was some in a drawer somewhere. The weekend had been hectic. She and Peggy had made a start on designing and making a dress by late Saturday afternoon and spent all day Sunday finishing it off, Charley having disappeared for three days. Then Jimmy turned up on Sunday night. His ship docked earlier than anticipated and Peggy scuttled off home.

An hour later at work, Ruby was making tea for herself and Mr Lerman. He was telling her about his vision for landscaping his garden and his wife's hankering for new furniture for the house, both of them seemingly at odds with one another.

Ruby waited for him to pause before asking, 'Do you have any plans for the small side window, Mr Lerman?'

'Not at the moment, Ruby. Why? Any ideas?'

'Umm, yes. I hope you don't think I'm being impertinent, but it might be nice to have a couple of ladies' items on display.'

Her boss stopped talking, furrowed his brow, then smiled. 'Alright, Miss Ruby Hodges, what did you have in mind?'

Ruby drew out her tissue paper parcel from under the counter where she had quickly hidden it when she came in earlier to open up.

'I made this over the weekend. Don't know if you or your wife would be interested. If not, please don't worry. It was just a thought.'

Her armpits feeling like smouldering coals and her mouth dry as a parrot's cage, she fiddled about with the parcel and held up the dress. She and Peggy had used some shiny blue fabric which had been all squashed up in Mam's wardrobe. It was originally a long dress, but they had fashioned it into a short Charleston style, with a dropped waist, floppy bows on each hip and on the loose sleeves. Peggy remarked that it looked like something you would see in a magazine or in a film and Ruby had to agree.

Mr Lerman took the dress from her and held it up to his shoulders, making a show of admiring himself in the cheval mirror. 'You asked if I would be interested, Ruby, but it's not quite my style. but I'm sure my wife will like it.'

Chuckling to himself, he put the dress gently back into Ruby's arms.

'You're a clever young woman. With a good business head on your shoulders. Rebekah will be dropping by this afternoon. And you two can work it out between you.'

Chapter Thirty

'S o, Georgie Porgey, talk to me.'

Bonnie stared at him as they were lying in bed one Friday evening. It was six days after meeting Alice outside church and he'd spent a couple of fervid nights wondering what his next move should be. Then the ever-bountiful Miss Fflett came along and knocked on his door two nights in a row and he happily obliged her. She certainly provided some action, but each time left him feeling somehow disloyal to Alice even though there was nothing between them. Not yet anyway. He had never come across a girl like her before.

He turned towards her, 'I was thinking maybe you could show me one of the hot places in town?'

'Well now honey, there's a plan. Seems like you could do with some livening up.'

She got out of bed and looked at her watch as she put on her robe.

'It's nine-thirty now, just give me a minute to get dressed and we'll hit the town, English boy.'

She hurried away, and he heard her slippers tapping away downstairs to her room. Fifteen minutes later, dressed and ready, he appeared at her door. She opened it wearing a bright pink dress in some droopy material which sashayed around her hips beneath a shiny belt. It made a change from the usual robe or towel. She twirled around on display for a moment before putting on a big coat. They linked arms, went outside and made their way to the Harlem Railroad.

It was the first time they had been out together. Out on the street. Walking along like a real couple. For a moment George imagined Alice walking at his side, but so what, needs must after all. And Bonnie was certainly a fun girl to be with.

She looked up at him: 'Penny for 'em, Georgey Porgey.'

'What?'

'You're in a world of your own. What gives, big boy?'

He patted her arm: 'Everything's fine. I was just thinking about where you might be taking me, you being more used to these parts.'

'Well, you'll have to wait and see. I know, how about we go dancing? Surely a fine fellow like you must be a whiz with your moves.'

Bloody hell, hardly one of his strong points.

'Sure, we can do anything you want, cutie-pie.'

'Then how about we go underground?'

'What's that?'

'It's a club you might like; small, hot and steamy. What did you think I meant? You're pretty distracted this evening, honey. Don't know what your problem is.'

The mood between them had taken a turn. George had heard about some of these places from Neville. It probably meant it would cost a few dollars to get in plus paying for drinks on top. And this gal was the type who would probably expect an expensive date. They got off the train and started making their way up to 135th.

Even though it was late the streets were humming with activity. A group of men were playing loadies on the sidewalk. One of the men looked up, muttered and scowled at George as they passed by, before turning his back. A few young women sat about on the steps or hovered in doorways, their intentions you may assume to be less than pure. But who would dare to consider themselves justified sitting in judgement on women with such limited life choices. Music drifted out from a basement apartment radio. The strains of Bert William's 'Nobody'. He wondered why his past insisted on leaping out at him. What did it all mean?

'Hey man, what you doin' up 'ere?'

Neville had come up behind them and touched his shoulder. He grinned at them both, raised his eyebrows, shrugged his shoulders and shook his head before strolling on by. George heard the familiar suck of his teeth as he went past.

'How do you know that man?'

Bonnie's voice sharp enough to slice his head off. She let go of his arm, stood stock still and stared at him. George shoved his hands in his pockets, his stance defiant yet anxious.

'I don't know who the hell he is. Maybe he's come into the building where I work a couple of times. Can't remember.'

'Well, he seems to know you. And honey, I may as well tell you now. I know who you are too.'

George said nothing, his hands clenched out of sight.

'So what, cat got your tongue, sweetie?'

He started to walk away in the opposite direction, although not too fast, unable to think quick enough to respond. Bonnie followed him and grabbed his arm.

'Don't walk away from me goddammit. Let's talk about this. You have to understand that you could be playing a dangerous game in this country. Maybe things are different where you come from.'

'What do you mean?' He turned back, eventually finding his voice.

She led the way. 'Look, we can still go out and have a good time, but let's go and talk somewhere quiet first.'

Resigned, he followed her as they went through a door further along the street. Trudged downstairs and into a small room where a few men sat at a makeshift bar. George wondered how she was familiar with the place. Despite exploring every inch of her pale body, he still knew practically nothing about this woman. He was thinking fast, feeling powerless and wondering how he could redeem himself and his pride.

The décor was similar to other illicit drinking joints: dingy, shabby and dark. The man behind the bar did not engage with anyone, just took orders or wiped the counter with a grubby cloth. There was no music playing and the drinkers sat quietly talking among themselves. The kind of place where a serious drinker could go unmolested to satisfy his appetite for strong liquor. He flushed as he recalled the look on Neville's face. The slight sneer and the shrug of the shoulders had said it all.

A couple of men looked up briefly as they approached before returning to their glasses. Bonnie took so much control that she even went up to the bar herself and ordered their drinks, before he could offer.

Man, this gal is certainly one tough cookie.

Like all the other women he had met in New York. Except for one.

They sat in silence at a corner table until after the barman brought across their drinks. George picked up his bourbon and gulped it straight down as Bonnie stared at him. He stalked back to the bar and brought across another for them both, banging them down in the middle of the table.

She seemed to be thinking about her words before speaking. The previous sharpness of her tone out on the street had gone, to be replaced by a quieter, more measured approach.

'Do you ever read the gossip pages, George?'

He wasn't sure where this was going, what did that have to do with anything?

'Well, yeah, course I do sometimes.'

'Are you aware of some of the things that happen to people who look like you but may not be, um, what they seem? It's a risky business.'

He recalled some gossip he had overheard of a rich heir to

fortune, whatsisname Rhinelander. It was rumoured he'd been dating a coloured woman, a domestic who was apparently passing as white. Nobody knew what the outcome would be. He had overheard a couple of the secretaries discussing it a few days before. Come to think of it, one of them was that girl from Lerner's that he'd messed with not too long ago.

Shit, that's all he needs at the moment.

His mind was racing with the implications of Mr Roberts' comments, 'A guy like you deserves better', and his warning about not inviting 'undesirables' to the house in Yorkville, the encounter with Neville, finding his place in New York. The signs had always been there, but he didn't want to reflect on it too much. Deep inside he had always been aware of his capacity to use any situation to his own advantage, right from when he was a small boy, encouraged by his mother and to the disappointment of his father. He knew that one day he would have to make what amounted to a public declaration.

'Well Miss Fflett, if you don't like it, you know what you can do.'

'Whoa there, Mr Big Man, I'm trying to be helpful here. You're not the only one who could be in trouble, you know.'

She was probably referring to the story about Jack Johnson, a coloured prize-fighter who had married a white woman, Etta Duryea, a few years previously. Etta Duryea was from a wealthy family in Brooklyn, a social butterfly who ended up killing herself after a couple of years. Ever since then she was held up as an example of the dangers of 'crossing the colour line'. But surely, it was different for him and Bonnie. With his looks, how was anyone to know?

Best to stay cool.

'OK, so if you knew, why were you so keen to get me into the sack? And boy, you made that clear from the start. Very clear.'

'I didn't see you complaining', she retorted. Quick as a knife.

George took his time with his second drink. He hadn't eaten

much earlier, couldn't afford to get drunk, and needed to be in full charge of himself. Dangerous ground. After all he liked the girl. Liked the fact that she was upfront about what she wanted, and she was right, he'd never said no. Quite the opposite in fact. He studied how she looked as her eyes flickered around the room. Eyes which were beginning to look damp, glassy. She had taken off her coat, the shiny dress clung around her middle, showing a glimpse of her breasts as she leaned forward for her drink. He noticed that her hands were trembling a little too.

Careful boyo.

'OK, Bonnie, so what now? Do you want to go home? Although that would be a shame, with you being all dolled up with nowhere to go.'

She smiled then: 'It would be a shame indeed. Come on, let's go and dance.'

She got up and pulled him to his feet. 'There's time for talking tomorrow.'

They went back outside and ended up in a lively joint just off 135th, where couples were swaying and leaning towards each other in ways George had never seen before. Hot and steamy was right. Before too long his arms were wrapped around the willing Bonnie as she showed him some smart dance moves.

Chapter Thirty-one

It was eleven-thirty. Alice lay in bed waiting for Florence who had been coming home later and later recently. Miss Kinsey came upstairs one night to ask where she was, leaving Alice unsure how to respond. When Florence eventually crept into their room, she was often distracted and unwilling to talk. They used to share many hours whispering in the dark until one or the other of them decided it was time to sleep. Florence knew everything there was to know about the world. Especially when it came to men. Alice was at first shocked by her revelations but still yearned for more. The girls she knew from church back home in Georgia never talked so openly, although occasionally one of them would disappear from Bible meetings only to be welcomed back into the church with a baby in tow.

It had been four weeks. Four Sunday afternoons of seeing George lounging against the wall outside church waiting for her. That first time they had walked right up to the top of St Nicholas Park; she stumbled on the steps she was that nervous. George took her hand to help her and didn't let it go all afternoon. His hands felt cool and smooth in contrast to hers which were hot and careworn. Florence advised that she rub them with olive oil every night before going to bed, also suggesting that she might soon need to rub it all over. Later, when Florence was asleep Alice ran her hands over her own body wondering how it would feel to be caressed by a man. By George. After some minutes, she offered up a quiet prayer seeking God's forgiveness.

★

Footsteps on the stairs. Efficient, intentional footsteps. It could only be one person. Alice opened her eyes and looked at the clock: it was five-thirty in the morning and the space beside her was still empty. She rushed to the door just as Miss Kinsey was about to knock.

'It's alright, Alice. Put your robe on, dear, before you catch your death.'

'Um, yes. Excuse me. Please sit down, Miss Kinsey.'

'I just wanted to show you this. It was delivered through the front door a few minutes ago.'

She sat beside Alice on the bed, handed her a note and watched her face as she read it.

Dear Miss Kinsey,

I need to tell you that I won't be coming back to the White Rose. Things have changed for me and I need to sort my life out. I am too ashamed to say what, but maybe you can guess. I just wanted to thank you for everything you've done for me over the years. Please tell dear Alice that I haven't forgotten her and will be in touch very soon. And ask her to get my things together so she can give them to me when we meet. You are a good woman Miss Kinsey and I'm sorry to let you down. God bless and keep you,

Florence

'I don't understand why she's leaving. She's my best friend.'

The older woman took her hand: 'I know, Alice dear, but sometimes folks get themselves into all kinds of trouble. Especially girls. Let's dry your eyes now. We need to talk.'

She used her own handkerchief to dab the girl's eyes. Alice thought that was just what her real mom used to do when she was real upset about something. She wept even more, holding her arms tight together and shaking. Miss Kinsey held her close and said nothing for a minute or two.

'You don't have work tomorrow do you, Alice?'

'What? No, it's Wednesday isn't it? Mrs Feldmann often stays home Wednesdays.'

'Alright then. Let's go downstairs to my parlour We can talk without disturbing any of the others. And I'll make you some coffee.'

★

'I know you and Florence are very close.'

'Yes, we are. She's very kind to me. Especially if I tell her I've had a tough day with the twins. She always wants to listen and makes me feel better.'

'I understand. And what does she tell you about her own life?'

Alice sipped at her coffee and picked at the tassels of the antimacassar on the arm of her chair, richly embroidered in Miss Kinsey's elaborate style. Coming into her private parlour was significant. It always signalled something special, serious, important or happy. Occasionally she invited a group of the newer girls in for coffee or soda, complete with home-made cakes. She talked to them about how to keep safe in the city and the sort of places they might like to visit. The meetings usually ended with a prayer, thanking God for His care and asking Him to help them do right.

The room was just about big enough to accommodate five or six people sitting down. There was a large horsehair couch with matching armchairs, all decorated in fabric which was once probably brightly coloured, now faded to a wilted collection of pale flowers. A couple of fold-up card tables leaned against the wall in one corner. On the opposite side was the bureau, sporting an array of photographs of past tenants of the White Rose and also a formal picture of Black Club women, patrons of the mission, looking upright and serious as they posed in keeping with their roles. You would have to look carefully to see a photo displayed behind the others of a girl who looked like a much younger Sarah Kinsey, on the arm of a dark-skinned man dressed in a military uniform. He looked straight ahead while she gazed up at him, oblivious of the camera.

Miss Kinsey pulled back the drapes. Day was breaking on the quiet street and a few people could be seen hurrying off to their early morning jobs. The men were probably security guards or porters and the women, with their hair carefully covered from the ravages of the morning mist were going off to clean offices, or to care for the homes and small children of those with the innate privileges of class and race.

'Alice, tell me about Florence.'

'Umm, she enjoys going out and seeing her friends.'

'What kind of friends?'

'All sorts really. She's a very sociable person.'

'And does she talk about these friends?'

'Yes, sometimes. We're usually too tired to talk much.'

'I've noticed the light under your door when I'm doing my rounds. Seems like you're still awake pretty late some nights.'

There were sounds from upstairs as a couple of the girls were up and getting ready for the day. Alice twirled her cup around in the saucer.

'How about some more coffee?'

'No, I'm good, thank you.'

Sarah Kinsey poured another cup for herself and continued, 'I realise that you girls are growing up into young ladies and have your own lives to lead and I'm happy for you to go out and have fun. But while you're under this roof I have a certain responsibility to take care of you all.'

'Oh yes, you certainly do that, Miss Kinsey. I'm so happy to be here and still can't believe my luck that you found me that day.'

'Yes, yes, well that's in the past, Alice. Let's talk about now. How are things? Your job? What you like to do on the days you're not at work. I notice that you've missed a couple of Sunday afternoon Bible classes.'

'Oh, the job has its ups and downs. It all depends on the mood the boys are in. They are very active kids. But I do care for them just the same. And Mr and Mrs Feldmann are kind people.'

'And on your days off? Sunday afternoons for example?'

Alice downed the last of her coffee and placed the cup back on the saucer. Her eyes flickered about the room. She looked hard at the window as she answered.

'Florence and me like to take a walk into St Nicholas Park after church. Especially if it's a nice day.'

'And what about the days that Florence decides not to accompany you? Seems like the last few weeks she's been upstairs getting ready to go out for the evening. Or maybe I'm wrong and she has extra weekend shifts at her cleaning job. Is that it, do you think?'

'Maybe.'

'So, do you walk in the park by yourself. Or perhaps you have someone else to accompany you?'

'Yes, umm, I do have a new friend. He's very nice.'

'A man friend? And how did you meet?'

Alice was beginning to get jumpy. She couldn't bear it if Miss Kinsey's questions made as if George was a bad person. Florence's little comments about what men are like sometimes made her nervous. She must remember that he was a decent man. An honest man. A man who made her feel special.

Miss Kinsey glanced at the big clock above the bureau. 'Looks like we better go and start the breakfast. I think you're on kitchen duty this morning, right?'

'Yes, Miss Kinsey. I'll go right on back upstairs to get washed up and ready.'

'OK. But, we'll need to talk later. Maybe after this afternoon's Negro Culture class.'

'Yes Ma'am.'

★

'Come in, Alice, thanks for coming back. Sit yourself down and have some lemonade.'

'Thanks, Miss Kinsey. I thought I shouldn't knock until your visitor was gone.'

'Quite right, quite right. And what did you think about her talk this afternoon?'

'I was very impressed. I never knew that there were such brave and clever ladies doing those things. Ladies who look like us, that is.'

Sarah Kinsey leaned forward and drew Alice's chair closer to her own.

'Yes, we were very honoured indeed to have Mrs Dawkins come visit and to speak eloquently.'

Alice put her head to one side: 'How did she get to do all those things? How did she find time to study, raise money and help others like she does?'

'She belongs to a Negro Women's Club. The lady who started it came from nothing, just like you and me, Alice. Just see what we can do if we work hard, stay positive and trust that God will help us along our path.'

Alice put down her drink: 'I like what she said about helping each other any way we can. And she's done so much. Learning a lot of things so she could teach little kids and raising money for poor families and everything.'

'That's right. It just goes to show what you can achieve if you stay focused.'

'You stayed focused, didn't you? That's why you're here helping all of us girls.'

'Yes, that's right. But you need to understand that it's not always easy. Sometimes some thing or some person might get in your way just when you're trying your hardest.'

174

'I would like to be like Mrs Dawkins one day. Especially the bit about helping others.'

'Well my dear, maybe you will. You already help as much as you can here. And the Feldmann family too. I went into one of their bakeries the other day and Mrs Feldmann was singing your praises and said her boys loved you to bits. And who knows, you'll probably have a little family of your own one day.'

'Oh, I hope so. I do try. And that's where Florence is so helpful in keeping my spirits up on the days I feel low.'

They paused.

Sarah Kinsey cleared her throat. She went across to the bureau and began tidying the arrangement of photographs. She started speaking with her back to Alice before slowly turning around.

'Do you know what she might have been referring to in her note when she said she was ashamed at having to leave us?'

'I'm not sure. Perhaps she got somewhere else to live? Or plans to live with one of her friends?'

'But that wouldn't be a reason to feel ashamed, would it, Alice? When you see her I'm sure you will find out. She will probably write you to arrange a meeting.'

'Yes, I expect so.'

'And you will tell me, won't you, dear?'

'Yes, I will. After all you've done, it would be only right and fair.'

She sat back down and looked straight into the girl's face. 'Meanwhile, remember what I told you. You have a lot of potential to help people just like the wonderful Mrs Dawkins does. But don't let anything or anyone get in your way.'

'I understand. I'm happy that you have faith in me. Can I go now and help with supper?'

'Yes, run along, dear. And think about what I've said.'

Alice nodded and left the room quick as any jackrabbit.

Chapter Thirty-two

'August in New York sure is hot.'

Bonnie got up and went off to the bathroom, leaving George to enjoy a post-coital reverie. They had spent the last couple of hours in her room. It was a humid Friday night, just getting dark outside and the first time they had got together for three weeks. Meeting her near the front door a few times was tense and awkward, leaving him unsure whether she was deliberately avoiding him or having second thoughts about their friendship. Earlier in the evening she came upstairs and knocked on his door just like old times. But instead of jumping straight into bed she invited him down to her room for supper.

She had clearly made an effort, serving chicken with collard greens and grits. He was curious as to where she'd learned to cook that kind of food. Yet another surprise about this woman he had known for nearly five months. Somehow her manner never invited any confidences and he soon stopped asking, preferring instead to make the most of their times together. For dessert she presented him with ice-cream in a tall, fluted glass and two long spoons so they could share. She even brought out a bottle of bourbon whisky from the bottom of her wardrobe with much pride. He looked around. It was the first time he'd seen the inside of her room properly.

The furniture and layout was similar to his own, but her touch was everywhere. A big green plant waved its soft fronds against the window. The top of her drawer chest was covered in jars and bottles with a feather boa pinned across the wall above and the headboard was draped in bright sequinned fabric. The pink dress she wore the night they went out dancing hung on the back of the door. It was good to be together again. Really good in fact, but what was she playing at? What was the score with the invitation to her room and the dinner? Just then she came back, smelling as sweet as a nut and began putting on the pink dress.

He turned over onto his stomach, leaned on his elbows, watching her, 'What's all this about, sweetie? You going somewhere?'

'Sure am, honey. And you're coming with me,' she said, as she sat in front of the mirror and started applying face cream.

He sat up then, 'Is that so? What's this evening all about anyway?'

Bonnie stopped what she was doing and came to sit beside him on the edge of the bed. She crossed her arms, leaned back against the headboard and sighed.

'I need to talk to you, George.'

'Talk to me? What about? Is it about what happened a couple of weeks ago? What?'

'No, it's nothing to do with that. Although it sure gave both of us a lot to think about. As I said at the time, you could be playing a dangerous game.'

She hesitated before continuing, 'I have to go away for a while and I want you to take care of a few things for me.'

'Go away where? And why?'

'Look sweetheart, I haven't been quite straight with you. There's a lot of stuff in my life which, well let's just say I need to take a break.'

'You still haven't told me why or where.'

He knew he was beginning to sound like a petulant child,

decided to change tack, got out of bed, wrapped a towel around his middle and started to look around for his clothes.

'Although you don't need to tell me anything, we're only friends after all. Bed buddies. No more, no less.'

'George honey, will you listen to yourself? The fact is that I'm going away. To see my folks in Cleveland. My pa's not well and my mom is worried.'

He relaxed a little then: 'Oh right, I thought maybe you were getting scared and running off.'

'No, no, it's nothing like that.' She looked away, carried on speaking to the wall, 'I really like you, George. You're a nice guy, even though you've still got a lot to learn.'

'A lot to learn? About what?'

'Oh, I don't know. Things. Anyway, enough of that. Let me tell you what I'd like you to do for me while I'm away.'

He stood still. 'OK, I'm all ears.'

'I don't want old Roberts to know that I'm away because he could decide to let out my room to someone else. This is where you come in, like sending on any mail that comes for me and paying my rent to him. I could give it to you to pass on, tell him I'm on a different work shift or something, anything, just make sure he gets it on time without fail.'

'How? Will you send the money on, or what?'

'Calm down big boy. I'm not going to leave you in the lurch, but you're the only person I can trust.'

'I'm sorry Bonnie, it's a shock that's all.'

She got up, went over to the wardrobe and pulled out a box from under some clothes.

'In here is enough cash for two month's rent. I've been putting it aside. From my earnings. When that runs out I'll send some more. That OK?'

He put his arm around her: 'No problem, sweetie, leave it to me.'

She sauntered over to the houseplant on the windowsill and drew her hands through its tender leaves.

'And you can look after this little baby for me. She likes to be watered every day, a few drips each time – not too much.'

'I can do that too, no problem. And what's with the dress? What do you have planned for tonight?'

She pulled at the towel, 'Well now English boy, you better get on upstairs and put some good clothes on. We're going dancing.'

'Sounds good to me. At the same place?'

'No, let's go a little upmarket tonight. Let's call it a farewell present. My treat.'

★

'Good evening Miss Fflett, good to see you again.'

The waiter was tall, his chiselled face white as a bone with black hair slicked back neat and sharp across his collar. George took a second look at him. He was very beautiful in a way that it was difficult to tell if he was a man or a woman.

He nodded politely to George before pulling out their chairs, 'Good evening, Sir, and welcome.'

He straightaway produced a small bottle of strong liquor, seemingly out of nowhere and whispered politely to Bonnie to place it carefully under the table 'as usual'. They sat down and George looked around. He had no idea what to expect when Bonnie led him up to the entrance of the club and under a bright red awning reaching right out to the kerb. The doormen, two young coloured men dressed in close-fitting red uniforms, stood to attention as they passed by. Man was he glad she had offered to pay. This place would be way out of his league. Little Miss Bonnie never ceased to pull something out of the bag. There was a gleaming brass railing around the dance floor and their table was up close to the front, so they could command a good view of the dancers and the band.

It was nearly midnight and the general atmosphere was one of impending excitement. Only a few couples were on the floor, holding one another and swaying to the music which was slow and melodic. The stage was surrounded by red velvet drapes and there were woven leaves and flowers painted in gold up all around the walls. The tables were close together giving George the opportunity to examine the style worn by those who could afford to frequent places such as this.

Most of the men were wearing highly polished two-tone shoes, button-down collars and sharp trousers with creases you could cut your finger on. Several of the women were bedecked in long, glittering beads and dresses made of bright fabric which clung to their hips. A woman nearby turned right around in her seat to pick up one of her gloves which had fallen to the floor. A large frill hung around below her smooth back which was bare to the waist. George imagined running his hands all the way down it when she glanced up and caught him staring at her and she gave him an almost imperceptible wink. Her slick of dark chestnut hair curled around one shoulder. He couldn't be sure, but she looked like someone he'd seen in a film he saw at The Capitol with Rachel. In another life.

A gaggle of brass instruments dipped and lurked, the drum-kit was bedazzled with glitter, all obediently waiting to be kicked into action. The whole band wore the same uniform: matching red tuxedos, tight pants and bow ties. The musicians were all coloured, in a collection of every skin tone. George smirked as he recalls how Neville used to describe the different shades from 'high yaller' to 'blue'.

'What's the joke, honey?' Bonnie smiled up at him and patted his knee.'

'Nothing. Well, yes some words that a friend taught me when I first came here.'

'And what might they be?' Her voice teasing and flirtatious.

He told her, and she laughed. It was obvious that she was familiar with those terms.

'Yes, that's true. And do you know that tonight you are my honey man?'

'Don't know what that means. Tell me.'

She laughed again, 'Don't worry about it, baby. Make the most of it while you can.'

She was clearly playing with him and he briefly felt piqued by her patronising attitude.

But hey, so what boyo, she's right.

He was going to enjoy it all. He sat back and watched the band as they quietly talked among themselves before the leader counted them in. A lone trumpeter played an introduction before the rest of the instruments joined in with a tune that George had heard on Bonnie's radio: Bugle Call Rag. Seeing it played live was a very different experience. Trombonists pointed their instruments into the air as they took their turn to shine, the drummer's hands juggled and pranced, his face gleaming with sweat. The bandleader's behind jolted in rhythm as he tried to control the abundance of sound and pulsating jubilance.

Before long people were on their feet. The extravagance of the music was matched only by their uninhibited dancing, the glamorous couples from the nearby tables given over to gleeful abandonment. As much as he was mesmerised by the whole scene, it somehow made him feel slightly uncomfortable. His father's maxim about 'slaving away for the big man' came to mind as he studied the band wearing over-wide smiles and playing their damndest to satisfy their white guests. All of them knowing that at the end of the night they would be obliged to creep out through the back door, to join the community of the unseen and disrespected as the sun rose over the unremitting New York skyline.

Bonnie's feet were tapping. Eventually she got up and dragged him onto the floor, but his limbs would not, could not respond, such were his feelings of vague uneasiness. She on the other hand was dancing as if her body was made of rubber. She slid, paused, jumped and wriggled her taut little body to the end, at all times looking at him, challenging him.

Come on boyo, let loose.

When the tune was over they sat down for a while and watched the dance floor.

George was drinking fast. Bonnie looked puzzled, 'What's wrong, sweetheart? You OK?'

'Yeah, yeah, of course.' He paused: 'This is a terrific place. Great idea. Thanks for bringing me.'

★

Four-thirty the following morning; they had danced, smooched and chatted the night away. A lot of people were taking a break at their tables as the band played a selection of slower tunes. Only one or two couples were left on the floor, holding one another in vague time to the music. The bandleader made a grand introduction, telling the audience that he was very honoured to welcome a very special guest. The pianist played an extravagant introduction, making much of broken chords and tinkling notes at the very top of the piano. George didn't catch the singer's name. A young woman walked onstage. She was small, dark and curvy reminding him very much of Alice. Dressed very simply in a white dress with a bunch of turquoise feathers pinned on one shoulder. She started to sing: After you've gone, a tender song about love, loss and regret.

Bonnie stood up and took his hand: 'Dance with me, George.'

So many feelings drifted about his head: the grandiose setting, the willing girl at his side, and something else he couldn't seem to shift. He took another quick gulp of his drink and they walked onto the dance floor. Bonnie put her arms around his neck as they moved together, and she sang the mournful lyrics softly in his ear about the pain of leaving someone you love.

He looked down and noticed that her eyes were closed. When she opened them the song was over, but she didn't want to return to their table just yet saying, 'Hold me, honey. Just hold me.'

★

A few hours later George watched as she grabbed clothes from her wardrobe and started throwing them on the bed. She had not looked in his direction once since getting out of bed a few minutes before.

'Can you reach up and get that suitcase down for me honey?'

'What?'

'The suitcase. It's on top of the closet, see?'

He got up and started dragging on some clothes, 'What's the rush?'

She did not respond, just carried on flinging stuff around.

'Bonnie? You OK?'

'Fine. I'm fine. Just get the goddam suitcase, will you?'

'OK, OK, I'm sorry. You've got a lot to think about, what with the worry about your parents and everything.'

'Yes, that's right: and everything.'

She hesitated for a moment and pulled out a suit of clothes from behind all her finery. A man's suit. Very expensive looking. Sharp.

'Here, you might like to have this.' She held it up for his inspection.

'And before you think about it', she continues, 'Don't ask, OK?'

Her eyes were bright as she shoved the suit into his arms. Too bright. He draped the clothes hanger over the back of the armchair and picked up each garment, which looked as if they had never been worn. He held the trousers up to his waist: the right length. He put on the jacket over his underwear: the right size. It could have been made for him. And slung over the whole outfit was a white silk scarf, more glossy and heavy than the one hanging in his wardrobe upstairs.

'Bonnie, I don't understand, why…?'

'I said don't ask, OK? Let's just leave it at that. Now, either you better help me get my stuff together, or get the hell out of my way. I need to catch my train.'

Chapter Thirty-three

George's evenings were long since he was on his own again. He spent a few weeks wandering around Harlem, listening to jazz in any of the speakeasies which were free entry. He chatted up a few women along the way, some white and some coloured. That was fun. But they all had one thing in common. Because he looked the way he did and talked in that 'cute' way, they all assumed he had a pocket full of dollars.

Jeezus what man wants to be described as cute for chrissake.

He grunted to himself. And as for the dollars, nothing could be further from the truth.

The days of fancy clubs were over now that Bonnie was not around to pay up front. It was time to pick up his sorry arse and start striking out on his own. He got talking to a few musicians in his wanderings. Although some of them didn't seem to appreciate his approaches. Maybe they could see, where others couldn't. After all Neville was quick to realise he was 'a brother' when they first met. He grimaced to himself as he recalled his arrival in this tough city. It was almost a year and so many things had happened in that time. Some good, some decidedly crappy.

★

Drifting around Harlem one Saturday afternoon he happened to drop into a library on 135th street.

'Hi, I'm looking for some information about jazz.'

The guy behind the counter widened his eyes and grinned. 'Well man, you're in the right place. You sound like an Englishman. You new around here?'

George softly blew out between narrowed lips.

'No, I've been here a few months and I've been to a few joints. Heard some great stuff.'

'Oh right, so what are you looking for exactly? You wanting to learn to play an instrument? I have a good friend who teaches trumpet, if that's your thing.'

'No, no, not at all. I first heard jazz back home when Jelly Roll Morton came to Britain. He invented jazz, didn't he?'

The young man gave a slight laugh, shook his head. 'Well, folks say it wasn't quite like that. You ever heard of Buddy Bolden?'

'Who?'

'He played the cornet, did that New Orleans kind of thing. Ragtime. You know about ragtime?'

'Of course.'

Guy must think he's a twerp.

'Look man, let me give you this. You can read for yourself. I'm rather busy right now.'

He searched around under his desk and produced a couple of pages torn from a magazine.

'Here's a piece about Buddy. You can have it if you want.'

George put the paper in his pocket. 'Thanks. I think I'll take it home to read.'

'No problem, man. Enjoy.'

With that, the young man turned away and started tidying some books on the desk as George walked out onto the street.

November 1914
'Thinking about you Buddy'

Charles Joseph 'Buddy' Bolden, was born thirty-three years ago on September 6th, 1877. Folks regarded him as the king of the cornet in New Orleans. He developed ragtime music with added explorations of his own making, including the use of blues and gospel to create his own unique sound. It was called 'jass'. People were going crazy for his style and it was said that when he played you could hear him all over New Orleans. By the time he was aged eighteen he was often called upon to play for parades and social occasions all over the city. But sad to say, Buddy became ill. Seven years ago, at the age of thirty he was committed to a mental institution. And he's still there. Lots of musicians are following in his wake including Jelly Roll Morton, Frankie Dusen, King Oliver, Bunk Johnson...

But, for me, Buddy's still the main man.

The writer's name was illegible.

George put down the article, leaned back in his chair and closed his eyes. Interesting piece. Just goes to show if you know your stuff there were always folk who wanted to read it. He often got good marks for his writing when he was a kid. Maybe that was something he could consider.

Chapter Thirty-four

The time was ripe to give the sweet Alice a try. A man has needs after all. They had known each other a while and he liked her from the start. It was clear that she liked him too. And she trusted him. Such an innocent little thing. Naïve. He thought about the times they spent together on Sunday afternoons. At night he fantasised about what lay beneath those buttoned up clothes and before too long he had worn himself out and fallen asleep, lightly snoring.

★

'Hey there, Miss J.'

There he was again. Same place. Same clothes. Same smile. Another Sunday had rolled around.

'Or can I call you Alice?' he said, grinning, as he left from lounging against the wall and came up close beside her. Alice was feeling vulnerable without Florence at her side. On the other occasions her friend gave George a polite nod before walking quickly away in the opposite direction. Alice once asked her why she wouldn't stay to be introduced to him, but Florence wouldn't be drawn, except to warn her more than once to be careful, leaving Alice baffled and quite hurt. Careful of what?

'Hello George. Good to see you again.'

She wasn't sure if she should add the last bit, in case he thought she was too forward. But oh my, it really was wonderful to see him again. Looked like he felt the same too as he straightaway took her hand and gave her a smile. That special smile. Just for her. He squeezed her hand and said nothing for a while.

'Alice, I would like to take you for a soda. Would that be OK?'

She couldn't believe it, he wanted to take her out just like a proper boyfriend She thought of her girlfriend from church back in Georgia who used to boast about going for drinks with her man. Once he gave her strong liquor by mistake and she disappeared for a while. That was until her baby came along and he took off. Alice was shocked and sorry. Although she recalled that her little baby boy was very beautiful.

'Thank you, George, I would like that very much.'

★

The bar was dark and cosy. They must have walked past it before, but Alice hadn't noticed the dusty blue door. You had to knock to be let in and there were steps down to the basement. So clever of George to know about a little secret such as this. It wasn't anything like one of those brightly lit places full of noisy people that she usually hurried past on her way home from work in the evenings.

When they got downstairs she was surprised to see folks lounging around drinking on a Sunday afternoon. In her experience people liked to be at home with their families spending quiet times together. She remembered how Pa used to enjoy sitting outside on the stoop relaxing after a hard week's work. She and Mom would be in the kitchen cooking and seeing to baby Eugene. After eating they would stay at the table and discuss what Pastor Williams had talked about at church. And they never went to bed without spending a few minutes reading from the Bible. Especially on a Sunday evening.

But New York was a big city, full of so many different people from around the world. That was one of the things she liked about it. After all, the Feldmanns were just one example and look what they had achieved in a country so far and so different from their own homeland.

'Penny for your thoughts, Miss J.' George was smiling at her as she paused on the stairs to take in the scene.

'I was just looking. I've never seen anywhere like this before.'

'Like what?' Speaking in a teasing way as he squeezed her hand.

'Like, well, different and kind of secret.'

'That's because it is. Secret I mean. And do you know why?'

'Why? Aren't these people supposed to be here?'

'Well, honey, it's a little more complicated than that. Look, let's talk about that later. Come and sit down and I'll buy you a drink.'

He led her over to a corner table and pulled out her chair before going over to the bar in the opposite corner. She looked at him as he walked across the room, his long legs, his slim, strong shape. She felt like she was in some kind of stupor. He had pulled out her chair. He had called her 'honey'. These were the kind of things she had read about in some of Florence's magazines, the stuff of dreams. Heady, throat-constricting, heart palpitating. She moved around to get comfortable and spread out her dress so that it folded neatly about her knees. She pulled at her bang and touched the back of her hair to check if the combs were tightly in place, the tortoiseshell combs that Florence had given her for Christmas.

George returned with a tall glass, full of something fizzy and golden. There was a slice of lemon stuck over the edge and a tiny paper umbrella poking out of some ice cubes.

'Here you are honey, a special drink for a special lady.'

He placed it carefully in front of her and watched her reaction.

'My, it looks so pretty George. What is it?'

Alice took out the umbrella, twirled it around before drying it with her handkerchief and putting it in her bag alongside her prayer book.

'It's got soda, gingerade, molasses and a little dash of magic.'

She took a mouthful. It tasted tangy and sweet, the bubbles tingling around her tongue making her giggle. She peered around as he casually put his arm along the back of her chair. She studied the other people, mostly men who sat talking quietly. Occasionally someone let out a loud laugh or a chuckle before returning to his drink. One or two women sauntered in and joined them for a while, but the men didn't seem that interested. Alice was shocked to see one woman come right up to one of them and sit on his lap, bold as you please.

It was almost evening by the time they got back outside, and Alice needed to get back home within a couple of hours in time for Sunday night prayers. She had drunk two of the magic drinks while George drank several shots of something from a small glass. He took her hand then put her arm through his as he led her along the street towards Bonnie's room.

Much later, after Alice had missed evening prayers, she lay in the dark, in the safety of her own bed, willing daylight to appear as she sent arrow prayers to God for His forgiveness.

Chapter Thirty-five

A lice came home after a tough time with the twins; it was seven o'clock and she was tired. On days like those she wished that Florence were still around. Some nights she went to bed pretending that her friend was still there, and she would have one-sided, whispered conversation with her. Especially after the events of the last three Sunday afternoons. Florence would have known what to say to make her feel less confused about everything.

On the second occasion George had given her a hand-written note on paper with little flowers all around the edge. Told her he had copied it from a Shakespeare play about two lovers. She took it out and read it as she had done every night since: 'My bounty is as boundless as the sea, My love as deep: the more I give to thee, The more I have, for both are infinite.' Imagine that: Shakespeare. It just goes to show that he was a proper English gentleman who truly loved her. Did this mean that they were properly in love? Getting married? What? Dear God, please let everything be alright.

She went upstairs to see a letter addressed to herself placed on the bed. It could only have been about meeting Florence. Even though she was anxious to see what it said, she took a few deep breaths and decided it was best to read it later in bed, when she had calmed herself down. She looked at the clock; there was just time for supper before Sewing Class which was always such fun when Florence was there.

She knew how to make everyone laugh. Sometimes she would wrap herself up in a length of fabric and dance about the room singing songs that she'd heard in one of the joints she frequented. No doubt they were the kind of places that Miss Kinsey would have disapproved of. Alice never asked her very much, in case it made her feel anxious or scared. Although it crossed her mind that Miss Kinsey certainly wouldn't approve of what she herself had been up to lately.

It was eleven o'clock by the time Alice got into bed. The building was quiet and all she could hear were the muffled sounds of the street. She picked up the envelope from the small table beside her bed and read the letter.

★

Two days later, Florence was already there, sitting on a bench overlooking the East River. She had suggested in her letter that they meet in Carl Schurz Park because it would be convenient for Alice after work. Alice recognised her friend from behind. She could see there was something different about her even from a distance. Her shoulders were slightly slumped and her back looked kind of broad. Her hair which was always piled high with fancy combs was pulled back low on her neck, stuck down beneath her collar. Alice called her name. Florence turned in her seat but didn't stand up.

As she got up close they hugged each other, and both started to cry.

'Oh, my dear, it's so good to see you.' Alice sat beside her on the bench, then pulled back to take a closer look.

'You too, honey. I've missed you.'

'Then why? What happened?'

'I'll tell you honey. All in good time. How are you?'

Alice noticed her folding and refolding the edges of her sleeves. What could be wrong?

'I need to know now, Florence. Something's not right. Miss Kinsey said you called in to collect your things from her office when we were all having supper last Friday. What's it all about? I can't bear to see you looking so troubled.'

Florence took hold of her hand and looked up properly for the first time since they met. 'I don't want you to think badly of me. Promise?'

'Florence dear. How could I ever do that? You've been my first and best friend since I came here. And you always will be, no matter what.'

Florence gazed out at the river: 'You will probably think differently when I tell you.'

'Don't say that. I might be able to help you. Same way you've always helped me.'

'Thing is, Alice, nobody can. I got myself into this mess and I got to get myself out.'

'What kind of mess?'

She looked back, shook her head: 'Oh Alice, that's what I love about you. You're such an innocent, sweet thing.'

It was Alice's turn to look away, thinking that she wasn't so innocent. Not anymore.

'Please tell me,' It was her turn to glance away, her voice quiet.

'Look it's like this: I met this guy a few months ago and well, we got involved. Properly involved. Know what I'm saying?'

'Yes, I understand. Perhaps too well.'

'Too well? You, of all people?'

Alice sighed: 'Yes me.'

'Not the guy from outside church, that George?'

'Yes, him. George. But I do so love him, and I know he loves me too. I feel so happy and yet bad at the same time.'

Florence put her arm around her. 'Nothing to feel bad about honey. It's called being human. Everybody needs someone special in their lives. Even you.'

'I know, I know. Anyway, I want to know why you're so miserable.'

'You notice that I'm looking different. That's because I became…I got…Alice, do I have to spell it out? Didn't Miss Kinsey show you my note?'

'Yes, she did. You mean you're having a baby?'

Florence shrugged: 'I was having a baby. But I'm not now. I did something bad. I thought he would be pleased for us. What a fool I was.'

'Are you saying what I think you're saying? And why would he be pleased that you lost your baby?'

'That's the thing dear. I didn't lose it. I thought he just wanted to be with me, without any other, umm, complications.'

Alice got up and went to lean on the railings. She watched the river heaving slowly along, each small wave following the other in perfect rhythm.

Florence came to stand at her side: 'I knew this would happen. That's why I didn't want to tell you, but I also didn't know who else I could turn to. Please don't think badly of me, Alice.'

'Everyone's entitled to make mistakes dear. I don't find it easy, it's true, but then who am I to judge?'

She clutched onto the railings as she was talking, thinking of what it says in the Bible about what it means to take a life. But surely God would understand why Florence needed to take care of herself? How else could she manage otherwise?

'I'm paying for it now though, believe me.' Florence spoke in a monotone. 'The quack I went to see said that I probably won't be able to have any more babies after the damage this has caused to my body.'

★

Hours later, after they had walked around the park and cried some more, Alice went home. She knew that Florence was spending her nights in a hostel and she couldn't bear to think of her being in such a place. She needed to act fast and find a way to help her friend. Which also meant that her own safe days at The White Rose were over.

Chapter Thirty-six

Summer had slipped away and there was a chill in the air as Alice came out of church. She was wearing the same dress she wore when George waited for her that first time. She was glad she thought to put on the jacket she had been working on at sewing class for two weeks. There was a length of navy blue galatea at the back of the cupboard that nobody else wanted, so she asked if she could have it. It was a sturdy twill more suited to heavy clothes, but she had tried to pretty it up by adding pink braid around the collar and cuffs and matching pink buttons down the front. It hugged her around the shoulders and fit close around the middle. She was conscious that George always looked so smart and dapper and she was fast running out of ideas of what to wear for him.

She'd had a lot to think about since her meeting with Florence a few days before and thought that he might be able to give her some helpful advice. She walked slowly, without looking behind so that she could pretend to be surprised when he came up behind her and put his hand on her waist. The game they played every time.

★

Her head swimming and weak with hunger and thirst, Alice had been trying to hold it together since the previous evening. She had hung around after church, pretending to look in her prayer book. A couple of the congregation asked if she was alright, as she stood alone by the wall.

He wasn't there. He was nowhere to be seen. She walked over to the secret bar and hung around outside the door. She climbed up to the top of St Nicholas Park. Nothing. It was as if he had never existed. She couldn't understand it. Maybe he had been hurt, injured, perhaps he was lying somewhere thinking of her and unable to reach her? Or God forbid, did it mean that he had stopped loving her? Is this what love is supposed to be like? This pain, joy, confusion, this feeling of being unable to eat, drink, or think straight when the other person's face looms up in front of you?

She ran over to the hostel where Florence was staying, her mouth dry, her heart pumping. The man on the door couldn't understand her, carrying on like he'd never heard of Florence. You would have thought she was speaking double-dutch. Kept on telling her to calm down. In the end she ran past him and shouted out Florence's name. Someone gave her a chair and a glass of water. She closed her eyes and leaned, shaking, against the wall. When she opened them, Florence was right there holding her hand, making her weep all over again. Florence said they should go straightways and talk to someone who might be able to help.

★

Both fell silent as they approached the front door, dreading her reaction. Sarah Kinsey sat them down in her office, brought them some coffee and waited. Florence stayed quiet and let Alice speak first. She talked about George, trying to tell Miss Kinsey in a roundabout way that they were in love and she hoped that they would one day be married. Then Florence took over and told her the bare bones of her own sad tale. The older woman started tidying the photographs on her bureau as they talked, saying nothing for a while. Without a word she got up and went out to the telephone in the hallway.

The two young women looked at one another. Was she so angry that she just walked away? Should they creep out of the door and hope they wouldn't be seen? Where could they go? A few minutes later Miss Kinsey returned. She sat opposite them as they huddled together on the couch and started to talk. She wasn't angry, nor even did she seem surprised when she spoke: 'I know that you two girls are very close. And you want to help each other?'

Alice, always ready to be positive, 'Why yes Miss Kinsey. I love Florence like she is my very own sister.'

'And you, Florence? What are you thinking?'

Florence's response, slower and more measured, 'Of course Miss Kinsey. Alice is the best girl I ever met in my whole life. She truly is my sister.'

'Good. Anyway, I had an idea while you were talking. I've been on the phone trying to arrange something for you both. Alice, Mrs Feldmann will talk to you when you go into work tomorrow.'

Florence got up and gave her a hug: 'I'm sorry if I've been a disappointment to you, Miss Kinsey.'

'Yes, me too,' said Alice, 'But sometimes, it's hard to make the right choices.'

'I know, dear. We all make mistakes, but that doesn't mean that we can't go on to lead good, proper lives to make up for it. You're both good girls at heart with a lot to give.'

They looked at one another, not knowing how to respond.

Miss Kinsey got up and opened the door: 'OK, let's be practical. Florence, I think you should stay here tonight. I'm sure Alice won't mind sharing. It will be just like old times. And remember, always take care of each other. A good friend is a precious jewel.'

★

They sat in Mr and Mrs Feldmann's parlour, looking at the rug. The twins had been put to bed. Alice's hands trembled as she picked up her glass of soda. Nobody seemed able to start the conversation. Eventually, Mr Feldmann shifted around on the couch beside his wife and cleared his throat.

'Alice, as you know Miss Kinsey has spoken to us.'

'Yes Mr Feldmann, thank you for talking to her. I know you're busy.'

He went across and touched her forearm: 'It's OK Alice, we all know why you're here. We need to talk.'

'Yes.'

'We know that your friend has a problem and needs somewhere to stay. Is that right?'

'Yes, sir.'

'And you would like to be with her too, jah?'

'Yes sir, because she is like my sister and we always help each other.'

'Jah, jah. Well, you've been to the bakery a few times, haven't you? With the twins?'

'Yes Sir.'

'You probably didn't know that we also have two rooms above the store where we keep our cooking things.'

'No Sir...I mean yes Sir...I didn't know.'

'It's alright, I understand. Miss Kinsey has become a good friend of ours since you've worked for us. You are the best girl we've ever had to take care of our boys and we would like to help you.'

Mrs Feldmann nodded her head but didn't look at either of them as the conversation went on around her.

'If you want, you two could share one of the rooms until you find somewhere else to live.'

Florence began to cry.

'Oh my, thank you, sir. You are good people.' Alice's voice was quiet as she lowered her head.

He put his hand up, 'There is only one thing to remember. Yorkville is our neighbourhood and everyone knows us and our business. We do not want any, erm, difficulties. Of any kind.'

'Yes sir, I understand.'

She nudged Florence who looked up, 'Yes, me too Mr Feldmann. Dear Alice always told me that you are the best. And she loves Felix and Leon as if they were her own kids.'

Mrs Feldmann nodded again and looked across at Alice, 'Jah, and my boys love her too. She is like a second mama to them.'

★

Neither of them spoke until they were outside and down the street a few yards. Then Florence threw her arms around Alice, holding her tight and rocking her from side to side. Right there on the kerb.

'Dear Lord, when you came looking for me, honey, I couldn't make any sense of what you were saying, you were that upset. And now this. You are an angel.'

'I was in such a state, wasn't I? And what would we have done without dear old Miss Kinsey?'

'That woman sure is a diamond.'

A couple of days later they were carrying their bags along First Avenue to the small room they would share for a while. Until things changed. Florence tried to engage her friend in conversation as they walked but for once Alice had little to say.

Chapter Thirty-seven

George was just about to take the stationery downstairs to stack away one morning when Mr Roberts sauntered across to his desk.

'Good morning, George. Do you have a few minutes?'

'Yes Sir, of course. I was just about to go downstairs and pack this away.'

'Yes, don't worry about that. This will only take a moment.'

George's mind was running overtime: maybe one of the other tenants had noticed him sneaking Alice into Bonnie's room.

Bloody creeps.

He'd done his best to be careful, asking her to wait on the corner for a few minutes so that he could pick up the mail, when in fact he was glancing around to check if there was anyone about. It was usually quiet on Sunday afternoons, but he had to make sure. Then the first time there was the thing of having to explain to her why he was staying in what was obviously a woman's room, what with all the frills and fol-de-rols hanging about the place. Told her that an elderly neighbour wanted him to water her plant while she was away for a few weeks. Said that he would forget unless he saw the goddam plant in front of him every morning. Well it was partly true, apart from the elderly bit. Although Alice seemed to swallow it. She was acting like she was stuck in the fog anyway.

It was strangely comforting to caress and hold her dark little body. And man, after a while she was certainly up for it. But he had to remember that she was inexperienced. It was refreshing to meet such a sweet and genuine girl. Perhaps it was time to make a new start as far as women were concerned. Thinking about Alice engendered new sensations. He couldn't put his finger on it, nor what it all meant. Just that it was different. Perhaps meeting her meant that life was on the up. He was feeling quite pleased with himself. Until Mr Boss Man asked to talk to him.

'You coming in or what, George?'

'Yes, sorry, Sir. Not quite with it today.'

'Is that right?'

George stood in the doorway. Waiting.

Mr Roberts sat down behind his desk, leaning back, his legs stretched out, his hands crossed behind his head.

'So, how's it going in your new place? You been there a while now. Things working out with the other tenants?'

'I've been there six, no, seven months. No problems. I don't see much of anyone else. They're all busy I guess.'

'And what about Miss Fflett? Seen her much?'

'Yes, once or twice. You know, coming and going, putting out the trash and everything.'

'Is that so? I gathered that you two were friends?'

'Well, yes, I suppose we are in a way.'

'And what way is that?'

'Pardon me?'

'In what way are you friends?'

'Well, we talked sometimes, that kind of thing.'

Mr Roberts leaned forward: 'Sorry George, should have said. Sit down, boy.'

George sat. He hadn't been addressed as 'boy' for a few months now, something was definitely up, and he'd better be ready, whatever it was. Sitting on the opposite side of the big desk, like a naughty schoolboy awaiting his punishment.

Any moment now the old sod could be brandishing his cane ready to give him a good hammering.

Mr Roberts continued, 'Thing is, George, I had a little chat with the guy who lives in the room next to yours. He's in town for a few days. Says he hasn't heard you moving around in the evenings, but he's seen you coming and going from Bonnie's room. Is that right?'

'Yes, she had to go away and see her parents for a while. Needed a neighbour to keep an eye on her room, water her plant and make sure her rent is paid on time.'

'Her rent? What do you mean?'

'She left the cash with me. Said to post it for her. Said she will send me some more if she needs to stay away longer.'

'Well, well, you two must be really close for her to entrust you with her hard-earned cash.'

George was wondering how much the old man had caught on. And why he should care anyway. As long as he got the rent, what was the problem?

He paused before responding.

'Umm, are you happy for me to give you the money on her behalf, Sir? I just wanted to help her out.'

'Yes, that's not the issue here. The thing is you may not know that Bonnie is the daughter of one of my friends. He asked me to keep an eye on her while she's in New York.'

'I see. I quite understand. She's a very nice person.'

'Yes, well be that as it may, I'd rather you didn't get too involved, George, friend or not. You know what I'm saying? I've given you a chance. Don't blow it. You can go now, we've both got work to do.'

He stood up, so George did too.

'Yes Sir. Thank you.'

For the rest of the day George wondered what he was going to do about Alice. As Dad would say, he'd been given 'the gypsy's warning'. Better be careful. At six o'clock he made his way downtown to Brooklyn instead of heading off home.

'The way I see it, man, you 'ave come to a kinda crossroads.'

George was sitting in the armchair in Grantley's room in Flatbush. Despite not having seen him for months, he knew that Grantley would at least give him a fair hearing, whereas Neville was still too hurt and angry. Especially since he had snubbed him in the street not long ago. Still, turning up out of the blue was taking a risk.

'Yes, you're right. The thing is I really like Alice. She's a sweet kid, but…'

'But what?'

Grantley stopped stirring the stew he was cooking for them both. He put the spoon to one side and sat on the kitchen chair. Drew up close to George who got up and went to the window.

Bloody hell, maybe this was not such a good idea after all.

'The thing is, when I came to New York I had certain ideas of what my life could be like.'

'And what did you think it could be like? Like the movies?'

George flushed and turned around, 'Sorry man, I shouldn't have come. It's not your problem.' He took his jacket from the back of the chair.

Grantley stood up and held him by the shoulder. 'Hey, take it easy, brother. You come to talk to me after all this time. So, let's talk, eh?'

'Sorry man, sorry.'

'You don't have to keep apologising. Not to me anyway. As I said, you 'ave to make a choice. Up to you.'

George patted Grantley's hand which was still on his shoulder. He was a good man. A fair man who wanted to give him a fair hearing.

'Tell me what you thought when you first met me?'

Grantley grinned: 'What I thought? You want the truth?'

'Yes, I do. I value your opinion. That's why I came down here tonight.'

'Well, to be honest me and Neville talked about this long ago.'

'You talked about me? With Neville? When?'

'Soon after we all started hanging out together. It was obvious that you would get to this point one day. I remember thinking that.'

He shook his head. 'To be fair, you didn't know what it was like in this goddam country. Don't think you're the only one that come here to get a better life, only to find out different. Man, these folks can be wicked.'

He shook his head, 'Wicked.'

'So, what do you think I should do? And what about Alice?'

'Well, it look to me like she's little Miss Innocent. Try not to spoil it. At the end of the day, it's up to you, brother. Come let's eat. Don't know 'bout you but I'm starving.'

They spent the next hour eating and laughing together. Grantley regaled George with tales of the women that he and Neville had been chasing. He included an episode in which a woman's husband came home unexpectedly. The woman made Neville lay on the floor by the bed, pressed up against the wall. When they heard the husband snoring downstairs on the couch, Neville climbed out of the window, shinned down the water pipe and ran for his life. Not an easy feat considering his shape and size.

It was almost like old times. Almost.

Grantley's warm face became serious. 'Take my advice, brother, do what you feel you 'ave to do to survive, but don't hurt that sweet gal you 'ave there. Remember none of us can 'ave everything we want in life. Wish you luck.'

When it was time to leave, George shook his old friend's hand, then paused before clapping him on the back. As he walked up towards the subway he wondered if he would ever see him again.

★

Around eleven-thirty that night, a young man walks along 136th street. He is tall and slim, dressed in a thin jacket as if the cold is of no consequence. He glances up at each building as he walks, obviously looking for a particular address. He stops outside a big house with a small sign on the wall: The White Rose Mission. He takes an envelope from his pocket, looks at it briefly in his hand before going up the few steps to the front door and posts it through the letterbox. He pauses when he gets back down to the sidewalk and looks up to the highest windows. At the same time an elderly woman moves aside the drapes on the second floor and stares at him before pulling them closed again.

Chapter Thirty-eight

George was stuck indoors. It was Saturday on a cold November night and he had nothing to look forward to. He'd spent the last few evenings thinking about Grantley's advice. His birthday had come and gone. He remembered being ready to take the world by storm at twenty. He wondered where all that energy and optimism had gone in little more than a year. This was not the life he had dreamed of.

Turned out to be crap. Pure crap.

He put on his coat and went out, heading nowhere in particular, but ended up walking around the familiar streets of Harlem. The whole of human life was on display, from women walking along linked up with their friends, men joshing one another on the sidewalk, smart-looking couples being transported along Lenox Avenue in big cars. The whole works.

Jeezus, need to check out what's happening.

As for Alice, it was a pity, but there you go. Cute she might be, but a man had to find happiness somewhere and better to slam the brakes on sooner rather than later.

Still a shame though.

He went back home and lay on Bonnie's bed for a while before planning his next move. Within ten minutes he was washed and shaved. He opened her wardrobe and took out the suit she had given him on the day she left. As he pulled it out a box fell from the shelf above. Papers and photographs scattered all over the floor. He started to gather them up and shove them back in, then paused.

No harm in looking, damn it.

Pictures of Bonnie Fflett, all done up as a dancer, plumes, feathers, sequins, silk and satin, the business, with lots of flesh on show. An exotic dancer. So that was why she had those fancy moves on the dance floor.

In some photos he recognised the background setting as the smart club they had visited on their last night together. Other pictures had been taken in different places, most of her posing alone and others within a group. Thing is they must have been taken a while ago, he thought: she didn't look quite so hot by the time he met her. No wonder that the weird waiter knew her by name. He had learned a little more about the mysterious Miss Fflett. She never seemed to be short of cash when they went out, maybe there was more he could find out, but he was not sure that he wanted to know. Either way, the suit fitted him like a glove and the scarf felt rich next to his skin.

He slapped his hand to his forehead as he was about to go out through the front door and went back into her room for a few minutes. A small loan from her rent stash should be OK for a couple of weeks. Just until next payday.

★

'Ah, good evening Sir. Good to see you again. On your own tonight?'

Same waiter, Mr Creepy-Features, pulled out his chair and made a deal of using a dainty silver brush to sweep non-existent crumbs from the white tablecloth.

Bloody idiot.

'Yep. All by myself.'

'Not for long, Sir, I hope.' George gave a little laugh in a way he thought made him sound like a man of the world.

Jeezus, the guy looked like some kind of black and white lizard in his uniform, what with the greasy hair and his pale womanish face.

Before he even had time to savour his second drink a girl came across to George and sat next to him, pulling her chair up really close. He'd noticed her when he first sat down; she was sitting on some guy's knee and pretending to twirl his moustache. He got the picture alright, he wasn't falling for that one. He may not yet be a proper New Yorker, but she needn't think she could pull the wool over his eyes, no sirree.

'Good evening, stranger. Looking for some company?'

'Don't think so thanks.'

'Wow, an English gent. Surely you want to buy a girl a drink?'

'Afraid not. I'm waiting for a friend.'

'Afraid not,' she repeated, screwing up her nose before she moved on.

Must think I'm a sucker.

The band members were quietly chatting and laughing in between numbers, when a drum roll signalled something special.

The bandleader made an announcement, 'And now for some very beautiful ladies all the way from Virginia. Let's give them a big welcome!'

An array of glittering blondes came shimmying onto the stage as the band launched into The Charleston. George was mesmerised by their flashing thighs which twitched open and closed in rhythm as their hands slipped across their knees. He noticed that they were all dressed in outfits remarkably similar to Bonnie's pink dress. Silver headbands supported proud feathers as their hips sashayed and their silky legs kicked up high. The bandleader pretended to join in by copying their moves in a deliberately clumsy style, making the audience laugh, clap and smile at one another. Except for George. He glanced around him.

The only saddo sitting alone.

He summoned the waiter for another drink, who gave him a

patronising smile as he dumped it on the table before rushing off to simper over a noisy group sitting nearby. Before too long he came back, gave George a note and stood there while he read it:

'Hi there, handsome. Looks like your friends have been held up. Maybe you would like to join our table.'

'Who sent this note?'

The waiter smirked, 'The lady on that table over there, Sir. The one in the blue dress. Think she's waiting for a reply.'

George looked across and sure enough, a woman in some turquoise get-up put her head on one side and raised her eyebrows. He nodded back.

'Tell her I'll be very pleased to join them.'

'Of course, Sir.' The twerp still stood there, waiting until George got the message and dug around in his pocket for a 50-cent tip.

Cheeky sod.

★

Several drinks later, encouraged by the friendly group at her table, he vaguely seemed to recall coming on strong to the dickty gal in the blue dress. Didn't even remember her name. Kept asking her if she was the one who dropped her glove and winked at him the last time he was at the club with Bonnie. God knows what else he might have said.

The rush of night air when they got outside ushered in some sense. He groaned to himself.

She must think I'm as nutty as a friggin' fruitcake.

Not that she seemed to care, she was all over him like a rash when they got in the back of the car. The party they were going to was on the upper west side, from what he could see on the drive from Harlem.

The doorman, lounging in solitary splendour in the marble hallway showed no surprise when they walked in and she declared that they were guests of Mr V. He gave a slight nod and showed them to the elevator.

The apartment was huge, twice as big as the family house back in Cardiff. The door was opened by a woman who introduced herself as something beginning with F. He couldn't remember, so overawed was he by the splendour of his surroundings. The floor was wooden parquet, with a few bright rugs dotted about, the furniture heavy and luxurious and there were apricot-coloured drapes at the windows. Paintings hung on every wall and crowded bookshelves from floor to ceiling graced one side of the room.

Even a grand piano in the corner for chrissake.

He was beginning to think he'd struck gold, when who should come up to give him a hug but old Creepy Features himself. He had changed out of his uniform and was all done up in a red outfit that looked very much like a lady's gown. His eyes were surrounded by dark make-up and a slew of crimson lipstick pouted on his lips. He fluttered around George as if they had known one another for years.

Takes all sorts.

'I'm just wild about Harry' was blaring out from the phonograph in the corner. Miss Blue Dress was obviously enjoying taking him around and introducing him to people, occasionally inserting Georgie for Harry along with the song. George instantly forgot all their names. They were loud, flamboyant, colourful, confident. He met the husband of the woman called F. who immediately stood back and scrutinised him. Then he stepped forward again, grabbed his shoulders and murmured in his ear before moving off into the crowd with a smirk:

'Don't worry deario, your secret's safe with me. Why don't you drop by tomorrow night and we'll have a little talk.'

Chapter Thirty-nine

His boss had given him a short break, so George decided to go out and take a walk. He stopped outside for a moment wondering which direction to take. He stood and looked up at the high, white façade of the building. Getting that job as a porter at the impressive Hotel Serena sure was a godsend. A pure stroke of luck. Their segregation policy for staffing meant that with his looks he was able to slip in, no questions asked. Although those rules didn't always extend to the clientele. It depended on who they were; some well known faces sometimes swept into the foyer, with all their bags and hangers-on, carrying on as if they owned the world, which they probably did.

He recalled the evening a few weeks previously that a big band leader FH turned up with some of his musicians. With the band was a young man carrying a cornet under his arm. He had very dark skin and a laugh which filled the foyer as they all strolled in. He was big time in New York. His loud voice sounded like a bullfrog sitting on a lily-leaf. King of the pond. Who knew what his future might be?

The band leader had a round honey-coloured face and sported a neat moustache and conked hair. He remembered Neville telling him that 'conk' was made with a mixture of potatoes, eggs and lye. It had to be combed through the hair for as long as the person could bear the pain then washed out quickly, often causing serious burns to the scalp.

Sounds like a flippin' nightmare.

His sister Ruby always worried about her hair. When they were kids, she used to like combing his own shiny curls. He blinked for a moment, took a deep breath and expelled. There was no use dwelling on the past. What's done is done. Since he first pitched up on Ellis Island more than a year and a half ago, life had been a crappy merry-go-round. He couldn't have predicted any of it in a million years.

He shook his head thinking of the palaver with Roberts. When he found out about himself and Bonnie he had given him until the end of the week to leave his room and quit his job. Probably the creep from upstairs had put two and two together and snitched on him. Or the French bloke. At least he was lucky to have a couple of days, Roberts could have told him to leave immediately. Those two days were hellish, all the bossman could go on about was how disappointed he was and how he'd given him a chance and so on and so forth.

Miserable old sod, pain in the neck.

Fortunately, he managed to get the cash together to pay Bonnie's rent by borrowing some to replace what he had used from her stash. Thanks to the waiter from the club who seemed to take a shine to him. Going by the name of Harvey.

And it was just before Christmas. The so-called festive seasons had not exactly been his best times. Locked in a store cupboard the first year and then sleeping on Harvey's floor last time. He wasn't a bad bloke after all was said and done.

He certainly saved his back from all the Roberts shit.

And good company when they went out together to one of the flashy parties on the upper west side. It was good of him to lend the cash too. Just goes to show you can't judge by appearances.

When Harvey suggested they find an apartment together, it seemed like a good idea. Sharing bills, cooking and keeping the place spick and span was important to them both. George soon caught on that his friend's occasional partners could be of either gender, but he wasn't quite sure at first. 'Ask me no questions, I tell you no lies', was their maxim when one or other of them disappeared for a couple or three days. He thought about the few women he'd come across along the way. The rich ones who enjoyed spoiling him were OK for a while, but man, they were tough, demanding and used to getting their own way. There's nothing for nothing as Dad would say. All good things come at a cost. He opened his lunch bag and sat on a bench to eat, watching people go by. For once it was a fairly quiet day.

A young nursemaid walked by pushing a baby in a stroller and with a small boy on a rein at her side. The kids were giving her a hard time, the baby's deafening cry enough to shatter the nearby shop windows and the other kid pulling and shouting while she tried to stay patient. Reminded him of Alice.

'Excuse me, Miss, can I be of any help?' Gave her one of his killer smiles.

The girl looked young, no more than about eighteen or nineteen years old. She was dark, like Alice, but not as curvaceous, her thin frame enveloped in an ill-fitting nursemaid's uniform of beige and cream, which had clearly seen better days.

'Oh, thank you, I just can't seem to get them to be quiet. I've tried everything…'

George bent down, smiled and raised his eyebrows at the small boy. Then he sang to him quietly: Ar Hyd a Nos… The child had to listen so carefully to George's unfamiliar words and quiet singing that he was obliged to be still for a minute. The baby stopped crying and looked on.

'Oh, my. I don't what you done, but it sure worked. Thank you. Guess we better get on now. Goodbye.'

'Glad to be of help. Bye.'

He stood and watched for a couple of minutes as the girl carried on down the street. He wondered what it must be like to be married and have kids of his own. Maybe a boy and a girl and a loving wife to come home to. That could have been him and Alice if he'd played his cards right. And after talking to Grantley, it wasn't as if he hadn't tried. Never got a reply to the letter he delivered that night. And there he was thinking she was keen. Shame about all that stuff. Just wasn't meant to be.

He went back inside to his post and put on a welcoming smile for the guests.

★

'Stick with me, handsome, and we can take on the world.' Harvey was in one of his adventurous moods. He had the night off and was keen to get out and have some fun.

George smiled, 'OK, what's on the menu for tonight then?'

Harvey waved a little card about in the air.

'You won't believe this, but clever old me managed to wangle an invitation for us to a very elite place on west 136th. A private club, no less.'

'You don't mean AW's? How come?'

Harvey tapped the side of his nose: 'It's all about who you know, sweetie. Oh, my dear, the things I do for you. Come on, let's get dressed and hit the town.'

★

'Honey, so good to see you again.' The hostess herself came up and kissed Harvey on both cheeks, adding, 'That's how they do it in Europe, ya know.'

George had never seen any woman dressed as magnificently or flamboyantly. Especially a coloured woman. Her outfit was a mix of African-looking and plain fabric in bright colours, clinging to her shapely figure. He wondered whether the jewels around her neck and arms were real diamonds. Judging by the elegant furnishings he guessed they might be the genuine article.

She was giving him the once-over. 'And who's your friend?' she asked Harvey, who stood by grinning.

215

'Good evening, A. It's gorgeous to see you too. This is my good friend George.'

'Good friend, huh? I see.'

Harvey laughed, 'No, really we're just friends. He's my roomie.'

She took George by the arm, and looked back over her shoulder to Harvey, 'Get the drinks in, honey. I need to introduce young George here to some of my guests.'

As they walked away, she whispered in his ear, 'To be honest, I don't remember your friend's name, although his face is familiar to me. I see so many people.'

'It's Harvey. We've known each other a good while. He's a nice guy.'

'Oh yes, of course. I seem to remember. He's a dancer I think?'

'Yeah, something like that.'

She introduced him to a few folks before drifting off again, her hostess duty done. The people he met were both white and coloured and they all seemed to be at ease with one another, exuding confidence and geniality. It was so different from the world outside. He felt as if he was swimming around in a bubble; it was all so unreal. There was a lot of chatter and loud laughter; he overheard words and conversations which meant little or nothing to him. Discussions about books, poetry, music and painting, a heap of stuff from a world so different from his own. Some of them looked vaguely familiar. A light-skinned man came up to him, 'Hi, I read your article in *The Messenger* last month. Thought you hit the nail on the head when you said that…'

'I'm sorry, you must have the wrong person. I don't know who you're talking about.'

'No problem, man. Pardon me.'

He moved away and started talking to someone else. George decided to ask Harvey what this Messenger thing was all about when they got home.

Some guys came in from the hall, carrying big bags and music cases. A few people applauded in anticipation and before too long most of them were dancing. The band whipped them up to a musical high, women and men partnering up as they pleased. Harvey took off into his now famed style of swaying, leaping and jerking, his long arms and legs taking up so much space that other dancers had to move aside until eventually he ruled the floor, singing along to, I wish I could shimmy like my sister Kate. Some guy called out, 'Yeah, I wish you could too!' Everyone laughed. Unfazed, he danced up to George encouraging him to join in who grinned, shook his head and picked up another drink.

Around three a.m. they heard a mighty kerfuffle at the door. Someone muttered that 'the royalty must have arrived'. Being curious, Harvey and George went out into the hallway to see a large coloured woman accompanied by a few other people making their way into the lounge. Shedding her fur coat and pinching the cheek of a man nearby, she was clearly feeling good. Harvey nudged him: 'Looks like our famous friend is either drunk or high. Let's hope she treats us to a song or two.'

Sure enough, the lady herself went straight up to the band, turned her back on the guests and gave the musicians her instructions. She launched into a blues in which she was telling her 'daddy' to pack up his things and leave because: 'I ain't gonna play no second fiddle, I'm used to playing lead.' Everyone went wild. After the jump-up of earlier in the evening, it set the tone for the pace to begin winding down. After just that one song, she mingled with the crowd for a while, picking up drink after drink as the waiters passed by. By four a.m. she swept out again, surrounded by her acolytes.

George was beginning to feel the effects of all the liquor, slumping on a chaise lounge in a semi-daze. The musicians had packed up and gone and the phonograph was turned down low, playing a selection of slow songs. A few guests were left, sitting about, talking or resting after their frenetic night. Two or three couples cuddled up together on the big sofas.

The hostess, looking tired and rather sad, decided to make an announcement: 'Listen up everyone. I would like to play a famous song for you by a dear old friend of mine, who passed away over three years ago. Let's make a toast to the great man.'

People raised their glasses as she went over to the phonograph and put the needle down. Bert William's voice filled the room with his song: *Nobody*.

George sat forward in his seat and started looking about for Harvey, who was draped on a couch on the opposite side of the room in deep conversation with another man. He took one look at George's stricken face, said a quiet goodbye to his friend and went across to help him stand up.

'Come on, big boy. Time to go home.'

Chapter Forty

On 134th Street, ten blocks away from where George had been serenading two small kids in the late afternoon sunshine Florence had just got home. She pulled off her shoes and rubbed her swollen feet. Her cleaning job downtown was no joke; the fay she worked for was hard work. Must think she was the only woman to ever have a baby. Although he was certainly a cutie. Those big blue eyes seemed to follow her around the room while she was putting up with Miss Hoity-Toity's crap. Always carrying on something stupid about how exhausted she was. How she needed to get someone in as soon as possible to take care of her little darling. How important her job was as a singer with some fancy orchestra. A soprano singer, too, doncha know. Whatever that was. How she missed her husband who was away in Europe playing his trumpet, violin or whatever the hell he played. He was probably glad to get away from Miss Moaning Misery for a while.

And then there was her voice. Man, she talked so quiet and moany you would never believe she could churn out that big sound when she sang. Insisted she needed to practise every day, to keep her vocal tubes warmed up or whatever. She usually went into another room, so as not to disturb the baby. It was a wonder all her fancy ornaments didn't leap off the shelves, she made that much noise. Of course, that's when the baby wakes up. Every goddamn time and didn't he have a hefty set of lungs on him too. Florence always had to stop whatever she was doing and try to shush him.

★

She padded into the bedroom. At least she had a real job. If it wasn't for dear Alice, she would probably have been a working moll by now she thought, grinning to herself. She and Alice had made a cosy little home of the two rooms they shared together. And dear old Miss Kinsey had turned up trumps yet again; she had asked around which of her friends could offer them someplace to stay. They could have ended up out on the street. As Alice always says, 'Just when you need Him, Jesus is near.' It had been almost seven months. Just the two of them. That was until three weeks ago.

Alice was sitting on the edge of the bed with a bundle in her arms.

'So, how's our little man today?'

'He's fine.' Alice gazed down at her son. George Junior.

Florence put out her arms to take him for a hug. 'And how are you, honey?'

'My chest is a little sore. Little George is a greedy boy.'

Florence humphed, 'Just like his daddy I guess.'

'Oh Florence, I know you didn't approve. But he is my son's father after all. And I hope that one day little George might meet him.'

'You're right, dear. I'm sorry. I know how much you loved that man.'

'I guess you must be hungry. I haven't had time to cook anything yet.'

'Don't worry, dear. Miss Fancy-Pants left me some food in the kitchen. Looka here, I brought some back for you too.'

★

Baby George was asleep in the crib which had been sent over by

220

some of the White Rose girls. He was swaddled in a white crochet blanket specially made by Miss Kinsey. They were finishing the leftovers which were warmed up on plates over pots of boiling water and Florence was soaking her feet in a bowl. She'd walked the twenty-four blocks up from W 110th street, to save on subway fare. She didn't want to tell Alice, but cash would be tight until she could go back to work after the baby.

Miss Kinsey had given her some domestic work at the mission until George came along, but what was going to happen next was anyone's guess. They had to leave the Feldmann's room above the bakery in the new year, once Alice started to show. After all, sure as hell they wouldn't have wanted not just one, but two scarlet women living in their place.

Alice washed the cups and plates and sat down while drying her hands.

'I've been thinking, dear. I should get back to work as soon as I can. There might be somewhere I can go and take George with me.'

Florence closed her eyes. Maybe Alice was right: 'God is good.'

'OK, let me tell you what Miss Fancy-Pants was complaining about today. Maybe we can work something out.'

★

Later in bed, Alice was sitting up feeding George and Florence was trying to get back to sleep after having been woken up by his crying.

'There's just one thing, honey. When you go and offer your services, promise me you ain't gonna stroll into that woman's house and call her Miss Fancy-Pants now, will you?'

Chapter Forty-one

Harvey had been gone for a few days. George saw him once when he turned up for some more clothes a couple of days previously. He came into the kitchen where George was making coffee. Saying nothing, he tapped one side of his nose with his index finger, raised his eyebrows and gave a quiet laugh. George shook his head and grinned. That was Harvey all over. They had lived together for almost five years. It worked well for both of them. If he wanted to bring a woman back for the night, Harvey didn't interfere. If Harvey brought back – well anybody for the night, he said nothing either. Although there had been a few moments when the person creeping out of the bathroom in the early hours was sometimes of indeterminate sex.

They spent many long hours talking about their pasts. Harvey was the only person who understood him. Since Mam died there had been nobody. Nobody. Like the song. There was that word again. Kept leaping up to haunt him. Sure, Mam meant well, and she was probably the only woman to have ever loved him for who he was. But it was no joke feeling like an outsider wherever he went. Cardiff. New York. He could probably travel to the ends of the earth and not fit in anywhere.

He had told Harvey all about Mam, his sister Ruby and his dad and even Rachel. In turn Harvey related the sadness he felt the day he left North Carolina bound for New York. How his

222

blooming sexuality had caused an uproar in his family and he had no choice but to run away. Similarly, the only person who seemed to sympathise with him too was his mother. At the end of one heavy soul-searching evening they had a toast to 'outsiders everywhere', followed by a few drunken tears from Harvey as George awkwardly rubbed his back in sympathy.

Things picked up after his discussion with Clarke V back in – how long ago was it? About five, six years ago. He had asked George to drop by the next evening for a chat and he went out of curiosity. After all, maybe an obviously wealthy man like that could help him get somewhere. They spent a long evening talking, and for a white man he certainly had his finger on the pulse.

★

'Come in, George, and welcome.' Giving him a hug and kissing his cheek at the same time.

Oh shit, not that one.

What was it with these guys?

'Look man, Clarke is it? I'm not sure what you meant by your comment last night, but I'm not what you think.'

'It's OK, deario. Don't look so scared. I'm not going to eat you. Although, come to think of it…'

He giggled like a girl and took his arm. Led him into the sitting room, all traces of the previous night's party had gone, and it was restored again to its pristine glory. He ushered George to the couch before draping himself over the piano. Dressed in high-waist pants and a white shirt with ruffles down the front, his sandy hair slicked back with pomade, and what looked like a trace of lipstick too. George rubbed at the side of his face.

He could either make a run for it or see what this weirdo had to say for himself. After the pansy pose against the piano he poured two shots of whisky from a glass decanter on a side table, brought both of them across and sat right next to him.

'Alright George, I'll be straight with you. You're an interesting man and I think we could work together.'

'Work together how?'

'Well, it's clear to me and probably others too that you might not be who you proclaim to be. Am I right?'

'Don't know what you mean. I'm a lady's man, if you get my drift.'

'That's not what I'm saying, and you know it. Look, let me tell you what I thought we could do.'

He took a couple of magazines from the bureau and pointed out a couple of articles that he'd written for them. Articles about jazz, art, social life in Harlem. That kind of thing. George recognised a couple of the musicians he wrote about, but none of the other people.

'You seem like a clever guy. You could write too. About your experiences, your adventures in New York. Things like that. And you would get paid.'

George shook his head. 'Now look here errr—Clarke, I appreciate your offer. But you must understand that I don't want anybody to know my "secret", as you put it.'

Shit, shit, double shit. Have to think fast.

He put down his drink and stood up. Angry yet frightened as a rabbit.

'Furthermore, your exact words last night were: your secret's safe with me. I may have had a few drinks, but I remember clearly what you said.'

Clarke stood up as well. 'Deario. You left out the last word. Deario.'

He grinned and touched George on the forearm.

'You could earn a few dollars writing under an assumed name or simply calling yourself "anonymous". Think about it. Take these books and magazines home and let me know by the end of the week. Your choice.'

He paused… 'Deario.'

It turned out to be quite an experience. George spent the next few evenings reading the stuff that Clarke had given him. Poetry, stories essays, plays, all written by coloured writers. So many of his own thoughts fell into place when he read the work of some of these clearly talented men and women. He started keeping a notebook to write down his own feelings and ideas whenever he found the time in his short breaks from work or at home in the evenings if he wasn't going out.

He rummaged around in the closet to find some of his early writings. He grimaced when he read the first one. Clarke had to amend it a little, so the words ran together better and made it sound more American. God forbid if anyone picked up on the fact that any of the pieces were written by an 'Englishman'. He was beginning to know quite a few folks in Harlem and he couldn't take the risk. But it wasn't bad for a first attempt. Clarke particularly encouraged him to write pieces that challenged the very heart and soul of America.

He found a piece which seemed to go down well at the time:

Reflections of a Coloured Man
September 2nd, 1925

If you were a fly on the wall you may wonder why I laugh so hard at her jokes.
If you were a fly on the wall you may wonder why I'm so anxious to please her.
If you were a fly on the wall you may wonder why she gazes at my body.
If you were a fly on the wall you may wonder why I avoid her studied gaze and look instead at the wall behind her shoulder.
If you were a fly on the wall you may wonder why I drop my eyes when the boss walks in.

If you were a fly on the wall you may wonder why I
hesitate and drop my voice when he addresses me.
If you were a fly on the wall you may wonder why I
rush to help him wearing a rictus smile.
If you were a fly on the wall you may wonder why I
spit on the ground after he's walked away.

Anonymous

Then he found one of his favourite jazz pieces. Not a poem,
not a story. Just thoughts about a special night he'd spent with
Harvey at a speakeasy they came across quite by chance. This
one was more recent.

Stardust in Harlem
June 20th, 1928

He comes downstairs carrying a trumpet case. Nobody
looks up from their drinks. Just another musician trying
to make his name in the hot world of jazz. There's a
man setting up his sparse collection of drums on a
pile of upturned crates acting as a makeshift stage. The
drummer looks up and smiles towards Trumpet Man
and another guy with a saxophone who has appeared
from the shadows. He fiddles with the valves on his
instrument, his fingers like dark worms, stretching,
bending, wriggling. Preparation for sweet times ahead.
Trumpet Man takes out a battered horn from his case,
warms the mouthpiece in his hands and gets ready. He
holds the instrument at his side for a moment, eyes
closed. Then lifts it to his lips. He plays a long solo
introduction. Soulful, sad, poignant. The notes sway
in a slow dance around the melody, but there's no
disguising what song it is: Stardust. Folk stop talking.
Put their drinks down. And listen. Saxophone Man joins

in, playing a quiet accompaniment to the tune, a few bass notes, a riff, a pause. He nods at the drummer who gently brushes across his drums. Like a caress. After the introduction, a young woman gets up from the table where she's been sitting sipping her drink. Her face warm and brown as a chestnut. Dressed in bright blue satin. She starts to sing as she walks across the room. The lyrics tell of languishing in dreams and haunting melodies as her heart lingers on past love.

Anonymous

Chapter Forty-two

Alice usually dusted the china on Saturday mornings. George Jr and Frankie Pierce were bosom buddies. They were quietly busy in the kitchen, drawing or playing with the toy soldiers or some such. Not always a good sign. Much too quiet for two lively six-year-olds; what were they up to? It surely wouldn't be long before they would need to go out, get some fresh air in their lungs and run around. She planned to take them over to Central Park after lunch if she managed to finish all her chores.

It was hard to believe it had been nearly seven years since she started working for Mr and Mrs Pierce. Both of them being classical musicians, she sometimes had to stay over if they needed to go away on tour with the orchestra. But Mrs Pierce tried to arrange it so she could be at home most nights. Even though Alice and George could use the attic room if they wanted to stay over, she preferred to take him home whenever possible so he could sleep in his own bed. Although it was tough on him if she had to wake him up after a late concert when he was all comfy and snuggled up. He could be a real grump.

She enjoyed the job, but it was time for a change. Mrs Pierce didn't need her so much anymore. Frankie attended a small private kindergarten three days a week, before he started elementary school and it would soon be time for George to start school too. She heard the Pierces discussing a possible move to Europe. Italy maybe. Guess their kind of music was a big thing over there. She didn't want to be left in the lurch. It was time to start thinking about the future. Maybe she and Florence could talk about it later.

Some evenings when the Pierces got home, they were so full of it that they made a little music for Frankie before he went to bed. She and George would sit and listen in the kitchen. Even though he was only a little kid, George would go into a kind of trance when he heard them. He cuddled up on her lap and closed his eyes. She had never heard such music. It gave her that special feeling like when the choir at church sang a beautiful song and she imagined flying up along with those angel sculptures that draped themselves so gracefully high among the rafters.

She still went to St Philip's every Sunday, although she was a little shy at first after George was born. She wasn't sure how other folks at church would be. But God is a forgiving God and He knew how much she loved her son. She still felt the occasional pang when she stepped outside holding his hand. She liked to think his daddy would be lounging against the wall waiting for them both. Stupid thoughts. Why would he suddenly turn up after such a long time? No doubt he had found himself some other poor girl to be taken in by his charms. But none of that mattered when she looked at her son.

★

Florence was already home when she got back. She had spread a newspaper on the floor and was going through it on her hands and knees. She turned around and got to her feet on hearing Alice and George come through the door. Her face had that look which Alice had long learned to mean that she was not happy. Real mad in fact.

'Hi honey, hello Georgie Porgey.' She squeezed his curls and then launched in.

'Honey I am so fed up dealing with white folk's crap. Yes miss, no miss, I simply adore cleaning up your crap, miss...' She tailed off as Alice took hold of George's arm, led him into the bedroom and shut the door firmly, her lips tight.

'Florence, I know how you feel, dear, but we must remember it's not nice for George to hear all this. He'll learn soon enough.'

Florence shrugged her shoulders: 'OK sweetie, I'm sorry. I love that boy as if he's my own you know that. Just wish I – well both of us, could work someplace else. We've been slogging away in this goddam shit place for too long. I've had enough. Enough, I tell ya.'

Alice said nothing for a moment before stepping up close and hugging her tight. They sat down on the couch and Alice took her hand. Since Florence left the Pierces' household she'd had a couple of domestic jobs and things always went wrong. There was the man who kept touching her behind or her chest when she had to pass him by. She tried not to take much notice at first, thinking he was doing it accidentally, and a job was a job after all. But finally, she had enough, went straightway to get her coat one day and walked out of his apartment, vowing that if she stayed one more minute she would have punched him. Or worse.

Her next cleaning job was for some uppity lady on the upper east side. Things weren't too bad until she realised that the only dishes she was allowed to use in the kitchen were the same ones that the dog ate from. That day she threw her food all over the floor and walked.

She went off the rails for a while after that. Started coming home very late at night. Said nothing when she got in, simply climbed into bed and turned her face to the wall. But she was always able to pay her share of the rent and the bills. Alice had prayed hard for her every moment she could find.

'Did something happen today, Flo? Anything in particular?'

Florence's shoulders sagged, she started twisting her fingers in her lap.

'No, not really. The usual stuff. It's the way that woman talks to me. She's either being nasty, finding fault with my work or else she patronises me. Like I'm some little dog that has to wag my tail if she's in a good mood. And be grateful for the crumbs she throws my way. I don't know which is worse.'

Alice got their food ready, called George in from the bedroom and they ate in silence. He always went quiet when Auntie Flo was being a grouch as he called it. Alice worried about the effect it might be having on him. They'd had such a lovely time at the park earlier. He and Frankie were running and climbing like two baby goats. Although she noticed how George had learned to be more distant with his best friend when his parents got home. He usually retreated to the kitchen with her and sat quietly until she had finished her chores and it was time to head home.

★

Later. George was asleep on his cot beside the big bed. He was getting tall and his feet drooped over the edge when he slept. One more thing for Alice to worry about. Florence washed the dishes and was looking out the window. The newspaper was still open in the middle of the floor.

'I heard Mr and Mrs Pierce talking again today about moving to Europe. For their music, you know.'

'Humm, what you gonna do for a job then?' Her tone curt.

'That's the thing I wanted to talk to you about. I had an idea on the way home. You may be interested too.'

'What's your plan?'

'Well, as we went past Harlem Hospital I got to thinking how much we enjoy taking care of one another.'

'Yeah, guess so. And?'

'Well, why wouldn't we try to get jobs where we could care for other people too? I don't mean kids. I mean looking after adults. In a hospital or someplace like that.'

Florence picked up the newspaper. 'Funny, I was looking

through this earlier, to see if there was something different I could do. Didn't see anything.'

'My old Pa used to say, "if you don't ask, you don't get". There's no reason why we couldn't go into the hospital and ask. Or somewhere else. I don't know. What do you think?'

Chapter Forty-three

Ruby was sitting in the back room of the shop resting her legs, her daily ritual after kneeling down on the floor, cutting and shifting pattern pieces and fabric. Her movements like a measured, solitary dance: leaning forward, rubbing her knees in slow circles, leaning back. Forward, circles, back. Forward, circles, back. It had been a tough six years since she'd been running the shop by herself. She'd read in the papers how terrible it was in America at the beginning of the decade, with people doing crazy things because cash had run out. And before too long the effects ricocheted across the world. The coal trade slumped, shipping companies in Cardiff were collapsing like dominos and loads of men were out of work and on the dole. Including Jimmy.

Maybe George too. Or maybe not. Wherever he was. She'd met one of his workmates in the street a couple of years after he left who told her that her brother used to talk about New York. Things he'd picked up from the cinema no doubt. Sounded like the kind of place he'd be attracted to. Ever since then she decided that's where he was. Probably living the high life, knowing him. Although God alone knows how he would have survived the journey.

Mrs Lerman had given her a bundle of clothes she wouldn't need any more since she and Mr Lerman finally decided to retire to warmer climes. To be with their daughter they said. Didn't say where though. Even though all that business with George had happened long ago, Rachel was hardly ever mentioned. Not in Ruby's hearing anyway. And she thought it better not to ask. It was all water under the bridge now anyway.

She thought about her life with Jimmy. They were married in April 1924 and baby Georgia made her appearance the following year. They valued family times together when he was home for a few days. Occasionally they would walk into town and saunter round Sophia Gardens, which was where Georgia learned to walk. Ruby would never forget that day. Dad came too. Baby Georgia had been practising for weeks, staggering around holding onto the furniture and Ruby could see it wouldn't be long before she took her first steps unaided. She prayed that Jimmy would be home to see it.

It was a warm day. People lay or sat around on the grass. Walkers passed by quietly chatting and even the children's voices were hushed and softer than usual. Dad brought a blanket and they sat on the grass with a picnic. Jimmy picked a piece of long grass, held it along his mouth with both hands and blew. He was trying to play a tune on it, without much success. Ruby remembered some of the bigger boys doing that when they were children, but when she tried, the sharp edges of the grass made her lips sore.

After they'd eaten, Dad got up with Georgia. He started walking behind her, holding both her hands in his. He carefully let go of one hand and then the other. She tottered a few steps before collapsing onto the grass, laughed and pulled herself back up. They all applauded her and for the rest of the afternoon, that's all she wanted to do. Even though she must have been tired that night, she was so excited they had difficulty getting her to sleep. Jimmy sat and rocked her and eventually he fell asleep before she did. Happy times.

★

Jimmy's spirits were low when he was laid off in 1932. He had to find work. And fast. It nettled him to see his wife juggling her business at the shop with her role as a mother. He tramped about looking for employment and finally got a job helping out in one of the pubs in Bute Street. His sociable manner behind the bar coupled with his ideas for improving business meant that the pub soon became one of the more popular haunts in the area.

He persuaded two brothers well known for their guitar and singing talents to perform regularly on Friday nights. They were from a musical family of Cape Verdean descent, both of them handsome, charming and gifted. Jimmy worked out that when the music started playing and customers already had a couple of drinks inside them they would be willing to pay an extra penny for their beer in order the pay the musicians. It turned out to be a master stroke.

★

Smiling to herself, Ruby thought of all the days and nights that they shared together. Warm, safe, secure. She remembered how some of her friends at the rag factory used to talk about hot passion, fireworks, the ups and downs of love. That had never been her experience with Jimmy. To hell with that. Sounded like too much hard work.

It was nearly five o'clock and Ruby began locking up the shop before she went to collect Georgia on her way home. Georgia spent an hour or two at Peggy's after school every day until her mother came. Peggy was usually doing her finishing work: taking up hems, sewing on buttons or adding braid to garments for the shop. It worked out well for all of them. But not so good when business was slow. As it certainly was.

Peggy was sitting on the floor, her back against the sofa. She licked the end of a piece of cotton before threading her needle, eyes squinting and hands trembling as she took aim. Not a good sign. The demon drink. Lately Charley made his life choices very plain to anyone who cared to ask. Turning up when he felt like it and then going off again without explanation. That was when

Peggy reached for the bottle. Ruby worried about the effect it might be having on Georgia, but at the same time was concerned for her friend's welfare. She gave her as much work as she could, some of which she could do herself. Something had to change.

She hugged Georgia and stood back to look at her.

Peggy smiled, 'Tell your mam your good news then, lovely.'

'What's that then? We could certainly do with some good news.'

Georgia's eyes flashed as she raised her eyebrows, 'I've been picked for the scholarship class, Mam. Starting on Monday.'

'Well done, my girl. Does that mean they will put you forward for Lady Margaret's?'

'Yes, Miss Pickard called some of us out of class to tell us. It means having special classes, preparing for next term.'

'There's my lovely girl. Not just beautiful, but clever too. Come here.'

Ruby held her daughter tight while Peggy concentrated hard on her sewing.

★

Ruby was lying in bed, looking about at the dark shadows in the room. Her dressing gown on the back of the door swung gently in the breeze from the open window. She heard the door open and close quietly downstairs, then Jimmy coming up the stairs. A heavy tread, meaning he had probably stayed at the pub for 'afters' and had one too many. He tripped and cursed softly. He undressed in the dark and slid in beside her, trying not to disturb the bedclothes.

'It's alright, I'm already awake.'

'Sorry love. Trying to be quiet.'

Trying to stifle a belch, he cuddled up to her. 'I know you like to make an early start in the mornings.'

'Don't worry, Jimmy. Got some good news.'

He sat up, turned on the bedside lamp and leaned on his elbow to look at her.

'Not the pitter patter of another chile? Maybe a boy this time? Yeah man.' His face bright as a young boy.

'Gosh no, not at my age. I'm an old girl pushing forty.'

He chuckled: 'You'll never be an old girl, to me Rube.'

'Yeah, yeah, I know. Anyway, the news is that our beautiful daughter has been chosen to go into the scholarship class at school.'

'OK, what does that mean?'

'It means that she's a clever girl and could be going to Lady Margaret's High School after the summer. So, there you are. What about that then?'

Jimmy lay back down, and she hugged up against his chest. 'Isn't that the posh school across town? Well, I'm not surprised. She takes after her clever mam.' He rubbed her head.

They talked quietly in the dark and Jimmy fell asleep. But Ruby lay awake a lot longer, wondering how they would be able to afford the smart school uniform. The straw hat, the blazer, the raincoat, gym slip, blouses... Plus she would probably need exercise kit and books. The list seemed endless. She was familiar with the uniform. Occasionally a couple of her clients were accompanied by their daughters after school. The girls were confident young women carrying an innate sense of their worth in the world. Quite a different one to that in which she had grown up.

Hearing the exciting news of Georgia's achievements was like someone bringing you a wonderful gift, only to have it fade from view as you put your hand out to receive it. One thing she knew for sure. She would do whatever it took to find the money. Her daughter would never have to work in the rag factory.

Chapter Forty-four

Alice and Florence had worked at Green Fields Nursing Home as Nurses' Aids for nine years, following their training at The Harlem Hospital.

Alice had been off sick for a couple of days and the residents were delighted on her return that morning when she came into the lounge. Heavier than she was in her twenties, her firm, rounded shape in the wrap-around pinafore always brought a lot of comfort. She was the one who was the first to notice if someone might need a glass of water or if they took on that blank look which meant they were probably in need of some human contact. She knew only too well that what you miss most when alone is just being held by another person. If only for a moment.

Some of the old men nodded or waved to her and one of them called out, 'Love ya baby!' She waved back and blew him a kiss as she passed his chair. Old Mr Miller had been at Green Fields for five years and once gave her a white flower which she pinned above her ear, just beneath her winged hat and wore it all day. She tried to remember to buy a flower from the stall at the corner of the street every time she was on shift since then. It didn't do any harm to try and bring a little joy into the lives of these elderly men who had to spend the autumn of their lives in an institution.

After all, Miss Kinsey used to tell her that she was good at taking care of people. She had never forgotten those words and tried to be that person ever since. You might be inclined to think that Alice's own life had not been all that fortunate, but if you were to ask her, she would smile and tell you about all the good things and wonderful folks she'd come across over the years.

You would never know that she suffered years of disappointment and hardship unless she was pressed to talk about it. Even then she'd be reluctant to tell you. She had a unique talent in maintaining a positive attitude, a strong hold on life, and an unwavering trust in the God she believed always walked beside her.

★

Lunchtime a couple of hours later, she went into the kitchen, took her sandwiches out of her locker and sat at the table. Florence was already there, shoes off and feet up with a cigarette.

'Hi honey, where have you been all morning?'

'Been upstairs on cleaning duties. I'm back on lounge rota afterwards. I always enjoy talking to the old fellows.'

'Yes, I know you do, honey. They like it too.' She groaned, 'Man, I get so sick and tired of hearing the same old stories. You have the patience of a saint.'

'Well, the way I look at it, the past is all they got left. That's the same for all of us.'

Florence nodded and smiled, blowing out a tobacco cloud, 'Honey, you're damn right. Remember all that bamalam we went through to train up for our jobs? If it hadn't been for dear old Sarah K, God rest her soul, we wouldn't be here today.'

'Yes, God bless Miss Kinsey. I'm sure she pulled strings for us. Remember when we turned up at the hospital to ask for a job? Both of us at the same time?'

'Yeah, like two old maids. When we pitched up it was obvious that Matron knew we were coming. Didn't look a bit surprised. Happened to mention she knew Miss K just as we were leaving.'

Florence laughed loudly, followed by her smoker's cough. Alice leaned across and patted her back.

Alice grinned: 'The training was pretty tough to begin with too. Do you recall how often we were sent to empty bedpans and clean up vomit and goodness knows what else?'

'Don't I just. We could probably fill a thousand trucks with the shit we've picked up over the years.' She laughed again, wiping tears from her eyes on her sleeve.

Alice tutted. 'Florence dear. Please.'

She paused. 'And as for being two old maids, we've not done too badly. I'll never forget dear Benny.'

'I know sweetie. But be honest, you never really loved him.'

'I did dear. Of course, I loved him, but I suppose I wasn't in love with him. There's a difference. Know what I mean?'

'Course I do, honey. He was a good man and gave you a few years of security before he popped off. But anyone could see he wasn't long for this life, what with his heart and everything. No surprise, being that much older.'

'Guess so. We took care of one another. And he was such a wonderful father to George when he was little. A good kind man.'

'Yep he sure was. I missed you after you moved into his place. And it wasn't long before I came across Jerry. Thought he was my last chance of happiness.'

She frowned. 'But that's another story. Never did make good choices when it came to men.'

'Mmmm. And here we are back to being like two old maids again. But you're happy now aren't you, Flo?'

'Yeah, guess so. Kind of.'

They looked at one another. Serious for a moment.

'You're off this afternoon, aren't you?'

'Yep, after my early start. Sure could do with a rest.'

Florence got up with a sigh and started putting on her shoes. Opened her locker, took off her pinafore and folded it ready to put away.

She turned back to where Alice was sitting. 'Ok honey-pie, you best get back to work. There's a whole bunch of guys waiting for you, although all of them are at least as old as Methuselah.'

Alice could hear her tittering at her own joke as she left the room and went off down the hall to collect her coat.

Chapter Forty-five

It was a quiet day at the shop. It had been that way since hell broke loose all over Europe. Ruby had just finished making a couple of pillowcases by using up one of the threadbare sheets that had seen the family through too many years to recall. She wondered what she might use to make a couple of items for the window display and thought it was time to take a look in the old trunk down in the basement.

The Lermans had been gone ten years. Hard to believe it was that long. And Ruby was still paying the same rent as she did when they first left. Mrs Lerman had tears in her eyes on that last day too. They were good people, no doubt about it.

She had stored most of the clothes in a cupboard in the storeroom, just taking one or two out occasionally if a customer wanted something special for a wedding or a christening. She used one of the garments to make a coat for Georgia. She was only six years old. Dark maroon it was in a warm, heavy fabric, lined with satin in different colours, scraps from her bag of bits. She'd so enjoyed cutting it down and re-designing it to fit her. Double-breasted, with pressed-in pleats which swung from the bodice. And there was even enough left to make a matching bonnet and a small muff. Georgia looked so pretty. Jimmy took them all uptown to Hansens to have a professional family photograph done. The photo was still on the wall. It was probably time to take another family portrait. Although without Dad this time.

★

There was a big crowd lined up along Bute Street on the way to St Mary's Church on the day of his funeral. April 9th, 1940. Barely four months ago. People joined in the cortege as his coffin passed by as was tradition down the bay. He was a well-respected man, although he probably didn't realise it himself. He'd been laid off from work due to an accident on his hand. He'd lost the top of one of his fingers many years previously, but this time it meant he couldn't do the heavy lifting and loading any more. A couple of years later his body was riddled with some malevolent, unexplained infection. Sixty was no age to die for a man as strong as Samuel Hodges had been. But he was never really the same man after Mam passed away all those years before.

The event passed with all the familiar rituals and camaraderie. His coffin was carried by six of his former work mates. Seeing them made Ruby yet more upset. His son should have been one of the pallbearers. And where was he? For all she knew he could be dead too.

Although he had the day off at the pub, Jimmy went behind the bar to help out, so many people had turned up. Everyone piled in there after church to make a toast in honour of Samuel Hodges. A lot of people had sacrificed some of their food rations to make a contribution to the wake and there was a lot of music, Pinkie's role having been taken over by a younger man, albeit he was not averse to being pulled up to his feet to give a rendition of the blues, even though his joints were not what they used to be. Drinks were passed out to younger children running up and down on the pavement outside. A proper send-off it was.

★

'You alright, Mam? Looks like you're daydreaming.'

Georgia had been sweeping the floor in the shop and came out the back to find her mother.

'Yes, I was. Thought I'd have a look at some of Mrs Lerman's things. See if we can concoct something fancy to put in the window. Mind you, folks are struggling these days.'

'All the more reason for us to make it look nice.' Georgia was holding a Fair Isle woollen jacket up against her shoulders.

'This is nice. Got plans for this one, Mam? Or not?'

Ruby laughed: 'Alright, lovely, I know what you're getting at. You can have it if you like.'

She paused. 'You remember the business we had getting your uniform for school?'

'Oh yes, I do. You did it though. You and Dad.'

'And you were worried it might not be ready in time for the beginning of term.'

'I was a bit. But I knew you and Dad would do it somehow. You and your creativity. Dad and his extra shifts. I want to be like you one day, Mam.'

Ruby raised her eyebrows.

★

She remembered it well. Mrs Lerman's trunk of stuff had come in useful. She was hunting around in it one day and found a bag right at the bottom, all tied up with string. Hadn't taken much notice of it before. When opened it turned out to be two school uniforms, belonging to her daughter Rachel. One of them being for Lady Margaret High School. It looked hardly worn. She sat back on her heels and thought about a conversation she'd had with Mr Lerman years before, shortly after she first started working for him. She recalled the tale of Rachel having started at Lady Margaret's, but they decided to take her out and send her to boarding school instead. She couldn't remember where. Perhaps it was north Wales. Somewhere quite far anyway. He hinted that Rachel had 'got up to mischief' as he put it and Ruby was too polite to ask what he meant.

Rachel was obviously very tall for eleven and rather more curvy even at that age. No wonder George had been attracted to the woman she grew into. She certainly knew how to flaunt it by then. Georgia was shorter and more finely built.

Ruby didn't want to alter the length of the gymslip too much. She could grow into it over her school years. It had a wide hem, which was taken down a little every summer. The trouble was, even after it was pressed with a damp cloth and a very hot iron, if you looked hard enough you could still see faint lines all around the bottom every time it was taken down. Then there was the problem of making the garment narrower while still retaining the box pleats running from the bodice and all the way down. The blazer was a massive feat of tailoring. Fortunately, she'd seen how Mr Lerman used to work and had some idea how to go about it. Then there were the blouses and the raincoat. She virtually remade every garment from scratch. When it was all done, it could only be described as bespoke. A word which Jimmy found very amusing and bandied about every weekend when she was getting the uniform clean and pressed for Monday.

Jimmy took on extra shifts by taking a cleaning job in an office uptown. Ruby found an empty biscuit tin with a picture of Cardiff Castle on the front, left over from one Christmas when she was a child. Mam used to keep buttons in it.

Every week for five years she and Jimmy both put any small change they could find in the tin. It had to cover the cost of Georgia's bus fare, lunches and any extras she might need for school.

A couple of hours later, Ruby and Georgia were both kneeling on the floor in the back room, with pieces of a dismantled coat laid out all around them. Plans had been agreed to make a two-tone matching skirt and jacket. If there was enough fabric.

Chapter Forty-six

It wasn't often that George and Harvey were both at home for the evening. Harvey had cooked them a meal and they were both enjoying an after-dinner cigarette. George was in pensive mood.

Harvey got up and went to his bedroom. On his return he made a show of holding something behind his back.

'Get the best glasses out, pretty boy.'

George was accustomed to Harvey's exaggerated appellations yet still groaned every time. He went to fetch the glasses and put them down on the coffee table. With a flourish and a bow, Harvey presented an elegant, dark blue bottle of some sophisticated liqueur and twisted off the cork.

'Wow, that looks swanky. To what do we owe the pleasure? Or more to the point, who did you have to pleasure to get it? Must have cost a few bucks.'

'Well my boy, let's just say there's no point in being a spoilt man, unless you can produce some evidence of the spoils.'

When Harvey laughed, his whole face lit up. No wonder so many people found him attractive. Of both sexes. George appreciated his beauty but had never felt tempted himself. Although he had always known he would only have to make one move in Harvey's direction and he would be all over him like a cheap suit. No, that was not for him. He loved women. Exploring their bodies was a compulsion. Each one was different and each one a beautiful fetish. That was until he got tired and moved on. The story of his life.

He smirked, 'Alright, say no more. Pour it out pronto, let me get a taste of how it feels to be spoiled too.'

'Now come on, Georgey Porgey, that's a joke coming from you of all people. What was the name of the last one? Can you remember?'

George put both hands up: 'OK, man, you win.'

They sipped their drinks. The taste was sweetly strong, like smooth treacle with a twist that left a tingle in your throat. Good stuff.

★

It was ten years since George had been writing anonymously for a couple of Negro periodicals. Ten years and still nobody ever discovered it was him. Coupled with his regular day job, he had been comfortable enough financially. That was until the last couple of years when there were less and less opportunities. Clarke had not given him much work. Shame, because his writing had improved over time. He kept a thesaurus beside his bed. The one that Harvey gave him when he first started out. And he still kept the old Shakespeare book too if he wanted to sound really flash.

Harvey put his glass down, the smile gone, looking as if he was ready to slit his own throat with a blunt knife.

What's up with the guy?

'I must tell you something, George.'

'Tell me what?' This was not looking good.

'I've told you about Pierre. Indeed, you met him once. Couple of weeks ago, remember?'

George grinned. 'Yeah, when he came out of the bathroom in his birthday suit?'

'Suit? Was he wearing a suit? Don't remember that.'

'Birthday suit, man. It means being naked. Like on the day when you're born.'

247

'Oh right! And what did you think?' Harvey had regained some of his twinkle.

'OK, let's not labour the point, Harvey. Tell me what's wrong with your darling Pierre?'

'Oh, nothing's wrong. It's just that he's had enough of New York and wants to go back to Paris.'

'Aw hell. I'm sorry man. You'll miss him. You've been seeing each other for – how long?'

'Six months. Six wonderful months. The thing is George, he wants me to go with him.'

'To Paris? What, forever?'

'Yes, we want to set up home together. He has an apartment there. His sister's been living there but she's leaving soon and it's the right moment for us to move straight in when she goes back to Toulouse.'

George put his elbows down on the coffee table. Covered his mouth and nose with his hands.

Could really do without this shit. Not Harvey. Stay calm.

'I can't say I'm not disappointed, man, because I am. But you must do what's right for you. You deserve to be happy and life is short. You've been good to me and you're my best friend.'

They embraced, holding one another tight. There were no words.

'I'm sorry to leave you with the responsibility for the rent and everything else but as you say, life is short. And who knows maybe one day you will come out to visit me and Pierre. We will show you the lovely city and the even lovelier French women.'

'Yeah man, that would be great. Let's drink to you and Pierre.'

★

Half an hour later, Harvey waltzed out to meet his French lover. George took out his notebook.

'When life seems full of clouds and rain, And I am full of nothin' and pain, Who soothes my thumpin', bumpin' brain? Nobody.'

You arrive. The journey's been long. Tortuous. And before you know it they're all around you, grabbing hands, loud voices, the smiles, the joy. What's all that about? You've been on your own for months and now this. That's when it starts. The love thing. Be careful. It's dangerous. Don't get me wrong you'll enjoy it. The charm and power of a mother's smile, its many guises. The love you feel for your family, your friends, your cat, your favourite shirt. That's when you know you've been sucked in. I'm not saying you should do without it. Hell no. They say it makes the world go around. How many times do you hear folk use the word? I love this song, I love your smile…

Then later you fall in love. The falling means you have no control. You. Just. Fall.

Into a barrel of sweet honey. You hold one another, lick, taste, smell, and touch. But at some point, you realise you have to get out. It's not easy. It's hard being in love and it's hard being out of love. Finally, you emerge, 'pick yourself up, dust yourself off and start all over again', just like the song says.

In the end you're alone. You came in on your own. You'll go out on your own. It's the same for us all.

'Who soothes your bumpin', thumpin' brain? Nobody.'

He tore out the page and read it aloud to the empty room. What a load of shit. Can't send that anywhere.

He folded the paper in half and shoved it in his wallet along with all the other detritus of his life.

Chapter Forty-seven

Oh, for God's sake, George, that's the second piece you've broken this week. This Haviland stuff don't come cheap, ya know.'

Lily marched over and started picking up the pieces of a china jug, lavishly decorated with gold flowers which had shattered onto the parquet floor as he got up from the couch.

He walked away and locked himself in the bathroom.

Shit, shit, shit. Her and her bloody precious things.

It was seriously getting on his wick. If he hadn't got away quick he didn't know what he might have done. He looked about in the cabinet, just for the sake of something to do. It was filled with all of Lily's paraphernalia: creams, lotions, rouge, lipsticks, face powder, hair combs. There was one lonely jar of the stuff he used on his hair and that was about it.

Just goes to show who's more important in this bloody apartment.

It had been the same ever since he moved in a couple of months before. Although to be fair, he didn't want for anything. Her apartment was located in a real swanky area, on the upper East side. It was big, comfortable and stylish. And she really knew how to look after him; it gave her a lot of pleasure to dress him up and ferry him around. It cut both ways; he certainly got to meet some different types.

Like the man he met at the Lilac Lounge. They were in the restroom and the guy came right up to him and started talking, said he was a writer and did all kind of stuff from poetry, to stories, essays and such. One of those intellectual types that hang around Harlem and bend your ear about the good old days when their stuff used to be published in some coloured magazine. He had pulled a pile of papers from his pocket and given them to George to read, a couple of essays they were. To be honest, he couldn't make much sense of any of it when he looked at them the following day.

They came across one another a few weeks later and had a chat, then he got a better idea what it was about. It reminded him of his writing days with Clarke. But that was then.

It really cut him to the quick when the guy finished by saying, 'I know who you are, man, and I know what you're doing, but we all gotta stop dancing to the white man's tune. If a few showy clothes does it for you, well, good luck.'

He went out and slammed the door. Minutes later George saw him annoying some other poor sod in the crowd.

★

He first met Lily when he was working as a porter at The Mark Hotel. Man, that was an amazing place. Done up in that Art Deco style that he'd read about. Some of the larger suites even had three bathrooms. Shiny gold taps, soft white towels: the full works. He was lucky to get the job. Saw it advertised and went for it. Nothing ventured, nothing gained. Piled on the English thing and the manager loved it. He could still lay it on thick when necessary. Got to use what you've got. He recognised some famous faces from the movies passing through. They liked the accent too.

It was strange that a move upwards in life actually meant a move further downtown. Especially to the Upper East side. It was a relief to get out of Harlem during the day. He was beginning to feel jumpy about becoming too well known in the area and he would never forget the comment from the guy in the restroom.

As for Lily, she made it clear from day one that he was expected to deliver more than luggage up to her room. The first time he'd knocked on her door, she made a great show of hunting around for his tip.

Wearing a towel for chrissake, which accidentally slipped from her shoulders.

All the while she chattered away, telling him that she regularly came up to New York from God knows where on business. One of the senior staff noted how long it took him to deliver her stuff and made a snide comment.

She moved into an apartment on east 77th a few months later and before too long he was servicing her as much as she wanted. He was her honey man. Suited him, particularly when she went off back to see her old folks or took the occasional trip to Europe. The writing work had completely fizzled out. After all, he had nothing to lose.

★

He sat on the edge of the bath and waited. That usually did the trick. Sure enough, about fifteen minutes later there was the knock.

'You still sulking, honey pie?'

He didn't reply, stood up, unlocked the door and gave her a hug.

She lounged in the armchair and watched as he knelt down to pick up the last few splinters of china sticking out of the rug.

He looked up at her: 'Don't want you to cut your pretty little feet, do we?'

She grinned, extended one foot towards him and wiggled her toes right in his face, like he was some puppy dog. He waved her off, stood up and went across to the window.

Really pushing it now, the arrogant bitch.

He turned back to face her: 'Although, it's not as if there's not plenty more where that came from, right?'

She raised herself up and walked right across to where he stood, eyes squinting, dribbles of saliva appearing at the corners of her mouth.

'Is that so? My Great Grandaddy worked damn hard for his money way back when. As his last surviving heir, I'm entitled to it and I don't need anyone telling me otherwise. But that don't mean I have to waste it.'

'I know. You've told me enough times. And we all know how he made his money, on the backs of others.'

He stopped.

Hell's bells, can't go too far with this one.

'So, honey boy, that's what it is, huh? Let me tell you it was your English forefathers were right there with us in all that shit, so don't try that one on me. Think about it.'

She threw a curve-ball over her shoulder as she stalked off into the kitchen, 'Maybe I'm wasting it anyway. Why don't you think about that too.'

★

'Did you have a dog when you were a kid?'

Lily sat in front of her vanity mirror, with her mouth full of hair pins as she tried to sweep her ringlets high on one side. They had just spent the last hour making up. That always worked.

'Sure, we did. We had three dogs. Big, black beasts. Needed 'em for protection.'

'And did they?'

'Did they what?'

'Protect you?'

She laughed, 'Course they did. That was their job.'

'How did you train them?'

The ringlets fell down as she spoke to his reflection in the mirror. 'What's all this about, George?'

'I was just wondering, that's all.'

'Wondering about what?'

'Your childhood. You don't talk about it very much.'

'Grew up in the country. My folks had plenty of bodies working the land. All that. You're not suggesting that we get a dog?'

'No, of course not.'

'Good, this is no place for pets. Although that nice lady on the top floor has a cat, but they're different.'

'How are they different?'

'Cats have their own mind. They don't do anything they don't want to.'

'That's true. So, what did you do to make your dogs behave?'

'My daddy used to give them treats, although always kept them a bit hungry. Just to keep them wanting. Taught them to sit up, beg, bark at strangers – that kinda thing. Trained them in the proper way.'

Her hair looking tidy, she was now intent on the rouge and lipstick.

'They got rewards for being good. Got whupped if they didn't,' her girlish laugh tinkling off the mirror. 'One time, my daddy got rather carried away, whupped that dog till he died. You wouldn't believe the blood – took the yard boys hours to clean the place up.'

Make-up complete, she went to look for a suitable dress for the evening, and called out as he began to get ready, 'Why don't you put on that new tuxedo we bought yesterday? I've got a nice surprise for you tonight, honey. Want you to look your best.'

★

They'd been shopping at the biggest store in town, at 59th and Lexington. Lily sat there like a queen bee while he tried on a selection of different get-ups. Paraded in front of her like some kind of prize dummy, running his hands along the collar and adjusting the cuffs. She insisted that it would be OK to buy off the peg just this once and who was he to complain after all? He had to admit that she was always right when it came to style. She rushed off afterwards to meet one of her girlfriends for afternoon tea, leaving him with a few hours to spare. He had an idea and decided to make his way to a small photographer's studio he'd noticed somewhere in mid-Manhattan.

★

'Are you sure you've come to the right place, Sir? I usually only take pictures of buildings.'

George had knocked on the door which was locked for some reason, making him consider that could hardly be good for business. Anyway, he thought he may as well see if the photographer was any good. The man who unlocked the door was small and pale looking, like he spent his whole life in the darkroom. He had a strangely large head and wore glasses which looked as if they'd been cut from the bottom of an old jam jar.

'No, that's not a problem for me. You're the professional. I just want a simple portrait taken to send away.'

When he got inside he saw why the man specialised in buildings. The place was a mess, hardly the kind of studio to impress clients, but if the framed pictures on the walls were anything to go by, he certainly knew his stuff.

'I see.' The man was looking him up and down. 'Looks like you've brought something special to wear in that bag. Am I right?'

'Yes, um, I have. Where can I go and change, please?'

'Go behind that curtain and I'll set everything up. Won't take long.'

★

A couple of hours later he poured himself a drink and waited for Lily to get home. Perhaps she was going to take him to a different joint for a change. He remembered their first trip to the theatre. Shortly after they first met. A year ago, when he was still living with Harvey, who had been highly amused when he told him all about it the next day.

★

After they had been shown to their seats George looked around while Lily adjusted her fur stole, meddled with her purse and generally fussed. The theatre was built in the modern style, all curved walls made of fine wood with a few geometric designs dotted around the place. Everyone was dressed to kill and looking like they were settling down for an exciting evening. No wonder Lily wanted him to look smart.

She leaned across and whispered behind her programme, 'Nice huh?'

George nodded and smiled, 'Sure is, sweetie. How come you knew about this play? And what's it all about?'

She raised her eyebrows, fluffed up her hair and paused before launching in. 'Well now, I was thinking you might like it, you being an English gent an' all.'

He wished she wouldn't show herself off. Talking so loudly a man sitting in front of them turned around and frowned.

'Why would I like it?' His voice a whisper as he patted her knee trying to quieten her down.

'You know that raggedy book you brought to show me that evening? That old Shakespeare book?'

'What about it?' His neck feeling hot as he willed the lights to go down.

She was wittering on as she always did, 'It's one of his funny stories, about folks falling in love with the wrong people and magic potion and silly stuff like that.'

'*A Midsummer Night's Dream*?'

'That's the one. Clever old you,' she said, pinching his cheek. 'Except that we do things different in America. This is our version. With lots of tunes and fun. Think it might be just up your street, honey.'

Voices faded as the lights went down and the curtain rose. The band opened with an up-tempo brassy number to set the tone for the evening. George recognised the faces of many well-respected musicians, including some of those he'd been lucky enough to see playing in local jazz clubs and restaurants. The most well-known of them all was playing Bottom, complete with horns and baggy pants. Same guy he'd seen once at the Hotel Serena. He lifted his trumpet up high and the audience went crazy.

Titania and the other fairies were all legs and glitter and Puck's high-pitched voice was instantly recognisable. George pursed his lips, shook his head and thought of his first introduction to Shakespeare, sleeping on the floor in the storeroom. Years ago. Another era, another planet. Over time, he'd read more of the plays and sonnets even though it was tough to have to keep referring to the notes. Mind you, the man himself certainly knew his stuff and the language sometimes sounded like music if you read it out loud. Lily liked it when he did that pretending to be some big shot actor type. Never in a million years did old Shakey imagine one of his masterpieces would come across like this.

Lily clearly enjoyed the music but when the talking started she got restless, twisting around in her seat and twirling her ringlets about her little finger. He looked around and saw that a few people even got up from their seats for a while until the music started back up. Mr Miseryguts from the seat in front left during the interval and didn't come back.

On their way out, he heard quite a few people complaining that they couldn't understand much of it. A few weeks later George learned that the production only ran for thirteen performances. Lily took pleasure in reading the review article to him out loud, which stated that lots of the audience thought there was 'too much Shakespeare and not enough hot music'.

Chapter Forty-eight

It was Saturday morning and sixteen-year-old George Junior was lying on his bed. His mom had gone to work. She had a long shift that day and wouldn't be home until late. A good opportunity to listen to some hot music. Dear old Daddy Benny, DB for short, had bought him a gramophone for his birthday a couple of years before and since then they had built up an impressive collection of music. They enjoyed listening to jazz together and had similar tastes. DB enjoyed bopping away while he cooked, usually to One O'Clock Jump. That was until Mom intervened telling him he must be careful of his heart. DB sometimes took him around to local bars to see some live jazz, insisting that on no uncertain terms was he going to buy him any alcohol. George was tall for his age, so nobody asked any questions anyway.

He often wondered what it was between him and Mom. Nice guy that he was, it seemed strange for her to marry a man that much older than herself. Twenty years older. Man, that was no joke. But to be fair, he did everything he could to make her happy and him too.

★

He'd had a good send-off the previous year though. Benny Baker was a valued church member and had sung for many years in the choir at St Philips. George would never forget the last hymn as his coffin was taken up and carried from the church.

Softly and gently, Jesus is calling, calling for you and me, See, on the portals He's waiting and watching, watching for you and me.

Everyone sang with a passion and fervour he'd never seen before. He thought the carved eagle on the lectern would surely fly up to join DB on his journey. Mom loved that man, but George always felt that somehow there was something missing between them. Since he'd got older and been interested in girls, he had a shrewd idea of what it probably was.

She always got a bit jumpy if he started in asking her about his real dad. Her usual reply was always, 'Benny is your dad. He's been a real daddy to you and don't you forget it.'

He would back off then, not wanting to upset her.

She enjoyed listening to music too, but one or two songs upset her for some reason. He searched about to find the song: 'I'll Be Tired of You' sung by Ella. That really got to her. The lyrics suggested that it would take the grass to stop growing and the birds to stop singing before you ever got tired of loving someone. And Ella's honeyed voice could make anyone's soul ache with painful joy. He often wondered who Mom thought about when she heard it. Maybe it was his father. His real father. He came across another that really cut her up, Billie Holiday singing 'The Man I Love', along with Lester's warm saxophone wrapping around her voice like a cosy blanket.

It was strange, when he heard Billie it took him right back to when he was five or six years old. He used to sit with Mom in Mrs Pierce's kitchen and listen to her sing, while her husband played the violin. Sure, it was a different kind of music, but when she started off, especially the long high notes, he cried and cried against Mom's warm chest. Didn't know why. The Pierces sat him down one evening and told him the name of the tune, from a longer piece called *Stabat Mater*, written by some Italian guy, named Pergolesi. Said it was written hundreds of years before. They told him all about their orchestra, the different singing voices and all the instruments. Maybe one day he would go to a proper concert hall and hear that kind of stuff himself. Who knew. No wonder they decided to go and live in Italy. Seemed like the Italians were really keen on all that highbrow malarkey.

And right here in America, there was Billie Holiday bringing out those same feelings in people. The musical stories of her sorrowful loving were enough to make anyone cry. Goes to show how powerful music could be. It digs right into your heart. Like it's done for hundreds of years for people the world over. Imagine that.

He took off the sad stuff and looked for some instrumental jazz. That was more like it. Then later the mellifluous saxophone of Coleman Hawkins playing 'Body and Soul' drifted around the room as he swayed from side to side while enjoying his morning coffee.

Chapter Forty-nine

Another evening at the Lilac Lounge. One by one the musicians walked onto the small stage. Murmurs of excited anticipation rippled around the room as L. mounted the bandstand smiling and nodding at the audience while he adjusted the strap on his saxophone. The musicians languidly prepared their instruments and a hush fell around them like a soft summer dusk. The bass player leaned across to share a private joke with his friends.

Quiet secret laughter as they took their places. Stillness.

George looked at the woman sitting at his side and she threw him a tight smile. Her little fur cape slid from one smooth white shoulder and she drew it around her without moving her eyes from the stage. The gems at her throat slashed red against her pale skin. He put his hand palm upwards to invite her touch. She briefly acknowledged the movement with an arched eyebrow before looking away again. He stared at her as she studied the musicians, her hungry eyes resting on each man in turn. His mouth quivered into a slight snarl as he picked up his drink.

So that's what she's after? What about me and all the years I've spent searching. And for what?

The band was ready. L. signalled with a slight nod of his head, the lights dimmed, and the first song unfolded: 'The nearness of you'.

George closed his eyes and concentrated on the voluptuous tones of the tenor player as he delivered the verse straight, the others gradually adding the sounds of their instruments to his. He thought about all he had learned and loved about jazz across the long years of his journey. He recalled his first live jazz experience so long ago: Jelly Roll Morton, with his sturdy style and powerful lyrics. And all the nights he'd spent at The Calico Club with one dickty gal or another, keeping his head down at the end of the show if any of the coloured musicians happened to catch his eye and stare at him with a little shake of the head. After giving a searing performance of first-class jazz for a whites-only audience, they were obliged to exit through the back door. And there he was, knowing he was witnessing music that would become respected, embellished upon and praised as time progressed. Music that portrayed levels of subtle sophistication and a smooth symmetry unmatched by any other art-form, or certainly none that he knew of.

The band promptly launched into an up-tempo 'Honeysuckle Rose'. People began to smile at one another in recognition of an all-time favourite. Before too long the music makers started to play ball. Grinning together, four bars each bounded and rebounded between them, every sharp soloist challenging the next. The drummer then took control while the rest stood back in respect and delight as he rolled, rocked, knocked and whispered across the various components of his kit. Then the musicians fell together again as one for a final hard-driving chorus. A man in the audience yelped in orgasmic joy as the last notes bounced off the walls.

The evening passed. A few drinks later Lily relented. Taking his hand across the table she let her auburn hair sweep against George's neck as she rested her head on his shoulder. There was a pause until a young woman appeared, seemingly from nowhere, to join the band.

She needed no introduction. To see her up close was a privilege.

Her songs were often about loss, sadness and the disappointments of love. Her face, tender, smooth and honeyed shone out beneath a slick of black hair pulled up and away from her forehead with a white gardenia pinned to one side.

Her stance declared her vulnerability to the world in tandem with the broken sweet sadness of her voice in 'Body and Soul'. L. gently held the verse with an underlying sensuality as she sang, then smoothly brought them both upwards into the bridge of the song. Following the melody through, she and the others melted into the shadows and the tenor player stepped forward to solo.

★

Eight bars in and George hears echoes of that old familiar story of heaving seas and human misery. Transported into an alien realm, pain and sorrow blossoms into a poignant tenderness that encircles all those who listen. And those who can hear.

Degradation, sadness and loss is re-fashioned as solitary beauty. Sixteen, twenty-four, thirty-two bars, and still the narrative unfolds. Wave upon wave of instant creation holds sway over an ocean of pale faces. When it is over a brief silence falls as each person present imbibes the truth of what they have witnessed. A susurration of quiet delight.

Then: applause, calls, yells. The weavers of magic smile and nod.

Decades tilt away as George proudly stakes his claim to a supreme rightness, clarity and the innate comprehension of that he has so long denied.

The singer gently takes the original melody, her voice like hands cupped around it, before fading gently to the final notes.

George unwinds his fingers from Lily's and lets them rest, abject on the white tablecloth. The singer is the first to leave the bandstand. She plucks the flower from her hair and places it softly in his upturned hand as she saunters past their table. He holds it to his face and smells its sweetness.

★

Back outside on Lenox Avenue Lily's driver was waiting on the corner of 125th. He unwound his large frame out of his seat as he saw them approaching. A coloured man, he was always careful to cast his eyes down as Lily approached, but usually met George's eye with a blank stare accompanied by a very slight lift of one eyebrow.

Bastard. He does it every time.

And he always made the biggest deal of opening the door like some kind of idiot. George knew his game. The creep gave him a headache.

The coupe rumbled down Lenox Avenue: one of Mr Henry Ford's prize machines. Lily slid her arm into his.

'You OK, honey? Gonna give your girl a good time tonight?'

He stared ahead.

'Honey, you OK? George? Speak to me, George.'

She shook his arm and turned his face towards hers. It was damp and hot. His beautiful face. One of his eyes had drooped downwards and his mouth was dripping with saliva. She punched the back of the driver's seat, 'Maurice, Maurice, you gotta help me!'

George's brain felt like mud. Not feeling too good. His arms turned to lead. Nothing working. And Lily's voice coming at him from the bottom of the sea...

★

Nearly four thousand miles away, walking along Bute Street in Cardiff around ten o'clock the following morning, you might come upon a small shop which you recall was once a gentleman's outfitters. But not now. There are two tailors' dummies in the window, and a sign on the wall which declares the clothes on display as being 'Perfect for the Well-dressed Lady'. One mannequin is dressed in what you could describe as an outfit suitable for wearing uptown. Perhaps to go window shopping in Howells, or to enjoy a Sunday afternoon stroll in Sophia Gardens. You might even wear it to a matinee at The New Theatre.

The dress is made of apricot-coloured cotton, with a full skirt and big white buttons from the hem right up to the neat collar. The three-quarter-length sleeves and collar are trimmed with white braid and a pair of white crochet gloves is set at a jaunty angle beneath. A sturdy twill navy coat, made of galatea perhaps stands beside the dress, the collar and cuffs trimmed with astrakhan and square wooden buttons down the front. You would never guess that both items were made from cast-offs that have been kept in an old trunk for more than a decade.

Through the window you may notice a middle-aged coloured woman sitting at the counter. Dressed in a smart suit and her hair, a little greying around the edges and pulled back in a bun. As you look ostensibly at the clothes on display you watch her take off her spectacles. She puts her elbows on the counter, holds them in one hand and rubs the other hand across her brow, eyes closed.

A younger woman, maybe aged about twenty sits beside her, sewing up the hem of another garment. She is very beautiful, her hair similarly pulled back, her face glossy and dark. She wears a plain green dress without adornments. She needs none. She notices the older woman's discomfort and stops her work. Standing up behind the older woman, she puts both arms around her and nuzzles her neck.

You hesitate briefly, wondering whether to go in and disturb such an intimate moment. Then you open the door and smile, as the older woman slowly gets up to take her coat and bag from a hook on the back wall.

'Think I'll finish for today, lovely. Feeling a bit queasy all of a sudden.'

'Got a headache, have you, Mam?'

'Don't know. Strange feeling like someone just walked across my grave.'

'Oh, never mind, Mam. You go on home. I can manage here.'

She looks at you with a wan smile. 'Welcome. I'm sorry I have to go but my daughter Georgia will be pleased to help you.'

Georgia hugs her mother who nods as she passes you by on her way out.

Chapter Fifty

Florence was in the kitchen. She stubbed out her cigarette as Alice came in humming to herself.

'Oh my, someone's happy today.'

'Hi Florence. Look what came through the letterbox this morning.' Alice waved a letter in the air and jigged from side to side.

'Another letter? Oh, I think that poor baby's missing his dear mom.'

'Yes, looks like it. I'll try and wait until I get home, so I can read it in peace. Don't want to rush it.'

'Good idea, sweetie.'

Florence picked up her bag, ready to leave. 'Whew, these early shifts will be the death of me. Ain't doing much for my social life either.'

'Oh Florence, why don't we swap over next week? I don't mind.'

'OK, honey, sounds like a plan. By the way did you see the new man yet? Came in this morning.'

'No, I didn't.' Alice was buttoning up her pinafore.

'Yep, he's pretty sick. The sad thing is he doesn't look all that old to me. Not as old as most of the others. Shame. And do you know, it's strange, I feel like I've seen him before but can't remember where.'

'I'll introduce myself when I go on duty. Thanks Florence. You go on home and get a rest now.'

'See you later, sweetheart.'

Alice went off to her afternoon shift. Passing through the hallway she saw Florence by the front door, talking to one of the porters. Lounging against the door jamb, one hand on her hip in a way that Alice had seen so many times before. She grinned and raised her eyebrows over the man's shoulder and Florence winked back.

★

She recognised him straight away as she went into the residents' lounge. His hair, greying at the temples, which was always coerced into a stylish pompadour when they met twenty years earlier now rested in the soft curls she had loved to fondle. His handsome face drooped to one side and his left eye wept as if grieving over some terrible loss. He was sitting in a wheelchair near the window, his long fingers resting on the blanket covering his knees. She used to call them his piano fingers because when he listened to music he would pretend to play along the base of her spine or across her soft belly.

★

'It's OK, Florence, you go on home now. I'll take care of her.' Matron, friendly yet authoritarian had taken over the situation.

'Are you sure? I don't mind staying for a while. She needs me.'

'Don't worry, she'll be alright. Our Alice is made of strong stuff.'

Alice was slumped in a chair in the corner of the kitchen, after falling into a faint in the doorway of the lounge. One of the other patients cried out and Florence dashed in to help the nurse who was trying to bring her around. She had been sitting with her head between her knees for some minutes, with Florence crouching at her side.

On hearing her friend's voice, she lifted her head, 'Florence, it's him, it's him. Oh, dear Lord.'

Her shoulders began to shake, and she wailed as if she'd been holding on to something for a long time and had finally let go.

Matron looked hard at Florence: 'Does she know our new guest, George Hodges?'

'Yes, they were close friends many years ago. Alice hasn't seen him ever since he left her in the lurch.'

'I see. I think I understand what you're saying. Poor Alice.'

Florence took Matron's arm, 'No, it's good, Matron. Don't you see? She thought she'd lost him forever.'

'But poor girl, to come across him like this. It's terrible.'

Alice's cries grew a little quieter as she heard George's name out loud and listened to the conversation going on between the two women. She kept her head down and covered her eyes with the corner of her apron, shoulders shaking, mouth quivering.

Florence stood up: 'Who came in with him, Matron? That's if you don't mind me asking. He looks very sick.'

'He was brought in by a woman. She said she has been visiting him in hospital ever since he took ill a few weeks ago, but can no longer spare the time. She will be paying for his care at Green Fields.'

'She can't spare the time? Jeez, what a selfish...did she give a name? Is she his wife?'

'No, she said he was her live-in house-keeper. Looked after things while she was on business. She obviously feels responsible for him.'

'Is that so? Very big of her, I'm sure.' Florence stroked Alice's shoulder and continued, 'She must be rich then. Lucky for him, I say.'

'Now Florence, I don't think such comments are necessary. Although I have to say, I did notice a very shiny car waiting for her outside. With a chauffeur.'

'No surprise there either,' Florence muttered.

Alice lifted up her head: 'Can I see him please, Matron?'

'I don't know, Alice. You've had a very severe shock.'

'Please let me see him, Matron.'

Matron looked across at Florence who gave a small nod and offered, 'I'll go with her, Matron. We'll sit together. I'll make sure she's OK.'

'Well, I guess so. But Alice, we need to have a little talk later.'

'Yes Ma'am.'

Alice stood up, her knees still trembling. She wiped her eyes, took a deep breath and held onto Florence's arm as they walked slowly back into the lounge. To George. He moved his head ever so slightly to one side and gazed at her as Alice approached. She took her handkerchief from her pocket, dabbed his weeping eye and took his inert left hand in hers.

Chapter Fifty-one

Four weeks passed by. For the first few days all Alice could do was try to make him comfortable. The left side of his body was completely motionless, but his right arm and leg sometimes twitched a little, as if he was willing them to move. He couldn't speak but she could tell by his eyes that he knew who she was as his gaze followed her around. His quiet stillness was so at odds with the man she remembered. If she looked too hard at his poor weeping eye, it brought tears to her own. Then she would busy herself with the blankets, cushions, anything for fear that he might notice. She had told Matron that she could take care of him without her emotions interfering with her work.

Matron changed the timetable so that she could do regular dayshifts and stay on with him in the evening in her own time if she wanted to. Every morning she took a deep breath and walked in wearing her familiar smile. She stopped at the florist on her way in and bought the white flower to pin on the side of her hat, just like she used to do before George arrived.

Mr Miller called out, 'Hey baby, I thought you'd forgotten all about me.'

She went across and gave him a quick hug, 'How could I forget about you? And where have you been? I haven't seen you for a couple of days.'

'Had to see the doc. My old body is falling apart at the seams.'

'You still look handsome to me. And how are you feeling now?'

'All the better for seeing you looking so fine and dandy.' He kissed her hand before she went to George who was in his usual spot by the window overlooking the park.

She sat with him during her lunch break every day and did her sewing, embroidering a cushion to put behind his back. It had a musical theme, with treble clefs and notes dancing around on a stave, a design she had copied from a picture in a magazine. George's mouth slowly dribbled as he dozed in his wheelchair.

She leaned across to wipe it and whispered in his ear, 'Wonder what you're dreaming about, George. Maybe our dreams are the same.'

Just at that moment the door opened, and Matron came in accompanied by a woman, who was chattering away quite loudly until she saw Alice leaning right up close to George.

'Alice may I introduce you to Miss Atkins. She's come to visit Mr Hodges.'

The woman, tall and pale, wore her chestnut hair tied back with a bow, matching her red mouth in a mean smile. She dominated the room with her presence, even the cuffs and collar of her striped shirtwaister dress were pressed into obedience and standing to attention. She put out her hand, her nails perfectly chiselled and ruby red. Her waist cinched in with a wide belt made Alice feel like a fat pumpkin. The sewing slid to the floor as she stood up, her palms sweating, to return the handshake.

'Pleased to meet you, Ma'am,' before scrambling about trying to gather up her things.

She recalled Florence's muttered comments about George and this woman. Surely if she thought so much of him why had she taken so long to come visit?

Miss Atkins looked her up and down before fixing her gaze on the white flower. 'Yes, you too. I'm Lily Atkins. George Hodges is my housekeeper. Or he was, don't suppose he'll be much good to me now.'

There was a pause before Matron spoke again, 'I'm so glad you're able to come visit us, Miss Atkins. We've been doing our very best for him. Haven't we, Alice?'

'Yes Ma'am.'

'Yes, well, I had to go away for a while, that's why I haven't been in before now. Lots to do, you know how it is.'

'Yes indeed.' Matron tightened her lips.

'Alice, would you like to take a break now?'

'Why, yes Ma'am, I will. Thank you.'

As she started for the door, Lily Atkins touched her arm. 'I can see that he's getting all the care he needs.'

★

Alice was sitting in the kitchen, slumped over the table resting her head on her arms, feeling like someone had clumped her with a jack-hammer when she heard footsteps coming along the hallway: Matron and Miss Atkins, whose voice got louder as she paused by the open doorway. Alice sat up. Alert, listening.

'I won't be able to come any more. My life has changed, and I will be moving away permanently.'

'I quite understand.'

'And don't worry about the cost. Me and George go back a long way and I'm very happy to fund his care.' She gave a tight laugh, 'I'll just have to put it down to one of life's rich experiences. Seems like the little Nurses' Aid – can't recall her name right now, is quite devoted to him anyway.'

Matron didn't answer.

'I'll show myself out. I'm sure you are busy.'

'Yes thank you, I am. Would you like me to keep you informed of Mr Hodge's progress?'

'That won't be necessary. You can write to me if anything happens.'

The older woman shook her hand. 'Just as you wish. Goodbye Miss Atkins.'

Lily poked her head through the kitchen doorway and smirked in Alice's direction, before walking away: 'He's all yours, honey. Guess he's more your type anyhow.'

★

Things had settled down again after Lily Atkin's visit the week before. Matron went into the staff kitchen where Alice was eating her lunch.

'I know how much George Hodges means to you, Alice, and I'm so glad he has a good friend in you.'

Alice wiped her chin. 'I'm glad too, Ma'am. Think I'm all he's got left. But there is something else.'

'I think I have an idea what you're going to say. Something to do with your son? Florence kind of hinted as much. Am I right?'

Alice looked down into her lap. 'Yes, Ma'am. You see, George Hodges is my boy's real father. As you know my dear husband Benny passed away four years ago and I...well I always let folks assume that he was the daddy.'

'I understand, Alice. I put two and two together that day he came to meet you from work. I thought he looked quite a bit older than you.'

'I was very lucky. And he loved my son as if he were his own.'

'There's no need to explain. Anyway, let me tell you some good news. Miss Atkins has sent some extra funds for George. She says he used to love going out and listening to jazz music. She wants us to buy a phonograph for the clients to enjoy in the lounge. I would like your help in choosing the music.'

'Oh my, that's a great idea. I would love to help. I notice how he gets a little excited when I switch on the radio. I kind of know some of the tunes he likes best by the look on his face.'

'That's that then.' Matron turned back as she went to the door, 'Perhaps Miss Atkins is not as nasty as she makes out to be after all, don't you think?'

★

George was sitting near the window when the tune came on. Alice was on the opposite side of the room adjusting Mr Miller's cushions, who sighed and blew her a kiss. She looked over at George and watched as he slowly turned his head in her direction. Maybe it was her imagination, but she thought she could detect a little smile twitching at the corner of his mouth. She finished with Mr Miller and hurried over.

'George? You like this song?'

His mouth struggled to find the words as the sounds come. The first words she'd heard from him ever since he arrived. Dear God, he was trying so hard. Thank you, Lord. The fingers on his right hand seem to be indicating that he wanted the sound cranked up. She turned up the volume dial and Fats Waller filled the room, singing 'Ain't Misbehavin' '. By the time Fats got to the line about singing the praises of kisses which were worth the wait, Mr Miller had joined in singing from across the room.

★

Over the next few days, George made more and more of an effort with his speech, and mastered a few key words when he needed something. The daily music session after lunch brought a lot of joy. Alice put on the records, did her sewing and kept an eye on everyone all at the same time. George's cushion was finished, and she was busy making individualised cushions for everyone else. Matron came in one afternoon and surveyed the scene: Mr Miller was trying to tap his feet in time with 'Jumpin' at The Woodside' and missing the beat every time by a split second. Alice usually put on something quieter just before everyone was taken back to their rooms for an afternoon nap. There was sometimes a debate over what to choose, Mr Miller usually asking for anything by Nat King Cole or Billie Holiday.

Matron went over to Alice just as Billie Holiday sorrowed over the past, singing 'Yesterdays'.

'I forgot to give you a parcel which Miss Atkins sent over a couple of days ago. It seems she's been packing up to move back down south and came across some of George's things. She said she was going to throw the box away but had second thoughts. I thought you might like to help him look through it all.'

'Oh, thank you, Ma'am. I think it's so sad that he doesn't seem to have anything or anyone in the world.'

'He's got you, Alice. And of course, his son. Have you told him yet?'

'No, not yet. Waiting for the right moment, I guess.'

Alice fiddled with the phonograph as she tried to consider how much more Florence may have told Matron. If she knew that she and Benny Baker had got married quietly one weekend soon after she started her job at Green Fields. How she kept her maiden name while at work, always being careful not to say too much for fear of Matron's disapproval. She was a devout Christian woman and if it had not been for her she and Florence would never have been able to juggle everything all these years.

'Alice? Would you like to drop into my office later and I'll give you the box.'

'Yes Ma'am. I will. Thank you.'

Chapter Fifty-two

It was a hot night. Alice's shift had ended a couple of hours before, but she decided to stay on for a while. Most of the residents had turned in early, including George. He was lying on top of the counterpane in his pyjamas, trying to move his head from side to side to get comfortable. His eyes were closed but every so often he opened them, checking to make sure she was still in the room.

It had been a tiring day. She took a letter out of her pocket and put it on the bedside table with the other things they had found in the box. His own Pandora's box of secrets. She spread out the papers and photographs on the floor and looked at them all again one by one. She recalled the different expressions on his face as she had taken out every item during the afternoon and how he tried to say a few words about each one.

There were five photographs: two of him in a tailcoat, holding a top hat and wearing a silk scarf. She remembered the scarf from the very first time he waited for her outside church. There were another two, taken a few years later of him wearing a tuxedo. There were a few theatre playbills and another old-looking photo of a pale woman with curly hair standing outside a tall house with a child either side of her: one looking very like George aged about four and another of a dark little girl two or three years older. When she held it up and pointed to the girl in the photo, he paused for a moment. He slowly took it from her with his right hand and put it next to his cheek. He stared into her face for a long time as he spoke, his voice low, hesitant: sister Ruby.

She had wept silent tears then as he tried to touch her hand and said: sorry. Right at the bottom of the box was a large envelope with an address of a street somewhere in Cardiff. She remembers George telling her once that was where he was born. It didn't mean much to her at the time. A place in South Wales, in the United Kingdom. It was addressed to Ruby Hodges, his sister. The envelope was not sealed and inside was a card with a picture of white flower on it and written on the back: To my own sweet sister. Sorry. G. and the date: March 22nd, 1944. Five months ago. She asked him if she should post it and he had nodded before turning his head aside.

Alice put a copy of each of the photos in with the card and sought permission to go out and post it immediately. It was only when she came back that she thought she should have put in a little note too, to let his family know that their son and brother was still alive. But what with the shock of it all, she simply forgot. By the end of the afternoon they were both in tears and Matron suggested she might like to take George up early to his room.

'Alice?'

'I'm here, George. Do you need anything?'

'Only need you.'

'I'm here. '

'Love you.'

'Oh George.'

'Brought you a note.'

'A note? What note?'

'Missed you. You were gone. Too late.'

What did he mean? Gone. Gone where?

Then: 'I left the Mission to be with Florence.'

The chatter from outside had stopped and all that could be heard was the background hum of traffic. Time stopped as the rest of the world went about their business. Gone. Alice said it softly to herself. A short, bundled-up word that sounded just like what it meant. Twenty years gone.

She spoke again: 'I went to look for you a while later. The person who answered the door said you were gone too.'

She needed to grab back the moment, bring back that closeness they had created over the last few hours.

'Take a sip of water, George. Let me make you more comfortable.'

She held the glass to his mouth and dabbed his forehead with a damp cloth.

'Tell me about – you.'

Where to start? How much should she tell? She knew all she wanted to know about him, so she thought she may as well spill the beans. She sat on the edge of the bed and related why she and Florence had to leave The Mission, how they had been roommates on and off ever since, sharing chores and money and helping one another out. She somehow managed to lighten the atmosphere by describing some of the weird and wonderful people they met along the way. He smiled, shook his head and sometimes his eyes looked moist whether with laughter or sadness she couldn't decide. She talked about her cleaning jobs and all the other dead-end things she had done to make ends meet.

She spoke affectionately about her husband Benny Baker and what a kind and thoughtful man he was. It was only right to let him know that she hadn't spent her whole life waiting for him to come back. After all, he had clearly wanted something more. And that certainly didn't include herself. He wept. Silent tears. Kept trying to say he was sorry. So, so sorry.

She went quiet after a while.

'There's something else too, George. Something real special. I need to read you this important letter. It came all the way from Cornwall, in England. Do you know the place?'

He shook his head, waiting.

'Sounds like it could be another planet away, don't you think?'

He gave a lop-sided smile.

'There's a heart with a little happy face on the back of the envelope. Look.'

She held it up to show him.

'That's a sign from a brave soldier to show that he's alright. Well, as alright as anyone can be when they're thousands of miles away from home. You know there's a war on in England, right?'

His expression became serious. He waited.

'And here in the US we have sent our brave soldiers to help them out?'

'A letter from your friend?'

'Just listen.'

She leaned over so close to him that the flower fell from her hair into his open hand.

She read the letter, her voice gentle, intimate. Almost a whisper.

★

Hi Mom,

Early June 1944

Thought I'd write you a quick note before we leave here tomorrow. Nobody will tell us what's going on, but the big guys in charge all seem pretty jumpy. I've learned a heck of a lot since we pitched up here last November. Because they said I'm good with engines our unit is responsible for keeping the trucks in decent shape and ready. Ready for what I don't know. We are stationed at a little place called Treliske which is so cute and green. It's just outside of Truro, a city with a beautiful cathedral. Different from back home. Nothing like Harlem! On Thursday nights we can go out to the bars, but here they call them pubs. Colored and whites on alternate weeks get leave to go into town – would you believe that? I guess you would. The folks in the street look at us like we're from Mars. We got our rations today and I hope to catch up with Elsie again soon. She's a girl I met in The Navy Arms pub last Thursday. She sure liked the chocolate and The Lucky Stripe smokes I gave her. Said she'd send me her photograph, so I can keep it with me for good luck. I'll put it in my kit bag along with your letters. Guess we'll be OK. I'm going to make you real proud of me one day, Mom. Who knows, I may even come home with a medal!

I'll write again as soon as I can. Take care of yourself. Give Aunt Flo a big hug from me. Pray for me, Mom. I miss you.

Your loving son, George Jnr. Xxx.

★

George seemed to be deeply asleep. Alice turned off the fan and went to open the window. Leaning out she watched the flickering lights of New York City stretching outwards and upwards into the night sky. One of those lights may be shining from the house on 136th Street that was once the White Rose Mission. Miss Kinsey had gone home to be with the Lord long ago and that was the last she and Florence heard about the old place. She wondered who was living there now.

And there were surely a couple of lights shining from the Feldmanns' windows. The twins, grown men, were perhaps helping their mom and dad prepare the bread and cakes for the morning customers. Down below in the yard a couple of the night duty nurses had crept outside for a quick cigarette. She recognised Florence's hearty laugh and a giggle from one of the others as they shared a private joke.

Chapter Fifty-three

I f you were walking along 135th Street, Harlem in the spring of 1946 you may have seen a young man strolling along looking at peace with the world. He is tall and slim, his skin the shade of a ripe conker, with thick eyebrows and a full mouth. He is casually dressed in high-waisted pants, a hand-knitted pullover in a harlequin design with a crisply pressed white shirt underneath. If you observed closely enough as you passed by you may have noticed a couple of mistakes in the knitting. A few dropped stitches perhaps, or the diamond pattern not quite matching up. But you imagine him to be the kind of person who is proud to wear it simply because his mom made it.

If you slowed your steps and followed behind at a respectable distance you would find yourself going along the street as far as St Nicholas Avenue up to the edge of St Nicholas Park. As the young man reaches the steps leading up to a bench on the grass surrounded by some tattered bushes you may decide to step back a little and observe as he greets a small dark woman standing at the entrance to the park.

She wears a white dress covered in red flowers, with a matching red belt around her generous waist. She holds tight to the handles of a wheelchair, in which sits a middle-aged man with a blanket over his knees. His features bear a strong resemblance to the younger man, except that he's a lot paler in complexion. In fact, he looks like a white man. He and the woman look at one another and smile as the younger man approaches.

He hugs them both long and hard before rolling up his shirt sleeves and pretending to flex his muscles. He holds the foot of the wheelchair as he and his mother, for it must surely be her, carry it up the steps, almost to the very top of St Nicholas Park. There they stop in the bright sunshine and gaze out across Harlem.

Epilogue

When you clear out someone's home after they have died, the most precious things they leave behind are usually found stuffed at the back of a drawer or cupboard in old boxes, tins or folders. Letters, notes, photographs, newspaper clippings, programs: these are the things which tell their real story.

A major part of my grandmother Ruby's life lies in a dented tin with a black and white picture of Cardiff Castle on the front. My grandfather Jimmy Jacobs kept it after she died, and it eventually ended up in my hands. I am named after his wife Ruby Jacobs who died in 1945, ten years before him. Her younger brother George left his family in 1923 and Jimmy always maintained that she never really got over his sudden departure even though he had tried his best to make her happy and they were blessed with a beautiful daughter: Georgia, my mother.

I look at the photograph of George. A man who left home without explanations or goodbyes and has been the cause of much speculation among the family for two generations. Tall and handsome, dark curls slicked with pomade, his expression is that of someone who took himself very seriously. His nose is straight, his eyebrows abundant and he wears a thick moustache over his full mouth. He is posed in front of a swag of velvet curtains. A professional photograph then.

Judging by his clothes I would venture that it was taken in the late 1930s or early 1940s. Yet this was a man who came from a poor home. That's all I know about him. And the fact that he left his impoverished background on a quest. He is wearing evening dress: a high-button collar and tailored jacket with a frock coat draped over one arm. There are two particularly striking items: a scarf draped in careful yet casual fashion around his collar and a shiny top hat which he holds between his gloved hands. This was clearly someone who felt that he deserved nothing less than the best and was prepared to spend whatever the cost may have been at the time. You might wonder how he came by the money he needed to fulfil his dream.

★

Columbus Day, October 2013
New York
Ellis Island: 'The isle of hope and the isle of tears'

A chill wind blows off the East River as I walk along South Street towards Battery Park. I've been coming regularly to New York for many years, but I've never done this trip before and I promised myself that I would visit the island one day. I pull my hat down over my ears and turn up my collar. The air is damp and cold.

Old and young, families, couples, solitary walkers like myself are all out on a jaunt for the national holiday. Gulls swoop and scream, searching for scraps around a hot-dog stand as people stand in line for their food. The birds are bold and fearless as they dodge between people's feet and legs.

I reach a big brown building and join the ticket line for the ferry which will take me to see The Statue of Liberty. And Ellis Island. The end of the queue snakes all around the park. Crowds everywhere. I'm not even sure where to stand. I am buffeted on all sides; different voices and languages shout and call across me. Like myself they are probably trying to find out what their long dead relatives may have endured. Movement is slow and sluggish. My head throbs and my knees are aching. Beggars and itinerant musicians approach those who look likely to part with a dollar or two. There is a momentary pause in our progress.

A black man, wearing long, dirty dreadlocks and a shabby, faded coat shuffles towards me. He looks like someone who has slept rough for many years. He might be seventy to eighty years old but could be younger due to harsh living conditions. Dark skin which is not tended with oil assumes a grey tinge over time and wrinkles make black lines on either side of his mouth. He stands uncomfortably close, but I do not step back.

He starts to play the *Star-Spangled Banner* on a dented tin whistle, staring hard into my face the whole time as if performing for me only. The irony of being here on the day that America celebrates the arrival of her most lauded immigrant does not escape me. But this man is no immigrant. No doubt his forebears were displaced. Not for them was there the hopeful spirit of the pioneer. Nor did they stake claim to a land already loved and inhabited. Hungry and homeless he is twice displaced.

The phrasing of the tune is halting, poignant, sad. He stops midway through to catch his breath. I reach into my pocket for a dollar and put it in the paper cup he holds out before I am carried along on a tide of people.

'Thank you sister,' he says, his voice a monotone.

Once aboard, I find a seat near the window. When we reach the Statue of Liberty, about half the passengers disembark. I decide to take a few photos from the boat instead, so I can spend more time on Ellis Island, the final stop.

When we get there, I am handed off the ferry by a polite attendant and look up at the gracious building that is the museum. Steps lead up into the huge open hall where a pile of trunks, boxes and battered suitcases are piled high against the back wall:

the first items in the exhibition. A young woman welcomes me to the grand tour of the Ellis Island Experience at the reception desk and hands me a pair of headphones and a map.

I mount the stairs to the Registry Room. My knees still ache despite having sat down for a while. But never mind, I'm here at last. Nearly four thousand miles and ninety years since George's disappearance. I stumble for a moment and lean into a large man beside me. Embarrassed, I apologise and move on to find out what's next on the tour. My headphones have slipped, and I adjust them to hear a nasal twang telling me to look to my left where I will see the Medical Room. I stop for a moment to look over the banister at the luggage pile. I need to rest but the last ferry back is at four-thirty and I don't want to miss it. There's so much to see and learn. I sit down on a bench nearby; a few minutes won't make much difference. I close my eyes and feel tears pulsing behind my eyelids.

In the Medical Room I read how people were tested for trachoma. Surely not: a button hook was used to raise their eyelids. The voice in my ears brightly informs me what happened at each stage of the immigration process and how men, women and children were poked, prodded and questioned repeatedly. I can't bear to hear it and let the headphones drop onto my shoulders. I look around instead to watch and listen. I wander about, losing track of the order of exhibits.

I sense an emotional weight in the air but is it just me that can feel it? I have been building myself up to this day for so long. I want to be closer to George. I want to know why he deserted his family and what he was yearning for. I have been fascinated by his photograph for a long time. I will never know his story.

I note how quiet and intent people are as they study the signs on the walls. If an 'alien's' clothes were marked with white chalk it signified that they were mentally unstable or physically unfit. Once labelled thus they were very unlikely to pass immigration into the New World. I see a wooden sign with words painted on it in gold lettering: Deporting Division. Families were destroyed, children lost their mothers, husbands and wives were separated from one another. Lots of people were sent upstairs to the infirmary where they languished and maybe even died while others struggled to make new lives in the city.

The photographs show people of every shape, size, shade and nationality. Children gaze blankly at the camera, some wandering desultorily on the roof playground, others sitting at long tables in the school room. The adults look baffled and unsure as they await decisions at the hands of the Special Enquiry Inspectors.

There's so much information about mental testing, food concession outlets, money changing, Christmas on the island, charitable organisations. I can't take in much more. There are photos of people from Immigration Aid Societies who were on hand to help with clothes, employment advice and sometimes cash. I wonder if George took advantage of any of the help offered. Or maybe he was too proud.

Back downstairs again, I go to the gift shop and buy some postcards and a couple of books. On the ferry some time later, I take an envelope full of papers out of my bag and open it. I search around for one particular item: an ornately designed card with a painting on the front of a glossy, white flower which looks like a gardenia.

There's a date on the back: March 22nd, 1944.

Inside is written in a flourishing hand: 'To my own sweet sister. Sorry. G.'

The New York postmark on the envelope shows that it was posted to Cardiff five months later: August 22nd, 1944.

Glossary of Terms

As referenced from: Allon Schoener and Henry Louis Gates Jr (eds.) *Harlem on My Mind, Cultural Capital of Black America, 1900-1968* (The New Press, New York: 1995)

'The language of the speakeasy.'

Dickty: Used to describe a high-class person, a good sport.

High Yaller to Blue: names given to different shades of brown skin tones from pale to very dark.

Honey man (or Sweet Man): A man who is kept by a woman.

Working Moll: A prostitute.

Monkey hugger: Used by American coloured people to describe those who come from the West Indies.

Fay: A white person

Notes/References

Chapter Two

Bert Williams was a black singer, dancer and entertainer who was obliged to perform in Blackface onstage as a degrading caricature of himself and his race. Despite his personal unhappiness, he was very successful between 1892-1922 as part of a comedy duo with George Walker. He was most well-known for the song 'Nobody', a refrain which runs throughout the narrative.

Chapter Three

The musician character of Tommie Pinkerton is based on a well-known man from 'down the Bay', Victor Parker, who presided at local funerals as well as performing in various venues.

Mento: Early folk music from Jamaica and a precursor to modern day Jamaican music.

Chapter Fourteen

Mme S: this refers to Mme Stephanie St Clair, the 'numbers queen' of Harlem. The numbers game was an illegal gambling racket. It brought in a lot of cash to the 'bankers', who were often highly regarded as friends of the community because they donated cash to churches and other community activities.

Chapter Seventeen

'Negro girls [...] if she is not to fail here.' Quote from the Annual Report: Booker T. Washington, The White Rose Mission and Industrial Association 1897-1943, December 31st, 1912.

'...was incorporated to establish and maintain a Christian home for coloured working girls where they may be trained in principles of practical self-help and right living.' (Reverend Adam Clayton-Powell, one of the Directors)

The White Rose Mission and Industrial Association opened in 1897 for coloured girls, most of whom had fled from the South. It was often funded by well-known performers, pastors and leaders of the Black community, such as Adam Clayton-Powell who became a US Congressman. (There's a reference to 'The Empress of the Blues' in Chapters 24 and 39: Bessie Smith.)

Chapter Twenty-three

Yorkville: A neighbourhood which was mostly inhabited by German Jews. It was famous for its bakeries on the Upper East Side.

Chapter Twenty-eight

Welfare Island was re-named Roosevelt Island, after Eleanor Roosevelt in 1971.

Chapter Thirty-one

Black Women's Clubs: The Black Women's Club Movement, began in the 1890s. There were hundreds of such clubs across the USA, being eventually organised by the National Association of Colored Women in 1896, in response to the anti-lynching campaign of Ida B Wells, a leading reformer and former slave, who also wrote for Black publications. The clubs devoted their efforts to political, social, educational and economic reforms.

Information as referenced from: http://decolonizingourhistory. com/club-movement/

Chapter Thirty-five

'My bounty is […] as boundless as the sea.' William Shakespeare, Romeo and Juliet, in Jonathon Bate, Eric Rasmussen (eds.) William Shakespeare Complete Works (Palgrave Macmillan, 2007)

Chapter Thirty-two

The smart night club being referred to in the text is Connie's Inn, the first White outpost in uptown Harlem. It was run by a bootlegger during The Prohibition (1920-1933) and was a very expensive hangout for a wealthy White clientele. Mixed parties were not permitted. Despite Prohibition, alcohol was available and clients were urged to keep bottles in their pockets and not display them on the table. The coloured musicians who entertained them would have arrived and left through the back door.

Chapter Thirty-three

The library referred to in the text is a reference to The Schomburg Centre for Research in Black Culture, which began as a small library on 135th Street. It has grown and developed over the years and now houses a huge library of books, artefacts, audios and videos. Part of the New York Public Library it hosts talks, events, socials, exhibitions and educational visits.

Chapter Thirty-eight

The party host is a reference to Carl Van Vechten, a white photographer, writer and socialite, and an admirer of black culture. His novel entitled *Nigger Heaven* generated a storm of controversy and criticism when it was published in 1926. It is Van Vechten's portrait of upper-class elites, their drunken parties, night clubs and eager discussions about black culture.

Chapter Thirty-nine

A reference to The Hotel Theresa, which was often frequented by celebrities of the time; the text refers to Fletcher Henderson and the young Louis Armstrong. The hotel became desegregated in 1940, becoming known as the 'Waldorf of Harlem'. Apparently, Fidel Castro stayed there in 1960 and hosted Khrushchev to a meeting. Important community groups met there too, including Malcolm X.

AW is a reference to Alelia Walker, later known as Madame C J Walker, a wealthy Black socialite and businesswoman who made her fortune in the creation of products for Afro hair alongside her mother. She died in 1931.

The Messenger: An African-American magazine written by black writers, very popular during The Harlem Renaissance in the early twentieth century.

Chapter Forty-seven

Swingin' The Dream: Broadway musical, based on Shakespeare's *Midsummer Night's Dream*, featuring a mixed cast and including many well-known Black performers, including Louis Armstrong as Bottom, Dorothy Dandridge as Titania and Butterfly McQueen as Puck. It featured music by such composers as Count Basie and Benny Goodman. Many of the songs are still performed as jazz standards. The musical opened on November 29th, 1939 and only ran for thirteen performances, one reviewer stating that it included 'too much Shakespeare and not enough hot music'.

Information as referenced from: https://www.bdb.com/broadway-productions

Chapter Forty-nine

The Lilac Lounge re-named in the text is a reference to The Lenox Lounge, a much-loved club where many of the great jazz musicians of the day performed, including Miles Davis,

John Coltrane and others. It was frequented by many notable performers, poets and writers, including Zora Neal Hurston, James Baldwin and Langston Hughes. In the narrative, the singer with the white gardenia in her hair is of course, Billie Holiday, being accompanied by Lester Young and his band. The Lenox Lounge opened in 1939 and was eventually closed as recently as 2017, to the dismay of New York jazz devotees. Lafayette Harris Junior played there for many years as the last resident pianist. He still performs at other New York venues and across the US.

Songs and Music

Nobody (Bert Williams, Alex Rogers, 1905)

The Mountains of Mourne (Percy French/ Dr W Houston Collisson, 1896)

Auld Lang Syne (Lyrics by Robert Burns in 1788 to a traditional Scottish folk song)

The Whistling Coon (sung by George W Johnson, the first known recording by an African-American, Victor Records, 1902)

All Through the Night/ Ar Hyd a Nos (Jones, John Ceiriog Hughes, 1862. Welsh lyrics added by Ceiriog Hughes in 1862)

Wait 'til the Sun Shines Nellie (Harry Von Tilzer, Andrew B Stirling, 1905)

Hill and Gully Rider and *Dis Long Time Gal* (Traditional Jamaican Mento music, early 20th Century)

A Good Man is Hard to Find (Eddie Green, 1919)

Crazy Blues (Perry Bradford, 1920)

On Moonlight Bay (Perry Wenrich, Edward Madden, 1912)

Jesus Loves Me (Anna Bartlett Warner, 1827-1915)

Lift Every Voice and Sing (James Weldon Johnson, 1905)

Whispering (Schonberger, Coburn, 1920)

When the Mists Have Rolled Away, (Annie H Barker, 1883)

Bugle Call Rag (Pettis, Meyers and Schoebel, 1922)

After You've Gone (Turner, Layton, Henry Creamer, 1918)

I'm Just Wild About Harry (Eubie Blake, Noble Sissie, 1921)

I Wish I Could Shimmy Like my Sister Kate (Clarence Williams, Armand Piron, 1919)

I Ain't Gonna Play no Second Fiddle (Perry Bradford, Bessie Smith, 1925)

Pick Yourself Up, Dust Yourself off and Start All Over Again (Jerome Kern, Dorothy Fields, 1936)

One O'Clock Jump (Count Basie, 1937)

Softly, Softly, Jesus is Calling (Will L Thompson, 1880)

I'll be Tired of You (Tierney Sutton, 1934)

Stabat Mater (Giovanni Battista Pergolesi, 1736)

Body and Soul (Heyman, Sour, Eyton and Green, 1930)

The Nearness of You (Hoagy Carmichael, Ned Washington, 1938)

Honeysuckle Rose (Fats Waller, Andy Razaf, 1929)